CW00550070

BETRAYAL

MYSTERY, CRIME, AND MAHEM

ISSUE SEVENTEEN

LEAH R CUTTER   JOSLYN CHASE

CHRIS CHAN   DIANA DEVERELL

ROBERT JESCHONEK   ANNIE REED

DONALEE MOULTON

DAVID H. HENDRICKSON

KARI KILGORE

KNOTTED ROAD PRESS

Betrayal
Mystery, Crime, and Mayhem: Issue 17
Copyright © 2024
All rights reserved

Published 2024 by Knotted Road Press
www.KnottedRoadPress.com

Cover art:
Photo 51147350 © Ayome Watmough | Dreamstime.com

Cover and Interior design copyright © 2024 Knotted Road Press
www.KnottedRoadPress.com

Troubled Water originally appears in Black Cat Weekly issue #75.

Never miss an issue of Mystery, Crime, and Mayhem! Get yourself
a subscription!

https://www.mysterycrimeandmayhem.com/product/mcm-
subscription/

*This book is licensed for your personal enjoyment only. All rights
reserved. This is a work of fiction. All characters and events
portrayed in this book are fictional, and any resemblance to real
people or incidents is purely coincidental.*
*No part of this book may be reproduced in any form or by any
electronic or mechanical means, including information storage and
retrieval systems, without written permission from the author, except
for the use of brief quotations in a book review.*

Essay: Erle Stanley Gardner and "The Court of Last Resort" © 2024 by Chris Chan

Colder Than Gazpacho © 2024 by Joslyn Chase

Foul Trouble © 2024 by Diana Deverell

A Thieving Rescue © 2024 by Kari Kilgore

Night of the Moto-Men © 2024 by Robert Jeschonek

The Leather Jacket of Doom © 2024 by Chris Chan

Freedom Day © 2024 by Annie Reed

Troubled Water © 2024 by donalee Moulton

Your Mother's a Whore! © 2024 by David H. Hendrickson

A New Q © 2024 by Leah R Cutter

CONTENTS

INTRODUCTION

Welcome to year FIVE of Mystery Crime and Mayhem, issue seventeen!

I keep calling MCM the little magazine that could. Year three was really good to us. Four stories were recognized in "best of the year" anthologies.

It's too early to know what will happen with year four, whether the stories printed in 2023 will bring the same accolades or not. (Fingers crossed!)

I know that I, personally, couldn't be more proud and pleased with the syndicate, the new players as well as the old.

For this issue, the syndicate had the theme *betrayal*. Their takes were wildly different, as always. Some went for a more narrow definition of betrayal, such as a betrayed lover or friend. Others took a much broader approach, such as betrayal of country or self.

Overall, I think the stories in this issue, as always, are fabulous and very enjoyable (even the one with the R rating).

In this issue I have a very special guest author, donalee Moulton, a writer from Halifax, Nova Scotia.

Please, enjoy this issue, and all that is yet to come from MCM!

Leah Cutter
Ravensdale, WA
2024 January

Essay: "The Court of Last Resort"

Chris Chan

For much of the mid-twentieth century, Erle Stanley Gardner (1889-1970) was one of the most famous authors in America. He was best known for his Perry Mason legal thrillers, featuring a brilliant defense attorney with a perfect record for getting his clients acquitted. Assisted by his loyal secretary Della Street and the effective private detective Paul Drake, Mason took on seemingly unwinnable cases and triumphed. Eighty-two Mason novels appeared over four decades, from 1933 to 1973, the last two being published after Gardner's death. Perry Mason inspired several movies based on the books, a radio drama (with minimal courtroom scenes), a classic nine-season television show starring Raymond Burr, a less-successful revival series with a different cast, numerous reunion movies starring Burr, and most recently, a two-season HBO series starring Matthew Rhys with only a tenuous connection to the original mysteries.

Gardner's prolific output went far beyond Perry Mason. He wrote thirty novels in the Cool and Lam series, featuring the bellicose private investigation agency owner Bertha Cool, and her dedicated gumshoe (later partner), Donald Lam, an ex-lawyer who was disbarred for finding a loophole in the law that could be exploited so people could get away with murder– he didn't want to use it, only draw attention to it, but he embarrassed so many powerful people that his legal career was ruined. Parodying tropes of the P.I. who tended to use his fists first and his brain second, Lam was a diminutive man who was usually badly beaten by a bully at least once per novel.

As Gardner wanted to present a positive portrayal of a prosecuting attorney, he wrote nine novels in the Doug Selby "The D.A." series, about a young, principled, newly-elected district attorney of a California county, who battled ineptitude and iniquity in the local institutions, including the police and the press. Whereas in the Perry Mason novels, Mason went the extra mile to reveal the truth, and the prosecutor Hamilton Burger cared more about appearances and beating Mason than justice; in "The D.A." series, Selby cared only about the innocent being cleared and the guilty punished, and the unscrupulous defense attorney Alphonse Baker Carr (A.B.C.), was, like *Breaking Bad's* Saul Goodman, not just a criminal lawyer, but a *criminal* lawyer.

As if all of these books were not enough, Gardner wrote a handful of other novels and scores of short stories in the pulps, initially using pseudonyms, though when the works were republished in the following decades, they would appear under his true name. These stories featured cultured master criminals and other skillful legal sleuths. In addition to his fiction, he wrote travelogues about his experiences across the Americas.

All of this legal fiction was inspired in part by Gardner's own legal experiences. Though he only went to an accredited law school for a very short time, Gardner studied law independently, and he was able to be admitted to the bar in California, where he took on cases for the poor and downtrodden, particularly minorities, like immigrants from China and Mexico. While the work was satisfying, it was not lucrative, which is why Gardner turned to writing crime fiction.

Always a champion of the underdog, and passionate about reforming the justice system, by the WWII era, Gardner realized that the nation's prisons were filled with wrongly convicted people. Fascinated by new scientific approaches to studying crime scenes and autopsies, Gardner decided to use his platform for educating the public about new advances in policework and flawed investigative practices. Many of his Perry Mason novels open with a dedication essay, where he honors a friend of his, such as a specialist in legal medicine, or a criminology instructor, or a medical examiner calling for new ethical standards in testimony.

The more Gardner learned about the American

criminal justice system, the more he tried to publicize miscarriages of justice. Much to his frustration, many individuals, often coming from poverty and inadequate education, were convicted of crimes, and evidence of their innocence was ignored by the criminal justice system.

The magazine *Argosy*, then a popular publication, ran an article about a case Gardner believed was a miscarriage of justice. A man named William Marvin Lindley (nicknamed 'The Red-Haired Killer") had been convicted of the horrific sex slaying of a teenaged girl. He was sentenced to die, but Gardner and his friends learned of the case through a concerned former public defender, and started their own investigation. They proved that the star witness against Lindley, who'd identified a red-haired man, was colorblind. The California State Supreme Court was not moved by the new evidence, and affirmed the conviction and death sentence.

Gardner was certain of Lindley's innocence, and a frantic battle in the courts and press seemed to be ending in a loss, as then-Governor Earl Warren refused to enter the fray. However, when Warren's brief trip out of state left the lieutenant governor in charge, Gardner took action. With less than a day before the execution, Gardner and his colleagues hurriedly reexamined the evidence and not only found another suspect, but went over the timeline of the crime and proved that Lindley had an alibi. Gardner appealed to the California Supreme Court and Attorney General, and Lieutenant Governor Fred Howser as well. After some justices of the California Supreme Court spoke with Howser, the lieutenant governor delayed the execution, going against Warren's wishes.

Warren was adamantly in favor of the execution, so Gardner wrote about the case in *Argosy*, and provoked a massive public outcry. In the wake of the pressure, Governor Warren used his executive powers and reduced the death sentence to life in prison. Though Lindley lived, the case does not have a particularly happy ending. The alternative suspect was lost in the wind, and the strain of the near-executions caused Lindley to have a mental breakdown. He remained confined, a broken man. After the book's second edition was published, Lindley was eventually released after two decades of incarceration.

Though the case's resolution was not wholly satisfying, it inspired Gardner. Harry Steeger, the publisher of *Argosy*, decided to allow Gardner whatever space he needed in the magazine to write about potential miscarriages of justice, and soon numerous cases where the law had gone wrong were being brought to the public's attention. Eventually, he would revise much of the material published in *Argosy* into a full-length book.

Gardner was America's bestselling mystery writer, but none of his scores of novels or short stories was ever nominated for an Edgar Award, the writing prize bestowed by the Mystery Writers of America. Gardner's one and only Edgar nomination —and win—was in 1953, when his full-length book *The Court of Last Resort* received the Best Fact Crime Edgar. Gardner would also receive the MWA's Grand Master honorific in 1962 for his long career of crime writing. The book version of *The Court of Last Resort* was initially published 1952, and was expanded with new details and stories in 1954. After being out of print for many years, the book was rereleased in 2017 in both print and ebook formats. The version available today is the updated second edition.

In the opening chapter, Gardner wrote:

"We realized early in the game that it would never do for a magazine with a national circulation to come out and say in effect, "This man claims he's innocent. He's been convicted of murder. Erle Stanley Gardner thinks there may be something in the man's contentions, therefore we want the governor to grant a pardon."

We knew that we'd need facts, and these facts would have to be presented to the reading public in a form that would incite interest. No matter how much space *Argosy* donated to some worthy case, no good would be done unless people read what was printed in that space. And, even then, merely reading about the case wouldn't help unless people became sufficiently aroused to *do* something about it.

Public opinion must be molded, but it must be an enlightened public opinion based on facts, otherwise we would be charged, and justly charged, with the tactics of the rabble rousers.

It is customary in legal circles to refer to the highest tribunal in any jurisdiction as "the court of last resort." Out there in the wide open spaces of Baja California, we came to the conclusion that in a country such as ours no officially organized tribunal ever could be the *real* court of last resort. The real court of last resort, we felt, was the people themselves. It was a new and daring concept, yet it was essentially sound."

Gardner covered several prominent cases in *The Court of Last Resort*, like convicted murderer Clarence Boggie, a Washington man with a personal history too improbable to believe...but the seemingly ridiculous claims Boggie made about being swindled out of a massive inheritance were, in fact, true to a large extent, as were his eyebrow-raising assertions of being a first-rate lumberjack and being wrongly convicted of bank robbery in the past. An investigation had already cleared Boggie's name regarding the bank robbery. When a prison chaplain called Gardner in to investigate, the warden proved surprisingly supportive. After a substantial investigation, the members of the Court of Last Resort discovered how an improbably comedy of errors, malice, and official misconduct led Boggie into a wrongful arrest and conviction. A long, epic battle in the courts and press led to Boggie's release, but Boggie's eventual fate was a premature death caused in part by two decades of rough life in confinement.

Gardner and his colleagues were also pivotal figures in the era's most talked-about instance of a wrongly convicted man: the case of Sam Sheppard, the doctor who was convicted of his wife's murder, who probably was an inspiration for the television series *The Fugitive*, though the show's creator, possibly out of concern for legal repercussions, denied that the real-life case played any role at all in the creation of the show. Gardner and his colleagues pushed for a polygraph, publicized the case, and supposedly helped to convince F. Lee Bailey to take over Sheppard's defense.

Gardner's real-life experiences would shape his fiction. In the Perry Mason series, District Attorney Hamilton Burger begins as a fair-minded, amiable prosecutor, but over the years Gardner altered him, warping Burger into a seething enemy of Mason, placing personal pride and a lust for revenge over the rights of the wrongly accused. Gardner dealt with many similar prosecutors and bureaucrats, who, even when a convicted person's innocence was provable, refused to help because they claimed that acknowledging a wrongful conviction would undermine public faith in the criminal justice system. Less publicly, these prosecutors feared that overturned convictions would crush their personal statistics for wins in court. Gardner was too fair-minded a man to argue that *all* civil servants fit this mold, and in his fiction and non-fiction, he would applaud the honest people who put truth and true justice over personal reputation and convenience.

The Court of Last Resort has power in part because it calls for sympathy towards its subjects. Throughout the book, Gardner profiles the effects of incarceration on people, especially men who preferred the wide-open spaces of the American West. Two brothers who were able to make a living off the land, gathering gold dust, were convicted of a violent crime. When Gardner and his allies theorized that the pair had been framed by a rival, they reconstructed a crime scene, where the brothers were accused of attacking members of law enforcement during an attempt at arrest. When the official version of events proved impossible, the Court of Last Resort argued that they had been framed and slandered, and eventually earned their conditional release from prison, but they were forced to stay in urban areas, far from the open-air natural settings where they were more comfortable. On numerous occasions, Gardner voices his wholehearted approval of self-reliant men who stand on their own two feet and make an independent living in rural or desert settings. This attitude is seen throughout the Perry Mason novels, where some of the happiest men eschew "civilization" in favor of simple lives of fishing, hunting, and scavenging to survive. Gardner glorified the rugged individualist, and his novels and nonfiction reflect how he felt that such an attitude not only made for better men, but it also proved critical in reforming criminals.

Much of the latter third of *The Court of Last Resort* is not about the group's adventures trying to clear wrongly accused innocents, but about how to turn the guilty into useful members of society.

Gardner was very interested in penology—the study of running prisons and controlling prisoners. Long before more recent challenges to the current prison system became trendy, Gardner was calling for smarter approaches to handling criminals, arguing that the main goal of incarceration should be rehabilitation, suggesting that life sentences often made for desperate men with nothing to lose, and decrying the death penalty. It was not just prisoners who received Gardner's sympathies. In one chapter of *The Court of Last Resort*, Gardner eloquently calls for better pay and working conditions for the police, and fighting the causes of corruption in the local government that led to low morale amongst law enforcement.

It should be noted that Gardner did believe that a significant number of criminals were incapable of being reformed, and that society was better off if they were permanently kept away from the innocent law-abiding populace. But wherever possible, Gardner called for a mindset of reform, particularly amongst juvenile offenders. Pointing out that many young convicts were brutalized and sexually abused in prison, Gardner suggested that under the current system, teenagers generally emerged from prison angrier, harder, and more traumatized than when they entered. Tying together his admiration for men of strong character in the American West, Gardner promoted an experimental ranch for wayward youths, which was set in the countryside, and never forced the boys to stay there if they didn't want to, though if they left, they were not allowed to return. At the ranch, traditions were stressed over rules, and juvenile delinquents were taught ranch work, horseback riding, and the value of being a member of the community. When the ranch's owner believed that a young man had overcome any anger and personal flaws that had turned him towards crime, that individual was encouraged to go back out into the world, hopefully to succeed in whichever endeavors he chose thanks to the character-building exercises he learned at the ranch. Though much of Gardner's book is devoted to advocating for more intelligent, humane, and cost-effective ways of fighting crime, the Court of Last Resort is best known for clearing the innocent, rather than advocating for improvements in public policy.

The Court of Last Resort caught Hollywood's attention, and during the 1957-1958 television season, the group's adventures were turned into a half-hour series. Over the course of twenty-six episodes, real-life cases were dramatized to demonstrate what had been done. Four of the episodes were released on a very grainy DVD, and restored versions of these episodes are available on YouTube, as are a few others in the series. "The Mary Morales Case," "The

Clarence Redding Case," and "The Jim Thompson Case" explain how innocent people can be caught up in false accusations of crimes through flukes of chance, and shows how various scientific and legal methods were used to clear their names. In these episodes, many of the names were changed for privacy and legal reasons, and the basic facts of the cases were streamlined, abridged, and often bowdlerized for television. In "The John Smith Case," the subject at the center of the narrative was indeed guilty of a double homicide he committed during a robbery as a young man, but after decades of incarceration, he had been a model prisoner, learned a trade, and served as a mentor to other prisoners. The episode covered how the Court of Last Resort believed that the man was reformed, and that no benefit to society could come from having a potentially productive citizen locked away at taxpayer expense. The legal battle for parole is dramatized, with the local press leading the charge to keep the now late middle-aged Smith in prison, and the now-grown son of the victims wrestling with trauma and the pressure to forgive the man who murdered his parents. Each episode opened with the narrator declaring that "It is you, the people who are...The Court of Last Resort," illustrating that the only way to achieve justice was through an active and determined citizenry.

The seven members of the Court were listed in the opening credits:

ERLE STANLEY GARDNER
Lawyer, Noted Author
HARRY STEEGER
Publisher,
Administrator of The Court
DR. LeMOYNE SNYDER
Lawyer, Doctor of Medicine
Medicolegal Expert
RAYMOND SCHINDLER
Celebrated Private Detective
ALEX GREGORY
Lie-detector Expert
MARSHALL HOUTS
Professor of Law, Formerly
With FBI
PARK STREET, JR.
Trial Lawyer, Chairman of Texas
Law Enforcement Foundation

The members of the Court of Last Resort came from different backgrounds, careers, and financial statuses, brought together by friendship, mutual respect, and a shared desire for justice, even if it cost them their spare time and a great deal of energy.

As the years and these seven men passed away, as did the age of popular magazines like *Argosy*, The

Court of Last Resort similar faded into memory. It would be replaced by other movements such as The Innocence Project, but the passion and righteous determination of Gardner and his colleagues is as fresh today as it was over seventy years ago. The achievements, lessons, and legacy of The Court of Last Resort are due for rediscovery and renewed appreciation.

Colder Than Gazpacho

Joslyn Chase

Cathryn stood, hands on hips, feet splayed on the wet sand, waves lapping at her ankles, as she gazed out over the western horizon. In the first days of spring, the sun set early, even in southern Spain, and its golden rays melted across the copper ocean like butter on a golden pancake.

She dug her toes into the cool grains beneath her feet. Though the day had been fine, the breeze feathering across the bay from Cadiz raised a slight shiver along the hairs on her arms, and Cathryn hadn't gone past her knees into the aquamarine water.

She might have picked a warmer time of year to do the research for her next mystery novel, but she liked the relative quiet of the off-season, offering long moments of solitude, perfect for pondering and plotting. Licking the slight salt tang from her lips, she gathered her things and began trudging along the slithering sand back to her rented apartment, one block from the beach.

Climbing the steps to the promenade above, Cathryn skirted a few piles of dog detritus dotting the sidewalk. Everyone in Spain, it seemed, owned a dog and the messes were shrugged off and accepted by the locals as part and parcel. Cathryn tried to adopt an equally casual attitude, grateful the aromatic lumps hadn't been baking all day under a scorching sun.

Entering the foyer of the apartment building, she scraped the last of the sand from her sandals on a nubby mat before starting across the marble floor. Water from a fountain at the center of the space splashed gently into a ceramic bowl, and the soft strains of a Spanish guitar floated on the air. Cathryn liked the building, and her apartment offered a spectacular view of the bay.

From the corner of her eye, she caught movement at the manager's counter and heard the slight murmur of conversation as she headed to the elevators. She jabbed the button and as it lit, a resounding crash echoed in the airy space, making her jump.

Turning, she saw a woman staring down at the shattered mess of a potted plant, her palms pressed to her cheeks. Cathryn dropped her beach bag and hurried to help.

"I...I'm sorry," the woman stuttered as León, the property manager, came forward with a bag to collect the broken shards.

"Are you all right?" Cathryn asked her. The woman was shaking, her face extraordinarily pale. "Can I get you a glass of water?"

Cathryn nodded to León who handed her the bag and went to fetch the water. The woman pulled her hands from her face and began helping with the cleanup. As Cathryn worked, she studied the woman from beneath her lashes. There was something familiar about her, and as León arrived with the water and a broom, it came to her.

"Paige?" she ventured. "Paige Kincaid? Is that you?"

The woman's startled eyes flew to Cathryn's face and she stared hard, her mouth dropping open. "Cathryn?"

The two college roommates embraced over the pile of scattered soil. "It's been thirty years!" Paige said. "How can you possibly still look the same?"

Cathryn laughed. "I'm sure I don't."

"Nor do I. But you recognized me anyway."

She sat back on her haunches and was about to speak when León shooed them both away. *"Por favor, señoras.* Go now. I will handle this."

Cathryn helped Paige to her feet and they walked arm in arm to the elevator, Cathryn retrieving her bag on the way.

"I'm Paige Morrison now," her long ago roommate said.

"Is your husband here with you?" Cathryn asked.

Paige sighed, shaking her head. "My Walter has passed on. Been almost five years now."

Cathryn squeezed her hand. "Six and a half years since my Ryan died. I guess we're kind of in the same boat."

Paige gave a wan smile. "Paddling along with you was always a good thing."

The elevator arrived and they stepped inside. "Which floor?" Cathryn asked, her finger poised over the buttons.

"I'm on six."

"And I'm on seven," Cathryn smiled.

"Come in for a drink?"

Cathryn regarded her friend. "I think I should," she said. "Something really upset you back there, and if there's any way I can help, I'd like to do that."

The sparkle went out of Paige's eyes, but she nodded, leading the way as the carriage arrived on the sixth floor. Like Cathryn, she wore sandals that made little slapping noises on the polished marble floor of the corridor. Inside the apartment, she kicked off her sandals and padded into the kitchen, opening the refrigerator and gesturing Cathryn onto the sofa.

"Did you ever take up drinking, Cath, or are you still strictly no alcohol? I have a passable cabernet I could open."

"No wine for me. I still prefer water over everything else."

Paige shook her head. "I never could understand that, but...good for you."

She brought two bottles and settled next to Cathryn on the sofa—one water and an amber-colored cerveza which she drained past the halfway mark in one long draft before speaking.

"I've read some of your books, Cathryn." She thrust her beer bottle out, clinking it against Cathryn's water in a sort of salute. "They're good. You've come a long way from Professor Darnell's English class."

Cathryn smiled. "I'm glad you enjoyed reading my characters' exploits." She paused. "I don't claim to be an expert at solving mysteries, but I like to think I can help an old friend. So, what's up, Paige?" she asked gently. "What happened down there in the lobby?"

Instead of speaking, Paige dug a crumpled note from her pocket and handed it to Cathryn.

What can one admire more than the honest and pure?

What can lift the soul higher than noble truth?
What can hold us with fervent allure,
More than the sweetness of innocent youth?

Enjoy my gift,
   Jane

Cathryn read the note twice, unsure what she should be taking from it. "This came with the plant?"

Paige bit her lip and nodded.

"It's a lovely poem," Cathryn said. "Why has it upset you so much?"

Paige clenched her fists in her lap and squared her chin. "The sender—Jane Lucas—couldn't have written that note." She raised her eyes to Cathryn's.

"Because I killed her, thirty-three years ago."

"Thirty-three years!" Cathryn exclaimed. Shock and disbelief washed over her in equal measure. "That was before we met. Why did you never tell me anything about this."

"Would you, in my place? If you were trying to put the awful past behind you and start a new life?"

Paige's hand trembled as she raised the beer bottle and downed another long swallow. "I wanted to forget it, pretend like it never happened." She paused. "I wanted to be somebody else. And so, I was."

Cathryn remembered that bright college girl of long ago, the wistful hopeful air she'd carried. There had been a brittle edge that Cathryn had sensed but never come close to breaking through. And now, more than thirty years later, she was about to take that plunge.

"Tell me," she said.

Paige set the beer bottle on the glass-topped coffee table with a hard click. "I was a stupid teenager with a brand new driver's license. After a school dance, I took a carload of friends out for a ride."

Paige's nostrils flared and she swallowed hard, her face twisting under the bitter taste of it. "I thought I was so cool, so invincible. Driving fast, pedal to the floor, the road like silk under the tires. My friends were laughing, cheering me on, and everything was wonderful."

Creases rose on Paige's forehead as she fought to control her riling emotions.

"Until I saw the girl."

Cathryn could almost feel the words sticking in her former roommate's throat, knew it hurt her to spit them out. But also knew she had to.

"She was just there. Suddenly. Out of nowhere. And I couldn't stop in time. I just mowed her over."

Paige's face crumpled. "The awful, haunting sound of it." She shook her head, unable to say more for several minutes. When she spoke again, all she said was, "Her name was Jane."

Cathryn moved closer on the sofa, taking her friend's hand, lowering Paige's head to her shoulder while the woman sobbed into the silence of a Spanish evening.

After a while, Cathryn asked, "What happened to you after that?"

Paige sniffed, reaching for a tissue from a box on the end table. She mopped her face, pressing her lips together to quell further tears. "I served nine months in juvie for vehicular manslaughter. The judge ordered me to write a letter of apology to Jane's parents. They never replied."

Cathryn frowned. "And now, after thirty-three years, someone pretending to be Jane sends you a potted plant?"

"It's not the only thing that's happened," Paige said. "I came here to get away from it."

Cathryn swallowed her surprise, realizing the tremendous amount of stress her friend must be operating under. "What else?" she prompted.

"About three months ago, I got an email from a woman claiming to be Jane's sister. She said she wanted to meet and talk about what happened, that it might bring us both closure."

"Did you agree?"

"Not at first. But after some thought, I decided to meet her. I went to the place we arranged, but she never showed up."

"What was the woman's name?"

"She just signed as Susan, and I remembered that Jane did have a sister named Susan."

"Did you ever hear from her again?"

Paige hesitated. "I'm not really sure. She never emailed again, but someone started calling me on my cellphone, whispering my name before hanging up. Sometimes, when I came home from church or running an errand, I'd find a poem tacked to my front door. Similar to the one that came with the plant. And then I got a friend request on Facebook from someone calling themselves Jane Lucas."

Cathryn felt herself squirming. This conversation was definitely making her uncomfortable. She couldn't imagine how awful it must feel for Paige to be going through it.

"Did you hold onto those poems?" she asked.

"The first time it happened, I tore up the blasted thing and threw it out. After that, I thought maybe I should keep them, in case...I don't know. In case the police needed them for evidence or something. I can dig them out for you."

"Sure" Cathryn said. "But later. Right now, I want to hear the rest of the story. How did you end up here?"

"I started to feel unsafe," Paige continued. "Like I was being watched or followed all the time. I just had to get away. Walter left me enough money to take a trip now and then, so I packed up and came to Spain. I thought I'd get a real break, and then..."

"Right. The plant. The poem."

"I'm scared, Cathryn. It seems like Jane's sister is set on making me pay for what I did."

Cathryn leaned forward, placing her water bottle on the table next to Paige's beer bottle. "But why now?" she asked. "After all these years?"

Paige slumped against the sofa, misery stamped on every feature. "You know what they say about revenge—it's a dish best served cold. Like gazpacho."

"That's one cold gazpacho."

Cathryn regarded her friend, noting the still-pale face, the trembling hands. "You need to eat," she said. "And so do I. Let's walk down to the Argentinian steakhouse."

After some persuading, Paige agreed and they exited the apartment building into the dusky evening, a long line of streetlamps sending spangles of light into the blue velvet sky. A couple of kids on skateboards sped past, their wheels setting up a rhythm on the squares of pavement.

The enticing tang of grilled meat drifted on the air and Cathryn felt her mouth water as she anticipated a tender steak, flanked by a medley of vegetables. The restaurant was just around the corner, but before they made the turn, a voice hailed them and a woman stepped from a tiny shop crammed with merchandise of every kind.

"Paige! I thought that was you. Are you headed to dinner?"

The woman cocked her head at Cathryn, smiling and holding out her hand. "Hi, I'm Anita. Paige's neighbor."

Cathryn shook the proffered hand. "Then you're my neighbor, as well. I'm Cathryn."

Paige gripped Anita's shoulder, a trace of excitement and pride in her voice. "Cathryn Harcourt," she told Anita. "The mystery writer."

Anita's hazel eyes widened and her gaze sharpened, appraising. "Really? How marvelous. I don't know how you do it. I can't string together a decent sentence unless it's steeped in code and executes a command."

"Anita is a software engineer," Paige explained. "Made a mint out of computer programming."

Anita nodded, grinning. "Maybe two mints," she agreed. "Which prompts my question—are you eating Argentinian tonight? That's where Gerald and I are planning to dine. Will you join us? My treat."

Without waiting for an answer, she swung her mane of long dark hair and hooked her arm through Paige's. They began walking. Cathryn fell in beside them, a little bemused by the woman's positive presence. She seemed genuine and friendly, and though her manner was a bit pushy, it came across as an odd sort of charm.

"Where is Gerald?" Paige asked.

"Oh, he ran down to that tobacco shop," Anita said. "He's discovered some kind of Turkish something-or-other to stuff in that pipe of his." She tossed a glance over her shoulder. "He'll be along any moment."

As she spoke, a man appeared out of the shadows of a side street, walking toward them.

"Speak of the devil," Anita said, giving her husband a fond glance and accepting his kiss on her cheek.

Gerald nodded a greeting at Paige and Cathryn as they rounded the corner to the steakhouse, the tantalizing aroma growing more alluring with each step. Cathryn's stomach growled, but as she moved forward, she bumped into Paige who'd frozen, standing stiff and staring.

Cathryn followed her gaze to something dangling from the arched entrance to the restaurant's patio, caught in a halo of light from a glowing streetlamp.

A pair of pink silk dancing shoes, almost like ballet slippers. Pretty things, with a delicate rhinestone-studded strap across the ankles. Quite lovely.

Except that they were slashed to ribbons. Gutted down to the leather soles.

Cathryn stood over the stove in Paige's tiny kitchen, heating a can of soup. She had to get some nourishment into her friend—she only wished she could've found something other than tomato soup on the pantry shelf.

It bore too close a resemblance to gazpacho, brought too blatant a reminder of the vengeance hovering over Paige's head.

It looked too much like blood.

She felt protective toward Paige, acknowledging a growing determination to find out who was terrorizing her old roommate and putting a stop to it. After finding the ruined shoes, she'd walked Paige back to the apartment, insisting that Anita and her husband stay at the restaurant and enjoy their dinner.

Cathryn finished heating the soup and poured it, steaming, into a mug, adding a splash of milk to mitigate the redness of it. Paige accepted the mug and sat warming her hands with it, staring blankly at the wall beyond.

"They were my favorite," she murmured.

Cathryn knew she meant the shoes and said nothing.

"I wanted to wear them a couple nights ago and

couldn't find them. I decided I must have left them at home, and I wore a pair of black heels instead. I never imagined..."

Sitting beside Paige, Cathryn rested a hand on her friend's shoulder as she sipped the soup, finishing it like an obedient child. Cathryn rinsed the cup in the sink and suggested it was time for bed. Paige didn't object.

Leaving the apartment, Cathryn went down to the first floor and knocked on the door to the property manager's rooms. After several moments, León answered her knock, dressed in pajama pants and a silk robe open to the waist. His chest was covered in curly black hair going gray, like a dusting of talcum powder.

"Is everything okay?" he asked. "Mrs. Morrison was *muy afligida*—very upset this afternoon."

Cathryn regarded him, taking in the dark eyes full of concern. Genuine concern, she thought.

"May I come in?"

"What, now? Like this?" He gestured vaguely toward his state of undress.

She smiled. "My intentions are purely honorable, I assure you."

His olive complexion took on a rosy hue. "I never thought otherwise."

He stepped back and she walked past him down a

marble-floored hallway, following the sound of a jazz piano to the salon at the back of the apartment. León followed, gesturing her into a chair and turning the speakers down to a faint tinkling.

"Your English is excellent," she told him, settling into butter-soft leather. "Where did you learn it?"

He shrugged. "Like most of us, I learned it from American movies and television."

Cathryn raised her eyebrows, inviting more, and he laughed.

"Okay, and I spent a couple of years on the beaches of southern California."

"Surfing?"

"What else, dude?"

Now they both laughed. A wooden cutting board with a glass dome sat on the coffee table between them, covering slices of Manchego cheese. He slid it toward her. "Have some," he suggested.

Cathryn waved a declining hand, and he leaned back in his own chair. "What can I do for you, Señora Harcourt?"

She decided to play it straight. "Someone is terrorizing Paige Morrison. I don't know who, or for what purpose, but I intend to find out."

León's brow furrowed, but he didn't seem to doubt her statement. Instead, he said, "You and she —you are old friends?"

"College days."

He nodded, understanding. "Then you must do all you can," he said simply. "What do you need from me?"

"I want to know how you came by that potted plant. Who delivered it?"

"*Vale,* that I can help you with. I know the florist personally, and she delivered it herself. I will ask her tomorrow."

Cathryn hesitated. "Can you ask her tonight?"

He rolled his eyes, pinning her with a wry gaze.

Leaning forward, Cathryn reminded him, "You said—very correctly, I might add—that I should do all I can."

Sighing, he pulled a mobile phone from the pocket of his robe and dialed a number. He spoke for a moment in rapid Spanish, then turned to Cathryn.

"She arrived at her shop this morning to find an envelope with a request for the plant to be delivered here to Mrs. Morrison, and the cash to pay for it."

Cathryn said, "What was the signature on the note?"

He relayed the question and shook his head. "No signature. Anything else?"

Cathryn lifted a shoulder. "Not right now. Please thank her for me."

"*Por supuesto.*"

Riding the elevator up to the seventh floor, Cathryn thought about the ragged bits of information she was gathering. It felt like the beginning of something, like when her first plot ideas came to mind, floating and formless until she shaped them into a cohesive story.

She hoped she could coax the true shape of things from what she was learning and find an end to this nightmare for her friend.

Back in her own apartment, she undressed and slid beneath the sheets, tired and still hungry. Regretting the loss of a fine steak dinner, she dreamed about it as she drifted off to sleep.

And woke an hour later to thunderous pounding at her door.

Cathryn pulled on a pair of sweatpants, wriggling into a T-shirt as she hurried to answer the frantic hammering. Paige stood in the corridor, her gray-blonde hair a tangled mess, dark shadows and creases beneath her eyes.

All of it punctuated by the reddening three-pronged scratch across her left cheek.

"She was there, Cathryn! Watching me while I slept."

Cathryn led her to the sofa, snagging the little first aid kit she kept in a drawer of the end table. Little beads of blood were oozing from the scratch and the skin around it was enflamed. Paige hugged herself, shivering, while Cathryn dabbed antiseptic over the wound.

"I heard someone whisper my name, right next to my ear. I felt her breath." Paige's voice cracked and trembled, like a warped and scratchy vinyl record. "I woke up and she was standing over me."

"Did you see her face?" Cathryn asked.

Paige closed her eyes. "No. It was hidden in shadows. Or maybe she was wearing a mask. I couldn't see. I was frozen in terror, and there was a peculiar smell in the air that somehow made everything more frightening."

Cathryn squeezed her friend's shoulder. "I'm so sorry, Paige. Can you describe the smell? Was it perfume?"

Paige shook her head. "I don't know what it was." She sniffed and her voice grew husky with unshed tears. "She leaned over me and I tried to scream, but I couldn't make a sound."

She broke off, shuddering, then gulped and choked out the rest of the story. "Her long black hair brushed my face, then she slashed me across the cheek and disappeared."

Paige caught at Cathryn's hand, held it tight. "Oh, it was awful! I can't take much more of this, Cathryn. What am I going to do?"

Cathryn kept her voice steady, her tone matter-of-fact. "I'm going to call the police."

Paige bit her lip. "Please don't," she said. "It's useless. I called them last week when I thought I saw someone on the balcony, trying to get in. They investigated and found nothing out of place."

"Well now—unfortunately—there's a little more for them to work with. This scratch across your face, for instance."

Paige still held her hand and Cathryn felt the trembling in her fingers. "Please don't call them. They think I'm loony. My Spanish isn't very good, but I know *poco loco* when I hear it. They won't take me seriously."

"*I'm* taking you seriously. Give me the key to your place. I'll investigate."

"No, Cathryn. Not tonight," Paige pleaded. "Let me stay here, and please don't leave me alone."

"I won't. I promise."

Cathryn tucked Paige into her own bed and curled up on the couch where she had line of sight to both the front door and the balcony slider. As she floated toward sleep, she reflected that she wasn't making much progress on her research project on crime in Andalusia.

Then again, maybe she was.

The click of the front door lock had Cathryn bolting from the couch as watery sunlight trickled in from the balcony. A woman with long dark hair was letting herself into the apartment. Cathryn's heart leapt into her throat until she registered the plastic bucket in the woman's arms, filled with spray bottles, sponges, and brushes of varying size and shape.

It was Wednesday. The maid's day for coming.

"Buenos dias, Señora."

Cathryn released her breath and ran a hand through her hair, smoothing it down. "Good morning, Soledad."

"You sleep on couch? Something wrong with your bed? I fix?"

"*No hay problema*," Cathryn told her. "I had a friend sleep over. Let's not wake her yet."

"*Vale, Señora*. I start in here."

While Soledad dusted and ran the vacuum cleaner, Cathryn scrambled eggs and made toast. By the time it was ready, Paige had joined her on a bar stool at the counter.

"I prescribe a day in the sun," Cathryn said. "Let's eat breakfast and go to the beach."

The day was fine, the salt air wafting on a gentle breeze as they descended the stairs to an expanse of shadowed sand. Gulls called overhead, their melancholy cries echoing against the rhythmic swell of the waves.

A woman in a blue bikini lay stretched out on an enormous rainbow-striped beach blanket, a shaggy golden retriever at her side. As they drew near, the dog rose, barking, and ran to greet them.

"Elmo!" Paige cried, sinking to a knee to give the dog a vigorous rub down. He wriggled with pleasure, tongue lolling as he followed them back to his mistress. The woman raised up on an elbow and removed her sunglasses, waving a welcoming hand.

"Come on in," she said. "The water's fine."

"How would you know?" Paige teased. "You never actually go in."

"Salt water makes me itchy." Shifting her long, well-tanned legs, the woman rolled into a sitting position and peered at Cathryn with curiosity.

"Kim," Paige said, "meet one of my oldest and dearest friends, Cathryn Harcourt."

Cathryn spread her beach towel out on the sand and Paige did the same. "Kim actually lives here,"

Paige told her. "Not just vacationing like you and me."

"Really? Cathryn asked. "What brought you to Spain?"

"US Navy," Kim said, waving a hand toward the nearby Naval base. "My husband's a Seabee, on the construction battalion. We're here for a three-year tour."

"Are you enjoying it? Doing any traveling?"

Kim replaced her sunglasses and stretched out on the blanket. "Charlie isn't able to get away much," she said. "But we've been to Morocco and Gibraltar, as well as Seville. They're close enough for day trips."

"Wonderful," Cathryn said. "I hope you'll get a chance to do more. In the meantime, you've got a lovely setup here."

"Mmm," Kim agreed, lifting her face to the sun. Cathryn watched the sweep of dark hair settle around the woman's shoulders. Shifting her gaze, she took in the well-manicured fingernails, long and red, entirely capable of inflicting a nasty scratch on vulnerable skin.

She didn't really think Kim could be Paige's night visitor, but she wasn't ready to rule it out, either. If Jane's sister truly was stalking Paige, intent on revenge, she might be hiding behind any innocent façade.

After a lunch of crusty rolls stuffed with crab salad, bought from a seaside bakery, Cathryn and Paige climbed the stairs, returning to the apartment building for a siesta. While Paige napped, Cathryn made a call back to the States.

Zach Dillinger, a PI she sometimes consulted, would just be starting his workday. After exchanging pleasantries, Cathryn said, "If an investigator, such as yourself, were to dig into a long-ago event, like a juvenile case of vehicular manslaughter, how would he go about it?"

"Is this research for a book, Cathryn?"

She hesitated. "Not initially, although it may spark an idea for a future plot. No, Zach, it's a bit more personal this time. An old friend is in trouble."

She heard him clear his throat. "As you are no doubt aware, juvenile records are sealed," he told her. "But sometimes there are ways around that."

"I'm not after the information in the file. I just want to find out who else might have accessed it."

She gave him Paige's maiden name, the approximate time frame, and any other information she thought might be useful. "I'll do some poking around and get back to you," he told her.

"Thanks, Zach. We'll talk later."

Ending the call, Cathryn peeked in on Paige and found her curled in a ball, gently snoring. Moving quietly, she let herself into the corridor and punched the elevator down button.

This time, when she found León in his daytime office, he was fully and properly dressed in slacks and polo, only a hint of his curly chest hair showing at the open collar. He greeted her with a grin.

"*Hola, Señora.* I am at your service. How can I help?"

Cathryn indicated the open door. "May I?" she asked, pulling it closed at his nod. "I'm sorry to tell you this," she said, sinking into a chair next to his mahogany desk, "but Paige Morrison's situation is getting worse."

"*Qué pasó?* What's happened now?"

She told him about the previous night's events.

"Did you call the police?" he asked.

"Paige preferred not to. She feels they wouldn't take her complaints seriously."

León pursed his lips. "As manager of this building, I could consider their point of view," he said, giving her an apologetic look. "I don't like to think crimes are occurring beneath this roof. Is this not perhaps the result of stress or an overactive imagination?"

Cathryn glowered at him. "Someone raked her across the cheek last night," she pointed out. "I've seen her face and it's no figment of the imagination."

He raised his hands in surrender. *"Vale,* I believe you. What do you suggest we do?"

We. Cathryn felt some comfort in having him come over to her side. She only hoped he would comply with her next request.

"These troubles followed her here from the States," she told him. "Which of your tenants booked their rooms in the days following Paige's arrival?"

He stared at her reproachfully. "I can't just dispense that information," he said. "My tenants have a right to privacy."

They locked eyes for a count of ten before Cathryn sighed. "Will you just verify, then, if any women with long dark hair fit that time frame? Anita Wilson, for example."

"I can at least set your mind at ease on that score. The Wilsons moved in before Paige Morrison's arrival."

"Really?" Cathryn said, surprised. "How long before?"

He shrugged. "A few days, a week." With a sly look, he said, "I will not consult the register on this. I am speaking only as an observant neighbor, you understand."

"I thank you, dear neighbor, for your quick and ready powers of observation." She paused. "And what about Soledad, the cleaning woman you recommended?"

"Soledad! She is the daughter of a close friend," he assured her. "Above reproach."

"That may be, but when did she start cleaning apartments in this building?" Cathryn asked pointedly.

León sighed. "Soledad has been working at another of my properties for more than two years. She transferred here just last week, about the time you arrived," he admitted. "But I am sure this means nothing."

"Did you initiate the transfer?"

He gave her a dark look. "No, it was at her request."

Cathryn rose. "Thank you, León. Can you tell me which apartment she is cleaning now? I need to speak with her."

Deciding to use the stairs, Cathryn climbed to the third floor. León had been reluctant to reveal the number of the apartment where Soledad could be found, but Cathryn had persuaded him with the argument that his friend's daughter must be innocent, as he believed. She might, however, possess information that could help lay this whole thing to rest.

Panting only slightly, Cathryn emerged from the stairwell and started along the corridor. Ahead she saw the sort of cart a bellboy uses to deliver luggage to the upper floors of a hotel. She knew the apartment building kept such a cart in the utility room next to the elevators for tenants to use.

The cart was loaded with bags of groceries and household items and stood next to an open apartment door. As Cathryn passed, she heard a murmur of voices from inside. She'd taken several steps beyond when the voices registered in her memory.

Anita and Gerald Wilson.

Cathryn halted and crept closer to the open door, staying close to the wall. Shamelessly, she strained to hear their conversation.

"...they can go on this bottom shelf," Anita was saying.

"Very well, my darling," Gerald replied, and something more that was lost amid a clattering of pots and pans. Then Cathryn heard, "Don't worry about the canned goods, my sweet Anita Sue—I'll take care of that."

"Way ahead of you." Anita's voice was suddenly loud in the corridor as she dipped forward to grip a bag of canned vegetables and saw Cathryn standing there.

Cathryn quickly assumed a pondering expression. "Sorry," she said. "I didn't mean to snoop, but the labels on those cans caught my eye. I'm not familiar with these Spanish brands. Have you tried that one? Is it any good?"

Anita broke into a smile. "Cathryn! Good to see you. How's Paige? We haven't seen her since...you know, last night at the restaurant. Is she okay?"

"Oh yes, she's quite recovered. Did you and Gerald have a good dinner?"

Anita snorted. "Have you ever had a bad dinner at an Argentinian steakhouse?"

"Come to think of it," Cathryn said, "I have not."

Gerald stepped out into the hallway. "Oh, hello," he said, lifting the bag from his wife's arms. "Did you come to visit?"

"No, I won't bother you. I was just passing by." Hoping to ferret out more information about Anita's movements the night before, she added, "Did you two do anything fun after dinner? Dancing? Moonlit walk on the beach?"

Gerald laughed. "Not a chance! We ate too

much, drank too much, and came straight home to sleep it off."

Cathryn flapped a hand toward the cart. "Well, I'll let you get back to it," she said. "See you around."

As she continued down the hallway, she reflected that while Gerald was sleeping off a slew of margaritas, Anita could have crept out without his knowledge. She turned the corner, glad to be out of the Wilsons' sight as she knocked at Apartment 342.

After a moment, the door opened, and Soledad's hesitant face peeked out. "Oh, hello Señora Harcourt. I'm sorry, the Cuadrados are not at home right now."

"That's okay, Soledad. I came to see you."

The hesitation turned to wariness. "Me? *Por qué?*"

"There are some things I would like to ask you."

The maid shook her head, the dark hair tumbling around her shoulders and Cathryn saw the door closing—literally—on this opportunity to question the young woman. She put out a hand, speaking quickly.

"I'll only take a moment of your time. Please," she added. "It's important."

Soledad gave her a stoic glance, squaring her shoulders. "What do you want to know?"

Cathryn wasted no more time. Getting right to

the meat of the matter, she asked, "Why did you come here, Soledad? To this building, at this time?"

The woman's chin rose a notch higher. With a touch of defiance, she said, "Why shouldn't I? America is not the only country whose people can do as they please."

Cathryn dipped her head in acknowledgement. "You are right, of course. But something brought you here and now. Will you please tell me?"

The woman's eyes narrowed suspiciously. "Did he send you?"

Cathryn blinked. "He? Who do you mean, Soledad?"

The maid studied her, and Cathryn sensed a shift in her attitude.

"No one sent me, I promise you," she hurried to say. "It was my own idea to seek you out. I have a friend in trouble and I'm trying to help her."

"You have nothing to do with José?" Soledad pressed.

"Nothing," Cathryn assured her. "I know nothing about this José."

The maid's shoulders relaxed, and her face softened. She regarded Cathryn solemnly, her dark eyes huge and strangely haunted. "I came here to get away from José," she admitted. "He does not respect my right to say no. He always wanting and wanting, and never leaving me alone. I had to escape him."

Cathryn nodded sympathetically. "I see. So, you asked for a transfer to this building. To get away from José."

The maid lifted a palm, her expression rueful. *"Cada maestrillo tiene su librillo.* Each of us must do what we think best."

"La verdad," Cathryn agreed. "I wish you success. Thank you for telling me, Soledad. *Adios."*

Back in the stairwell, Cathryn finished her climb to the seventh floor just as the phone in her pocket jingled. Pausing to catch her breath, she tapped to accept the call and greeted her PI contact.

"Zach, how's it going?"

"Good, Cathryn. I managed to unearth some information for you."

"Wonderful. Let's have it."

"I called the local courthouse, but the cagey clerk wouldn't give me anything. So I contacted an associate who lives in the area and he agreed to go in person and see what he could dig up. Turns out a woman calling herself Susan Fleming attempted several times to access the juvie file, claiming she was the sister of the deceased and had a right to know what happened."

"Susan Fleming? Paige did mention a sister

named Susan. Was she granted access?"

"Officially, no. But my associate questioned the clerk in charge during this Susan woman's last visit. He suspects money might have changed hands for a peek at the file."

"I see," Cathryn said. "Thank you, Zach. Send me a bill for your time and give my thanks to your associate."

Cathryn entered her apartment and went to the glass slider overlooking the beach. She gazed out at the distant horizon where the setting sun spread a copper mantle over the shifting water, turning it into a molten sea, matching the ideas in her brain.

She thought about the women she'd met over the last two days who fit the age range of the dead girl's sister and the physical description of Paige's attacker.

Despite Soledad's long dark hair and access to the building's apartments, Cathryn crossed her off the list as being too young. And she had no discernible motive for terrorizing a middle-aged American tourist.

That left Kim, Paige's friend from the beach. She had the requisite hairstyle and a set of claws capable of inflicting the sort of wound marring Paige's cheek. She could conceivably be the sister in question, be-friending Paige on the beach for reasons of her own.

Anita Wilson fit the bill, as well. And probably a

dozen more women in the vicinity.

Who, if any of them, was tormenting her old college roommate?

And why?

Cathryn slept late the next morning. She'd looked in on Paige the night before and found her friend white-faced and distraught. Paige had gratefully accepted Cathryn's offer to sleep on the couch, to be on hand if anything else occurred.

The couch was long enough, and the pillow and blanket Paige provided were comfortable. But Cathryn woke with the sort of crick in her neck that would be with her all day. As she sat massaging the muscles in her shoulders, she heard the flush of a toilet and seconds later, Paige padded into the living room.

"Good morning," Cathryn said. "Did you sleep okay?"

"Yes, fine."

The dark shadows beneath Paige's eyes said otherwise, but Cathryn didn't challenge her on it. Instead, she asked, "What are your plans for the day?"

Paige walked to the balcony slider and pressed the button to raise the heavy persiana shades, letting the weak morning sun dribble into the room. The day was overcast, gray-tinted clouds roiling in the distance, seagulls winging in the foreground, their plaintive cries faintly audible through the glass.

"I wanted to go to the gypsy market and look for those little—"

She broke off with a strangled gasp, standing frozen at the window, her face twisting in anguish. Cathryn jumped from the sofa and dashed to her friend's side. The balcony afforded a spectacular view of the beach, a wide swath of pale brown sand stretching out beneath, waves creaming up along the edge.

And written in large block letters on the slate of sand, it said:

I AM JANE.

"That's it," Cathryn said. "Enough of this nonsense. We are getting to the bottom of this. Today."

She put an arm around Paige and led her to the sofa, wrapping the blanket, still warm from her own body, around her friend.

"Let's get some breakfast," she continued. "And then I am going to talk to all the women on my suspect list, starting with..."

A sudden memory flashed across her mind, raising a flag that suggested here was something she needed to pay attention to. Focusing, she tried to hone in on the thought that fluttered at the edge of consciousness. She recalled the snippet of inconsequential conversation she'd heard yesterday while passing the Wilson's apartment.

Anita Sue. Gerald had called his wife sweet Anita Sue. Could Anita be the Susan she was looking for?

"My first stop will be the Wilsons," she announced.

Paige's stricken eyes grew wider. "Anita? No, Cathryn. She was already here when I arrived. They didn't follow me."

"Someone keeping close tabs on you, as it seems Susan is doing, would know your plans and act accordingly, staying a step ahead."

Paige shuddered. "I can't endure much more of this."

"And you won't have to," Cathryn assured her.

After a hasty omelet, Cathryn and Paige took the elevator down to the third floor and knocked at the Wilsons' apartment. After several moments, Cathryn tried again, but no one came to answer her knock.

"Let's try the beach," Paige suggested.

"Good idea. We might find Kim there as well."

"Kim? You suspect her, too?"

"Right now, I suspect everyone."

As they hurried along the sidewalk, Cathryn spotted Gerald Wilson strolling the promenade, puffing on his pipe. They rushed to meet him.

"Good morning, Gerald," Cathryn said. "Where's Anita?"

"Back at the apartment. She's not feeling well today."

"We stopped by the apartment," Paige said. "No one answered."

"She was probably sleeping. She pulled the persianas in the bedroom before I left. Is there something I can help you with?"

"Maybe," Cathryn replied. "Did Anita have a sister named Jane?"

Gerald stopped walking, his eyes wide and startled. "No, you're not going to talk to Anita about Jane," he said decisively. "That would be far too upsetting for her. Jane died years ago, and Anita doesn't like to remember it. She never even told me about her sister's death until after we were married."

"How long have you been married?" Cathryn asked.

"We just celebrated our first anniversary last month."

Cathryn heard a faint whimper from Paige and noticed her old roommate was hugging herself, her face a mask of misery. She looked like a piece of china about to break.

Making her voice firm, Cathryn said, "Gerald, we need to speak with Anita right away. I don't want to distress her, but it can't be helped."

"I don't like this," he grumbled, putting out his pipe. "But I'll see if she's willing to speak with you."

As they walked, Cathryn put her arm around Paige. "Are you all right?" she asked, feeling the tremors in her friend's fragile bones.

"No," Paige said. "I have a dreadful feeling. A sense of doom. I feel it in the air."

Gerald let them into the apartment and motioned them onto the sofa before disappearing down the hall. A moment later, Cathryn heard an anguished cry.

"No! Oh, no. Please, no."

She rushed to the bedroom, stopping behind Gerald's petrified form. Over his shoulder, she saw Anita Wilson sprawled on the bed, an empty pill bottle by her side. Pushing Gerald gently aside, she felt for a pulse but knew by the frozen rictus on Anita's face that the woman had passed beyond any help she could offer.

In the dim light seeping in through the chinks in the shades, Cathryn saw something clutched in the dead woman's hand. Without touching anything, she bent to peer closer. It was a photograph of two young girls together, laughing in the sunshine.

And on the back of the photo, she could make out a single word.

The name Jane.

Cathryn watched the last rays of sun streak across the ocean and melt into darkness as she stood at the window in Paige's apartment. Paige sat curled in a chair, her feet drawn up, arms locked around her knees, silent and shell-shocked. Gerald slumped on the sofa, hands splayed on either side, palms up, his face blank, eyes staring.

All three of them jumped when a sudden loud knock sounded at the door. Cathryn went to answer it, admitting a pair of blue-uniformed members of the Policía Local. Both held their hats in hand as they entered, solemn-faced, and expressed their condolences.

Cathryn, Paige, and Gerald had already given their statements at the scene before retiring to Paige's apartment to commiserate and wait for what came next. The older officer, a slim gray-haired man with an impressive Roman nose, approached Gerald and spoke in a soft, melodious voice.

"I apologize for intruding at such a time like this," he said. "But I must clear off a few matters before we can proceed any further. Is okay?"

Cathryn saw the Adam's apple bob in Gerald's throat as he swallowed. "My wife," he said, his voice coming out in a croak. "I didn't know, I didn't think she would..."

His words trailed off and he swallowed hard again. The officer held out the photograph, bent and crumpled, that had been clutched in Anita's hand. It was encased in a sheet of plastic, but the handwriting on the back was clearly visible now.

Summerhill, Susan and Jane.

"The girls in the photo?" prompted the officer. "Your wife, and...?"

"Her sister, Jane. She was killed decades ago by an out-of-control teenage driver. Anita never got over it and recently she's been...brooding on it. But I never imagined she would harm herself. I didn't realize how badly it was affecting her. It happened so long ago."

"These things catch up when someone is already depressed," the officer said. "Everything stacks up together. *Entiende?*"

Gerald sank his head into his hands. "Yes, I understand," he murmured. "I just wish I'd done something to help."

"Do not blame yourself. We found a box of old pictures similar to this one." He turned to Paige. "As well as several recent photos of you." He paused. "With red X's marked across them. Do you know why this may be?"

Paige's answer was so muted that Cathryn barely heard her say, "Because I killed her."

The officer frowned. "Are you confessing to murdering Mrs. Wilson?"

"No!" Paige burst out, her pale face going red. "I was the out-of-control teenage driver. I think Anita wanted to kill *me*." She choked back a sob. "And I don't blame her!"

Gerald stared, speechless. Cathryn went to her friend huddled in the chair and bent to put an arm around her. She'd caught a glimpse of that box of photos. An open shoebox on the bed beside Anita's body. She'd seen those red crosses.

And she'd seen something else she'd like to get a closer look at.

A sheet of pink paper printed with wedding bells at the top and a scrawl of writing down the page. She'd be willing to bet Gerald and Anita had written their own wedding vows and that the pink paper contained Anita's composition.

And that the blue paper behind it held Gerald's own vows.

An awkward silence fell in the room, broken only by a periodic sniffle from Paige. The officer in charge made a slight bow from the waist.

"It should not take long to wrap this up," he said. "Again, I apologize for the intrusion and I'm so sorry for your loss."

The officers departed and Gerald let out a long, mournful sigh. He looked at Paige. "I don't hold you responsible for Anita's death. She clearly had mental issues I didn't know about."

Paige gulped, looking small and miserable. "I'm so sorry."

Gerald made a brushing motion with his hands, as if to push the whole thing from his sight. "I'm glad to hear they'll soon close the case," he said. "I'm ready to go home."

"Yes," Cathryn said. "Once they find the private detective and confirm the details, I'm sure they'll complete the file and let you leave the country."

"Private detective? You've lost me, Cathryn. What are you talking about?"

"Anita would have needed help to discover the identity and current whereabouts of the woman she held responsible for her sister's death." She paused, watching Gerald closely. "You arrived here a week or so before Paige—how did that come about?"

Gerald seemed at a loss for words. Finally, he said,

"I don't even remember. We were in the south of France and suddenly Anita said she didn't want to be there anymore. She suggested Spain, she made the arrangements, and...we came."

Cathryn nodded. "She must have received word from her PI, letting her know where to find Paige."

"No," Gerald said, anger tinging his voice. "We got here first. Paige came after."

"Yes, but...Paige, how much time passed between when you booked this apartment and when you actually arrived here?"

Paige had unspooled from her curled up position. She stared at Cathryn, puzzlement in her eyes. "I had to wait almost two weeks for all the arrangements to come together," she explained.

"Plenty of time for Anita's investigator to discover your plans and pass on that information. And then," Cathryn added, "someone must have helped her write those poems."

"What poems?" Gerald asked. His face had grown florid, his brow creased.

"Paige, do you still have those poems Anita left for you? Your wife," she said to Gerald, "has been terrorizing Paige for some time now." She raised her eyebrows. "You knew nothing about it?"

"Nothing."

Paige left the room and came back moments

later, holding a plastic bag containing several cards computer-printed with the poetic verses. Gerald glanced at them and gave an aggrieved shrug.

"If, as you say, Anita wrote those poems, I'm sure she composed them herself. She was quite an eloquent writer, you know. And now, if you'll excuse me, León has prepared a room for me to stay in until this miserable business is over."

He left the apartment, shutting the door a little more firmly than necessary. Cathryn watched his exit, her gaze fixed on the door long after he was gone.

"I'm sorry for bringing you into this Cathryn, and ruining your vacation," Paige said.

"I'm not on vacation," Cathryn replied. "I'm doing research, and you've helped me immensely. You have nothing to apologize for."

Paige gave her a bitter smile. "I have a mountain of a mess to apologize for. A woman just committed suicide over something I did. It's just so...sad."

"I disagree," Cathryn said. "Sad is not the word. It's wicked. Anita Wilson did not kill herself. She was murdered."

"What! Oh, Cathryn—what are you saying?"

"I'm saying Gerald Wilson murdered his wife. I just need to find a way to prove it."

Later that evening, Cathryn let herself out of Paige's apartment and made her way down to the fifth floor. She'd been busy in the interim—talking, determining, arranging. Once more, she'd prevailed upon León for information, and after a few half-hearted sputters of protest, he'd told her where to find Gerald.

Reaching the apartment, she raised her fist and gave an authoritative knock. Gerald opened the door, his questioning face turning hostile when he saw who'd come calling.

"What do you want?" he growled.

Cathryn eyed him levelly. "I want to let you know that I'm going to the police first thing in the morning. I plan to tell them everything I know."

Gerald gave a derisive snort. "What could you know? We met you only two days ago. My Anita was alive, and now she's dead. I don't think I want to hear anything you have to say."

"You may want to listen to this," Cathryn warned. "I'm a writer, Mr. Wilson. I know that a person's style of writing is distinctive. Not as definitive as a fingerprint, perhaps, but a style analyst will easily determine that the woman who wrote those wedding vows in the box taken by the police is not the same person who wrote the notes and poems to Paige."

Gerald's eyes narrowed, but he said nothing.

"Anita told me herself that she couldn't string a decent sentence together unless it was written in code and executed a command," Cathryn continued. "I'm willing to bet an analyst, comparing those poems to the wedding vows you wrote—also in the box held by the police—would conclude it was you who wrote those poems."

Gerald's lips curled in a nasty grin. "That's thin, Cathryn. Really. I doubt it would hold up in a court of law."

"Maybe you're right," Cathryn agreed. "But when the police speak with the PI you hired to find the driver responsible for Jane's death, I believe the pieces will start adding up to something more substantial."

Eyes smoldering, Gerald moved to slam the door, but Cathryn planted her foot in the way.

"You are an evil man, Gerald Wilson. You married Anita for her money, planning all along to find a way to get rid of her. When she told you about her sister's tragic death, she handed you the key to her own demise. You made it look like Anita was deranged and out for revenge. And when she couldn't stand the pain any longer, she killed herself."

"Apparently that's what happened," Gerald said, his eyes taunting her. "And you can't prove otherwise."

"I won't have to. You're not as clever as you think you are. I'm sure you left plenty of indicators behind."

"Such as?"

Cathryn shrugged. "Perhaps strands of hair from that wig you wore when you attacked Paige in her bedroom. Or traces of your Turkish tobacco in the wound you left on her face. It's just a matter of time before the pieces fall into place and you're arrested for the murder of your wife."

"You're crazy!" Gerald snarled.

Cathryn removed her foot from the doorframe. "Goodnight, Mr. Wilson."

Turning, she walked down the corridor, keeping her pace even and unhurried, showing she wasn't afraid.

But she was.

Her heart pounded painfully inside her chest and her palms, clammy with sweat, shook like leaves in a windstorm. When she turned the knob on the stairwell door, her hand slipped, and she had to tighten her grip.

Glancing back, she saw no one. The hour was late, and the hallway was deserted. Her footsteps echoed eerily in the barren chamber of the stairwell as she walked to the top of the marble staircase and stood looking down, breathing deeply to calm herself.

She stood motionless, staring down the long flight of hard stone and listening hard. After a moment, she heard it—the metallic click of the door opening behind her, the padding of soft-soled shoes. The hairs on the back of her neck rose like tiny sensors as she felt the presence of another person at her back.

"You shouldn't have meddled, Cathryn. Without you sticking your nose in, this all would have worked like a charm."

Cathryn braced herself, felt the rough hands grip her shoulders. But she was ready for it. Crouching down, she clutched the banister rail and held on tight. She heard a scuffle and shout behind her as the two police officers grabbed Gerald and pulled him off her.

León helped her to her feet and wrapped his arms around her, steadying her.

"Ay, caramba!" He spoke the words against her hair. "Are you okay?"

"I'm perfectly fine, León. You needn't hold on to me so tightly."

He grinned. "My intentions are purely honorable, I assure you."

Cathryn felt her face go red. She laughed.

"I never thought otherwise."

The next morning, Cathryn walked once again with Paige on the cool sand of the beach. The sun shone lemony yellow up on the promenade, its rays yet to reach and warm the stretch of shingle rimming the murmuring waves.

A freshening breeze carried the smell of salt and seaweed, reminding Cathryn of something that had danced at the edge of her awareness ever since they'd accosted Gerald on the promenade above.

"Do you remember how you felt that sense of doom yesterday?" she asked Paige. "Right before we went up and found Anita?"

Paige shivered. "I'll never forget it."

"I think I know why you felt that way."

Paige gave her a sidelong glance. "Are you trying to tell me I'm clairvoyant?"

Cathryn smiled. "No, something much simpler than that." She paused. "You smelled trouble."

Paige wrinkled her brow. "So, I'm a bloodhound?"

"No. Gerald was smoking his Turkish tobacco when we encountered him. I believe you smelled that same odor on him while he was leaning over you in a wig and nightgown."

Paige gasped. "You're right! Now that you say that, I can smell it again and it brings back that sense of terror." She let out a long breath and patted herself on the chest. "You have no idea how much better I feel now, Cathryn. Thank you so much for rooting out my demons."

Cathryn heard a shout and looked up to see León loping toward them, kicking up sand in his wake.

"I wanted you to know," he said when he reached them. "When the police hinted that you had a recording of your conversation with him last night, Gerald made a full confession. He'll be extradited and tried in the U.S. for first degree murder. And thanks to you, Cathryn, the prosecutor ought to be able to make the charges stick."

Paige nodded her head vigorously. "Fantastic!"

Cathryn gazed out over the blue-green horizon, hazy with mist, and pondered the fate of Gerald Wilson and others like him. She shivered.

"So callous," she said. "So calculated. He'd planned it for months, knowing Anita had to die in a way that would make him appear blameless. He hired and bribed and cajoled his plan into action, all the while playing the adoring husband. That's cold!"

Paige hooked an arm in hers. "Colder than gazpacho," she agreed.

León turned, peering up at the apartment building looming above them. "Sadly, I've got to get back to my desk, ladies. I'll see you later."

Cathryn watched him retreat across the sand, the backs of his calves' brown and well-muscled, covered in curly dark hairs. To match the rest of him.

"Ugh," Paige grimaced. "Let's talk about something cheerier. I'm glad my Walter left me with a lot of good memories. I can think of him with sincere fondness. Right to the end."

"Same goes for my Ryan," Cathryn added. "Here's to good husbands. Not perfect men, but good men who tried hard and lived well." She paused. "I still miss mine so much."

"Me too," Paige said. "Terribly sometimes."

Cathryn let her gaze wander once more to the far horizon, the farthest point before the sea dipped out of view and the unknown began.

"Times like these," she agreed.

FOUL TROUBLE

DIANA DEVERELL

FBI Special Agent Dawna Shepherd perched on one of the two metal chairs in the front half of Copenhagen's Italian Corner Pizza Shop. She inhaled the delicious scent of yeast dough baking in a hot oven. Her mouth watered, though she knew that pizza would be hours old before she got a taste of it.

She sat with her back to the tiny store's show window and glass entry door. A metal table with a foot-diameter round top separated her chair from the empty one.

A cooler only a few inches shorter than her six-foot-three-inches sat to her right. It displayed bottled soft drinks and beers for sale. A small waist-high freezer chest sporting an ad for Snickers Ice Cream Bars sat beside it.

A chest-high counter separated the customer area from the pizza prep and sales section at the rear of the room.

High on the back wall, a colorful menu listed the pizzas and sandwiches for sale. Below, to the left, was a wooden interior door.

Dawna figured that behind the wooden door lay a restroom, supply storage area, and cleanup station. The counter was open at the end in front of the door, allowing the chef access to the front half of the shop.

A five-foot wide metal pizza oven sat beside the

door. On the oven's other side, a vertical rotisserie kept a huge piece of roast lamb in proximity to what appeared to be a heat lamp.

Zulfiqar, the sixty-eight-year-old owner of the shop, had his back to her. He bent over the counter, cleaning up for the next order. He wore a white bib apron over his black T-shirt and brown corduroy pants.

Short and scrawny, he came up only to Dawna's shoulder and she guessed he weighed less than a hundred pounds.

Dawna glanced outside at the cloudy sky. Today was the second Saturday in February and she'd dressed for the fifty-degree weather in her usual winter workout outfit. Black zip-front fleece-lined and water-resistant jacket over her sweat-wicking black T-shirt, matching leggings, and black running shoes.

Her blonde curls were covered by a black cuffed knit cap sporting a tiny gold applique with TEXAS LONGHORNS centered above a tiny map of her home state. She'd played basketball for the Lady Longhorns for four seasons and remained loyal to her alma mater.

She didn't need the cap indoors, but headgear was part of her cover today so she kept it on.

For the same reason, she had her cellphone in

hand, video and audio recording, with an open line to her team leader, hidden nearby. Nic Nygaard would hear every word spoken in this shop during the next hour.

He'd be listening for her to utter the code word Valentine, calling for immediate intervention.

The shop was located on her path between the fitness center she'd joined for her eight-week posting to Denmark and her temporary lodgings.

She'd popped into the place in January, on her first Saturday in Copenhagen, and asked the owner to recommend a pizza for her to take home for a post-workout lunch.

Zulfiqar obliged. He had dark hair and golden-brown skin. He looked like he might be Italian, though she soon learned he'd been born farther east, in Pakistan.

He'd taught English in a Pakistani high school before emigrating to Denmark five years earlier. He told her that his native language was one of more than seventy spoken in Pakistan and he was also fluent in Arabic.

Zulfiqar insisted she'd love his shawarma pizza and he was right. The tender bits of roasted lamb, topped with chopped lettuce and sour cream dressing, had delighted her taste buds. Though she had to be cautious with the small covered plastic cup of fiery chili sauce he added to her order.

His terrific pizza, his friendly manner, and his excellent English made Dawna his regular Saturday noontime customer.

While fixing and baking her pies, he practiced his English with her, testing his Britishisms against her slang. He'd been appalled by her casual approach to grammar and charmed by the basketball lingo that spiced her stories of life in Texas.

Both enjoyed the back-and-forth.

And Dawna, especially, liked the pleasant contrast with the special assignment that had pulled her away from her official position in the Counterterrorism Division at FBI headquarters in DC.

Dawna was in Copenhagen on temporary duty with the office of the Legal Attaché at the American Embassy.

Her focus for the past year had been on threats posed by terrorists carrying counterfeit US passports. In January, she was posted to Copenhagen to assist with a Danish National Police investigation into falsification of Danish passports.

Counterfeit documents recently captured by the Danes had the same covers, paper, and stitching as authentic passports. Each also met the international standard for a machine-readable one-hundred-percent polycarbonate data page with imbedded bio-metrics.

The counterfeiters were clearly using top-grade passport finishing equipment to create fake passports that were hard to distinguish from real ones. Clearly a quality product for which they could demand a high price.

Terrorists had to be a significant segment of buyers able and willing to foot the bill.

Danish passports were attractive to terrorists because Denmark is a member of the European Union. Danish passport holders can live and work anywhere in what is called the Schengen Zone for an unlimited time.

Once inside the Schengen Zone, without showing a passport or a visa at a formal border crossing, holders can travel to twenty-two other EU member countries, plus associate members Iceland, Norway, Switzerland, and Lichtenstein.

Four hundred and twenty-three million people live in the Schengen Zone, making it more populous than the US. With half as much square mileage as the continental US, the Zone is densely populated and includes hundreds of airports and maritime ports and land crossing points.

Bad guys with counterfeit Danish passports can

easily stay under the radar in crowded Europe as they plot to create havoc in metropolitan areas.

That the Danish National Police asked for FBI assistance with their investigation told Dawna they were treating theft of their country's identity documents as a grave problem.

She agreed with their assessment.

Dawna'd been thoroughly briefed on the counterfeit passport problem by the time she made her second visit to the Italian Corner Pizza Shop three weeks ago.

She'd been sitting on the same chair and wearing the same outfit, when a glossy white Mercedes cargo van parked on the other side of the glass.

She had a perfect view of the words ROMA RESTAURANT SUPPLY stenciled along the driver's side of the vehicle. The artist could have used Maron Brando as the model for the pizza chef pictured below. The mustache and lumpy jaw were a perfect caricature of the Godfather.

That face made her think of the Corleone's olive oil business—a cover for other illegal ventures.

The man who got out of the van wore a Navy peacoat over his no-name jeans. He was her height, but heavier and broader through the shoulders. He moved to the rear of the van and opened the left-side rear door.

Effortlessly, he pulled a tray of dough mounds and a five-liter container of sauce from the van, and carried his armload inside.

He set both tray and sauce container on the counter beside the credit card reader and laid his open left hand beside them, palm up.

Wearing his usual bib apron and brown corduroy pants, Zulfiqar pulled a fistful of bills from the cash drawer beneath the counter and slapped them onto the waiting hand.

Delivery Guy closed his fist, stuffed the bills into the left pocket of his coat, plucked a receipt from the right pocket, and departed.

Still musing over the Corleones, at first Dawna thought she might have witnessed a protection racket in action. Maybe, to stay in business, pizza chefs had to pay extortionate prices to Roma for their ingredients.

When she got Zulfiqar talking, she discovered the scheme was more sophisticated.

Had he known that Dawna was in law enforcement, he might not have been so open with her.

Dawna was a seasoned interrogator. She knew that when people speak a language that's not their own, they can't pick and choose their words, finessing their meaning.

Caught up in the linguistic adventure, the savvy

Pakistani gave Dawna a clearer picture of the scheme than he likely intended.

Dawna deduced that he paid discount rates for the ingredients he bought from Roma though his bogus receipts showed he was paying premium prices. Roma's additional phony receipts confirmed that he was also regularly replacing his oven, freezer case, and soft-drink cooler with top-of-the-line equipment.

Given the high expenses he could document, his business never showed a taxable profit.

And the criminal boss behind Roma Restaurant Supply got his dirty money laundered. Using the fraudulent paper to legitimize funds earned in other, possibly shadier, ventures.

If any government authority checked the paperwork at the store level, they'd find muddled bookkeeping and suspect only that the shop owner was cheating on his business taxes.

Dawna imagined that little arm-twisting was required to get shop owners to cooperate. They had a financial incentive to cook their books.

Still, participation wasn't voluntary. As Zulfiqar had learned the hard way when he started using his own tomato sauce recipe and buying pricier mozzarella balls from a different vendor.

When he got to that part of his story, his right

hand went to a lump on his nose where a break hadn't been set properly.

Delivery Guy's weekly visit to the Italian Corner Pizza Shop had turned violent that Saturday.

Because Roma didn't allow freelancing. A small shop owner selling pizza in Copenhagen bought his supplies only from Roma if he wanted to stay in business.

At that point in Zulfiqar's account, Dawna saw a possible connection between Delivery Guy's treatment of the shop owner and her investigation into counterfeit passports.

Because the money being laundered through the pizza shops could have been generated by lucrative passport fraud.

The following Monday, Dawna took her brainstorm to Officer Niclas Nygaard, head of the National Police task force investigating the counterfeit passports.

Dawna's mention of Roma Restaurant Supply startled Nic. He hadn't expected Dawna to encounter Roma on her own and connect the company to passport counterfeiting.

Though the National Police strongly suspected Roma was a front for criminal activity, they'd been unable to determine the precise nature of Roma's involvement. They'd probed for tax fraud and sanitation violations at the company's warehouse but uncovered nothing that gave them the right to search the premises thoroughly.

Nic was intrigued by the possible link between pizza shops and money laundering. He suggested busting the Roma employee enforcing control over Zulfiqar. With luck, they could turn the street-level thug and get him to testify against his bosses at Roma.

But they'd need Zulfiqar's cooperation.

Dawna wasn't comfortable involving her friend in a risky police operation. Yet, she realized that he had no better way to get Roma off his back.

When she put the offer in those terms, Zulfiqar reluctantly agreed to work with the task force. On condition that Dawna also took part in the operation.

Dawna wasn't eager to go undercover in an international capital where she couldn't converse in the native language.

Still, she admired the gutsy Pakistani, a Muslim chef in a country where pork roast was the national dish and the natives spoke an unfamiliar language. She reminded herself that she'd brought Zulfiqar into the operation. She had to help him through it.

Nic had planned to place a Danish police officer in the restaurant. Dawna persuaded him that she'd be an equally good witness to Delivery Man's intimidation tactics.

Plus, she was a known customer. Delivery Guy had seen her in the shop last Saturday.

She'd make sure he saw her again the following Saturday. When the op was up and running, she'd be a restaurant fixture.

Today, the second Saturday in February, was the day. Zulfiqar would play the part they'd rehearsed, the rebellious pizza chef.

Delivery Guy would retaliate.

And Nic's team positioned nearby would arrest him for violent assault.

Except that wasn't what happened. Because someone in Nic's shop sold them out.

Which meant that on this critical Saturday, when Delivery Guy pulled up in the van, instead of carrying in supplies, he had with him an equally tall man, twenty pounds heavier, with hands as big as a two small pizza pies.

Dawna's open phone line was sending no message because neither man said a word.

Their behavior told her they knew that the location might be wired and the cops could be listening.

Dawna's anklebone felt naked minus the Velcro-and-polyester holster she normally wore when working undercover.

But she had no law enforcement authority in Denmark, no right to carry a firearm.

Besides, her skin-hugging outfit wouldn't conceal more than the two pair of flex cuffs she'd looped around her middle, beneath the waistband of her leggings.

She'd have to rely on them and her wits to save this op.

Delivery Guy pushed behind the counter, grabbed Zulfiqar, and began dragging him toward the door. The overhead light glinted off the steel in Delivery Guy's hand.

Lifting her phone to her lips with her left hand, Dawna said, "Valentine."

Muscleman's fingers circled her wrist with a clawlike grip, forcing her to drop the phone to the floor. From behind her, he trapped her right arm under his.

Sour breath warmed her neck. She registered the prick of a metal blade beneath her chin.

She knew without looking down that the prick had drawn blood.

Muscleman poked again, silently urging her through the door after Delivery Guy and Zulfiqar.

The Italian Corner Pizza Shop had a prime intersection location near an elementary school with many eighth- and ninth-grade customers for after-school slices on weekdays.

On this cool Saturday afternoon, the sidewalks were empty.

Muscleman pushed Dawna to the right, toward the cargo van double-parked on Aarhusgade with the passenger side facing the pizza shop.

Muscleman swiveled to put Dawna in front of him as he backed toward the van. Shielding himself behind her, the knife stayed against her throat.

She heard the rasp of metal against metal, the sound of the side door sliding along its track.

From the corner of her eye, she saw Delivery Guy shove Zulfiqar through the opening.

A heavy object thudded against bone. Dawna heard Zulfiqar sigh, followed by a thump like a bag of laundry hitting the van's metal floor.

The van's springs squeaked, the engine turned over.

The knife blade left her throat and a knee came up to the base of her spine.

Dawna could picture what came next. Her sprawled on the sidewalk, the van roaring away, Delivery Guy and Muscleman taking off with Zulfiqar.

Planting her pivot foot, she yanked her body around, intending to tumble Muscleman into the vehicle with her body pinning his.

A male voice shouted from the sidewalk. His words were packed with the staccato rhythm of a command she'd recognize in any language: *Stop or I'll shoot!*

Muscleman realized he still needed her as a shield. Using Dawna's own momentum, he pulled her with him into the truck and flipped her to the rear.

She landed on Zulfiqar, her cheek pressed against his.

He grunted without opening his eyes. Pulled away from her. Curled up more tightly.

She guessed that Muscleman had hit Zulfiqar with some version of a blackjack. She had only seconds to prepare for the same treatment.

She'd learned how playing basketball at the University of Texas. The Lady Longhorns hadn't been ladylike. Tough women, they used their bodies in ways the ref didn't catch

A college ballplayer learns to deal with it. She sees an elbow coming that can't be dodged, she does her best to choose where and how to take it.

She protects the base of her neck. She moves away from the force instead of into it. She still goes down—but maybe she won't get concussed.

Dawna made her last-second shift and the weapon hit the back of her skull.

Intense pain shot through the space behind her

eyes. Instead of disappearing, the pain persisted. She wasn't going to slip over the edge into unconsciousness.

She imitated the sigh she'd heard from Zulfiqar and went boneless.

The truck rolled forward and the side door slammed shut.

The vehicle lurched down Aarhusgade.

Dawna peered between slitted eyelids. The knife had vanished from Muscleman's hand, replaced by an ugly pistol.

Dawna eased her arm between Zulfiqar's head and the gritty floor. She caught the scent of cardamom that always surrounded the Pakistani.

Seconds later, that aroma was overpowered by the yeasty smell from the trays of pizza dough racked across the back end. Tubs of sauce and cases of soft drinks lined the far wall. An ice chest sat behind the driver's seat.

She and Zulfiqar lay in the aisle between the side door and the stack on the far wall.

The truck made a tire-squealing turn to the left, followed by another to the right. Centrifugal force flung Dawna and Zulfiqar toward the pizza ingredients and away again.

The truck swerved and crunched over a graveled surface. Turned again and slowed, the vehicle's interior dimming. Engine noise echoed off concrete until the motor stopped.

Up front, the passenger door rattled open. Muscleman leaped out of the truck.

Dawna heard the distant thrum of a different motor and saw the reflection of fluorescent light from a smooth cement floor. They were inside a warehouse.

The driver's door chattered open. The van rocked as Delivery Guy heaved himself out.

Dawna inched forward to peer around the ice chest and out through the windshield.

Her gaze moved across five yards of bare floor to focus on dozens of pallets stacked high with cardboard boxes. Shoved closely together, they looked like a stockade fence.

In the nearest stack, twenty replicas of the Godfather-Chef graphic beamed at her from the sides of the boxes.

This had to be Roma's warehouse.

The drone of a distant motor continued. Neither Delivery Guy nor Muscleman was visible.

She eased her body closer to the front and peered out the open passenger door.

The van was parked in what appeared to be a two-lane canyon cutting through the center of warehouse between mountainous stacks of pizza supplies. Beside them was another van, twin to their own.

A loaded forklift at the rear of the van was silent, the driver's seat empty, as though the operator had left midway through supplying the van.

A lighted passage extended beyond the forklift, ending at a plywood partition rising ten feet high. A door stood open.

Dawna realized she was looking at an area of the warehouse sectioned off to create office space. She saw the back of a computer flatscreen and part of a desk. A ringtone chirped.

Motion caught her eye. She made out the hulking shape of Delivery Guy, pacing near the office. Likely, Muscleman had gone straight to the boss.

Delivery Guy was probably supposed to be guarding her and Zulfiqar. But Delivery Guy had lost his cool after Muscleman threw her into the van. Driving like a maniac to get the easily identifiable van off the streets, he'd foolishly sped to the one place where the cops would expect to find a Roma van.

The Roma boss would not be pleased.

At this point, Delivery Guy was more interested in saving his own skin than in dealing with two unconscious abductees.

Dawna turned her head the other direction, trying to see how the van had gotten inside the warehouse. She spotted a tightly-closed garage door in the wall to their rear. No easy exit that way.

She had to search for a side door out of the building.

She slithered back to Zulfiqar and patted his face, hoping to rouse him.

He moaned and settled deeper into sleep.

She eased the side door open quietly. Grunting, she tugged Zulfiqar to her back. Leaning his chest against her spine, she looped his skinny arms around her neck.

Swinging her legs out of the van, she planted her feet on the cement and grabbed his wrists. Crouching, she eased the Pakistani's lightweight body onto her back.

She scuttled in the direction the van was pointed, toward the pallets, eyes searching for a way between them.

Loud voices sounded from the office area. She couldn't understand the words, but she knew what she'd want to happen if she were the mob boss.

Delivery Guy and Muscleman should have disappeared Zulfiqar without a trace and left no witnesses behind.

The boss would probably order Delivery Guy and Muscleman to escape in different vehicles. He'd assign other thugs to get rid of Dawna and Zulfiqar.

Putting himself in position to pin the whole mess on Delivery Guy. The boss would insist he knew nothing of Delivery Guy's private dealings with the pizza shop owner.

Dawna plunged into a narrow path between pallets, eyes scanning for an opening to the left and away from the office.

What she found, only two pallets deeper into the warehouse, was a wall.

A thick, steel-clad wall with a solid metal door centered into it. She recognized the layout from a summer job she'd had stocking the frozen food section in a supermarket. Her brain identified the humming sound she'd heard as the compressor for the warehouse's subzero storage.

Shoe soles slapped against concrete. The blast of foreign words was loud, sharpened by alarm. Someone had discovered the van was empty.

Dawna clung to Zulfiqar with her right hand, fumbled with her left to find the door handle and shove it down.

The door swung inwards.

She fell through, dropped to one hand and her knees. She let Zulfiqar slip gently to the floor.

Balancing on her backside, using her feet, she shoved the door closed. The click of the latch was hidden by the compressor noise.

Darkness was total and she smelled chilled steel and her own sweat, rank with fear.

Staccato gibberish sputtered beside her. Likely, the language Zulfiqar spoke with his wife and children.

She slid a hand across the floor until she felt the coarse cotton of his apron.

"It's me, Dawna," she whispered.

"And it is I, Zulfiqar," he retorted.

Dawna heard his slight emphasis on the *I*. The icy temperature had slapped him back to consciousness and into schoolteacher mode.

A match flared in his hand.

She stood. "Come on. We have to hide."

"That would be the wiser move," he agreed, rising to his feet.

She glanced around the tightly-packed freezer unit. Cartons of Snickers Ice Cream Bars rose higher than her head, no gaps between the boxes.

She pulled the top three from the nearest stack to see what lay behind them.

Zulfiqar lit a second match, revealing only a new barrier of cartons behind the first.

Dawna narrowed her eyes at the boxes in the next row of stacks. Those boxes had no contours, no edges.

The falseness would have been invisible in the

glare of a fluorescent light. But the softer light from the match flame revealed she was looking at wallpaper. Its smooth surface was broken only by the rectangular, door-shaped outline.

The match guttered out as Dawna slid her hands over the flatness, her fingers finding the door's edge. She pried it open and the compressor noise doubled.

She stepped over the threshold and the floor vibrated through her shoe soles.

Zulfiqar slipped in behind her and she closed the door.

He lit another match.

They stood in the narrow gap between the sub-zero storage room and the warehouse's concrete exterior wall. Only the square yard of floor on which they stood was bare.

The thundering compressor filled the remainder, blocking a doorway that must have once led to the outside. The door was missing, the opening bricked up.

A jury-rigged metal ladder rose from where they stood, climbing up and over the unit, before disappearing into darkness. She guessed it gave access to service technicians.

The compressor's drone was a steady bass. For a second, Dawna heard a shriller sound that might have been a muffled siren.

The National Police coming to rescue her and Zulfiqar? She hoped so.

Delivery Guy and Muscleman had probably left the building. Which meant the task force had no witnesses to nail whoever was running this operation. No prosecutor could make a case against them.

Dawna glanced at Zulfiqar. If she got him out of this mess today, he wouldn't be safe.

Someone in the National Police had leaked Zulfiqar's name to Roma's boss. Revealed everything but the precise time of the bust and Dawna's role in it. Instead of bringing supplies as usual, on this Saturday, Delivery Guy had teamed up with Muscleman to silence the snitch.

The leak had to be as obvious to Nic as it was to her. When this mess was cleared up, they'd identify who'd sold them out.

The bad guys panicked when the cops showed up and they'd ended up taking her, too. Chalk it up to collateral damage.

The compressor motor ratcheted down its grumble but the siren noise was gone.

She heard the mutter of male voices from the freezer side of the door.

"Gotta move," she whispered to Zulfiqar.

He scrambled up the metal rungs into the void

above the compressor. Likely a dead end, but at least they'd be out of view for a few seconds longer.

She fumbled her way up and found herself on a narrow catwalk running the length of the compressor. The metal grid bounced and though she couldn't see Zulfiqar, she knew he was hurrying ahead of her.

She narrowed the gap between them and smelled his aura of cardamom. Her fingertips reached out to rest on his shoulder.

Zulfiqar stopped with his arm extended. He must have reached the end of the catwalk.

"Look at my feet," he whispered.

His words made her realize that light was coming from somewhere. She peered at his shoes. Beyond the toe, a narrow band of light striped the catwalk.

He drew back, allowing Dawna to slide past him.

She realized the light came through a small hole in the wall to her left. Her fingers explored the surface, found a keyway shaped to take an old-fashioned metal skeleton key.

Above the keyhole, a hollow metal doorknob stuck out. Her fingertips found it scaly with what must be rust.

At this end of the catwalk was a lockable wooden door. It must open to the attic above the freezer room.

Could be a store room, but she'd seen no windows in the warehouse walls below. Unlikely they'd have skylights in the roof. No, the light had to be from an artificial source.

She crouched, putting her right eye against the empty keyway. She saw no stored goods, only bare space. Her field of vision was too narrow to offer more detail.

Her fingers found the doorknob again. She turned it carefully, felt the latch bolt retreat. This appeared to be an unlocked office with the lights on. Had to be someone inside.

The space around her brightened.

"They are coming through the door below," Zulfiqar whispered.

Armed pursuers would be on top of them in less than a minute. They were better off surprising whoever was in the room.

"Follow my lead," Dawna whispered. "When we get through the door, close and lock it. After that, translate everything I say to Arabic."

She came through the door, exaggerating the posture of crime-film cops busting bad guys.

The door clicked behind her. The two men in the room gaped at Dawna. Both were physically unfit office nerds in long-sleeved white shirts.

Harmless, she concluded.

They stood in front of four waist-high stations of

white-painted metal. Each station was marked by a red and green stop/go light atop a six-foot tall pole.

A different machine was centered at each station and Plexiglas panels linked the four stations.

She saw a pile of what appeared to be reddish-covered finished passports in a tray at the left end of the tray. While the brand on the equipment in front of her was not familiar, the setup was a miniature version of equipment she'd seen at the GPO, the Government Publishing Office, facility in DC.

The two men were operating a four-module passport machine system.

"We are the police," she announced and pulled the flex cuffs out from under her waistband. "You are under arrest. Anything you say can and will be used against you in a court of law."

Zulfiqar turned from the locked door and spoke in Arabic.

She motioned him toward the older, gray-haired man.

Unarmed, speed and intimidation were the best tools they had.

She went for the undernourished twenty-five-year-old.

He'd been refilling the paper tray and for a second too long, he continued clutching the ream of expensive paper in both hands.

She got the flex cuffs around his wrists, kicked him hard in the right knee. Watched in satisfaction as he crumpled to the floor, still hanging onto the paper.

She heard a yell and whirled toward Zulfiqar.

He'd grabbed the older man's hands and was struggling to control him.

She stepped in close, jerked the second pair of cuffs tightly around the man's wrists, and shoved him hard to the floor.

Zulfiqar frisked the younger man and pulled a cellphone from his pocket. He tossed the device to Dawna.

The knob rattled on the door through which they'd entered. The lock held. A fist pounded on the sturdy wood.

Was it sturdy enough to last five minutes?

She'd memorized Nic's personal cellphone number. She punched it into the phone.

"Nygaard—"

She cut him off. "Dawna. I'm at the Roma warehouse."

"So am I," he retorted. "How do I find you."

She guided him into the cold storage where he spotted the route through the wall of Snickers cartons which had been left open by the pursuers.

"Hurry up that metal ladder. You need to over-take some bad guys between the freezer and me."

"Keep this line open," he ordered.

She turned to Zulfiqar. "Cops are on the way."

"Open up," the phone sputtered.

"You got it." Dawna strode to the door and opened it.

Nic was on the other side, his pale face sheened with sweat.

She gestured at the space behind her. "Looks like this is where Roma's been turning out passports to supplement their pizza sauce income."

Nic took in the whole room in one long sweeping gaze. His irritated grunt told it all. What four, no, five times he'd sent teams to this warehouse and found nothing.

And Dawna'd wrapped it up in a single visit.

Dawna kept her game face on, totally cool, totally professional.

She didn't want to come across like she deserved credit for the bust. Nobody liked that side of the FBI.

"Hey, I got lucky," she said. "I popped to the ball, didn't know what to do, except take it to the hole."

"What language are you speaking?" Nic demanded.

"The language of basketball," Zulfiqar informed

Nic. "Another way of saying her result was due to good luck."

Zulfiqar's leathery face broke into a smile. "She is exceptionally fluent in her second language."

Dawna had lived and worked too often in foreign countries with conversations swirling around her in Danish or Hungarian or Romanian or another tongue she didn't understand. Felt like she was walking the streets in a bubble of white noise.

At last, one non-native speaker of English got her meaning instantly.

She let a grin split her face. "Excellent translation, Zulfiqar. You're pretty good at speaking basketball yourself."

A Thieving Rescue

Kari Kilgore

Paul Roberts put on his best fake smile as he walked out of a blustery southern Illinois October into the crowded student union building. He was having one of those days where it was easier to try to fit in than answer questions about why he was in such a piss-poor mood.

Well, not a *day*, not really.

A long stretch of days that easily added up to a month.

One he was afraid would stretch into another rotten freaking year.

The turd-brown brick barn of a building was at least as old as his parents should have been in the endless year of 1989, with all the squared-off and bland architecture of the 1940s. The interior wasn't much better despite overly optimistic remodels that already looked outdated.

A huge open space off to the right featured a sprawl of beat-up wooden chairs, desks, and tables probably salvaged from high-school discards, but not quite enough of them to hide the unfortunate puke-green carpet that had to be a survivor of the 70s.

A bunch of kids around his ripe old age of twenty lounged, flirted, or argued, producing a dull roar that never seemed to change no matter the time of day.

Paul had never understood how anyone could

study in the din, but a bunch of the off-campus students somehow managed to get all their work done between classes before they fled back home.

He envied them that escape.

The days when he would have enjoyed joining them, and smiling and laughing and having fun along with them felt like another lifetime.

One he was afraid he'd never find his way back to.

He was similarly unimpressed by the cramped cafeteria wedged along the wall straight ahead, with rows of green plastic picnic-style tables currently almost empty. The thick aroma of some kind of meaty stew let him know dinner wouldn't be any more appetizing than lunch, if he could afford the splurge. But every seat would be full by six o'clock and stay that way until nine.

His backpack served as his own personal cafeteria almost every day. Hardly the most inspiring meals, considering he was limited to his tiny dorm fridge and whatever he picked up on sale from the tiny grocery store in town.

Still his belly, his general health, and his tight budget managed on a steady diet of cereal, sandwiches, and salad, probably better than they would have overpaying for greasy hamburgers and overcooked vegetables.

The only reason he ventured into the union at all

was the smallest post office he'd ever seen, taking up only about ten feet of the concrete wall to his left. A student clerk behind a sliding glass window offered the most basic services like cashing small checks or selling stamps and envelopes.

The most important thing the campus PO offered Paul was a free mailbox—one of about fifty little metal doors lined up in a neat rectangle.

He wasn't expecting a letter from home or a birthday card, not with both parents lost in a boating accident three years ago. That had been a high school graduation present he could have done without.

But they'd left behind enough insurance money to keep him scraping by in college as long as he kept up his grades for the scholarship that covered his tuition and basic fees. Not quite enough to swing the meal plan in that dubious cafeteria, but he was fine with that.

He *wasn't* fine with Jerry, his jerk of an older brother, still being in charge of disbursing that money.

When he bothered to.

Which was rarely on time, partly because Jerry'd gotten it into his head that Paul's stubborn pursuit of a computer science degree was a waste of time and money.

After all, Jerry had gotten a job at the massive

printing plant in their barely-on-the-map small town right out of high school, worked his way up to shift supervisor, and made enough to support *his* family. Between their seven-year age difference and Paul's continued refusal to accept a janitorial position at the plant, their distant brotherly relationship had deteriorated from cool to frigid.

Jerry lording such a humiliating difference in their job titles over him would have been intolerable on its own. And Paul was convinced he'd already seen the future of printing, and maybe publishing, when he'd helped the campus newspaper install both Page-Maker and QuarkXPress.

Tie himself to abuse from his brother *and* an industry likely to go through tremendous upheavals with the power shifting to computers instead of gigantic operations like Jerry worked for?

No thank you.

Right now dear brother Jerry's check was two weeks behind, and Paul's supplies were running as low as his patience.

Working at the campus library and helping out with other general computer stuff was about all he could do and still keep his scholarship. And his bare-minimum-wage salary hardly covered getting an attorney to help rattle his brother's stingy cage.

Again.

Thankfully he only had to get through until his next birthday before he'd finally be in charge of his own money. Some of which hopefully waited for him right that minute.

Paul had his stubby mailbox key out when someone called his name over the chatter.

He turned to see his buddy Tammy trotting toward him, and Paul's mood lifted as his smile turned into the real thing. His friends were the best part of school and living on campus, aside from putting a blissful number of miles between himself and his brother.

He'd known Tammy for ages, and she was the one most likely to brighten up even the most frustrating of days.

She wore one of her usual unusual outfits, either scavenged from the thrift shop or home-sewn. Often both. Today's featured a skirt and shirt made of what looked like a pile of blue scarves that fluttered around her long, slender arms and legs like ocean waves.

About as far as anyone could get from Paul's monotonous uniform of jeans and a plain green T-shirt, in other words.

Her brown hair bounced in perfect curler-waves around her shoulders, and a huge bag covered with old red and blue handkerchiefs banged against her thighs.

Tammy had moved into shared housing this year, which wasn't much cheaper than a dorm as far as Paul could tell. He knew the collective and overly friendly chaos he'd seen when he visited would drive him nuts in short order.

"What's the good word, Paulie? Finally decide to join us time-wasting commoners?"

"Not just yet. Still holding on to my monkish existence. Anything worth paying attention to in the scrum?"

Tammy rolled her eyes and glanced over her shoulder. A group of kids Paul knew through her—some of them her housemates—sat intently focused on some kind of card game, apparently using plain potato chips for currency. A pot cheap enough that even he could buy in if he bothered to learn the rules of the game.

Too bad the thought of handling chip-greased cards made his skin crawl.

"Not a damn thing," she said. "I'm about to dash to my biology class. Care to join me?"

Paul jerked his chin toward the post office, where a bored guy waited at the counter to see if anyone needed his expert-level assistance in applying a stamp.

"Can't. I've only got a minute, so I'm trying not to get my hopes up that my beloved brother finally sent me this month's check."

"That *ass*hole." Tammy scowled. "He deserves to spend a few cold, lonely nights in jail over this. Need cash? Or my dinner pass when I'm not using it? We can always pull together some kind of potluck study night at our house. Not exactly gourmet, but filling. And no one will know why."

"Not just yet, but I might take you up on that before long." Paul used his key on box twenty-seven, held his breath, and opened the just-bigger-than-palm-sized brass door on the shallow, overstuffed box.

A white envelope stood out from the rest of the marketing trash and general campus junk, which had all but disappeared at the beginning of the semester. One of those too-good-to-be-true things, because now his mailbox was stuffed with as much crap as ever.

He knew getting his hopes up about a single non-obvious trash thing was even more foolish, and likely to end in disappointment.

Tammy leaned close against his arm.

"Is it there?"

Paul sorted through the garbage, dumping it into a dented metal can someone had dragged over for that purpose. Then he finally turned the envelope over and snorted.

"Of *course* not. It's yet another reminder from

the Baptist church back home about my immortal soul. Probably along with a note about how much they miss my parents, without mentioning what they really miss is their butts in the pews and their cash in the collection plate."

Tammy put one arm around him in a quick, awkward half-hug.

"Listen, I'd bet we can find a law student who can help with this. And I'm not even sure a real lawyer would bill you if you just call, would they?"

Paul shook his head and tried to hold on to his temporarily better mood.

"No idea. The truth is I can't think about it right now, you know? I've got to work extra hours this week to help the library with a mainframe upgrade. The good news is they usually call in pizza for us, so there's one meal handled, right?"

Tammy frowned, but thank goodness she seemed to realize Paul wasn't up for a discussion.

"Okay, but promise to let me know if you need a food rescue. I meant it about dinner at our house. If I find out you've been skipping meals or scavenging somewhere, I'll take my revenge."

"I know you will. And that you've got bio and I've got a Pascal class right now, so we'll talk about it later."

"See if you can program your way into your brother's bank account while you're at it."

He watched her strolling back toward her housemates and the card game, wishing he had the guts to stop by for a minute and risk being late for his class. But his dislike of ending up at the computer with the half-broken keyboard and fear of missing a word of the professor's rapid-fire instruction got him headed out the door.

If nothing else, it might be time to spend the quarter on a pay phone to remind his brother that even people wasting their time on nonsense like learning needed to eat, too.

And he wished the idea about hacking Jerry's bank account wasn't so damn tempting.

———

Two rainy days later, Paul made another trip to the union, this time early enough in the morning that the thick smell of bacon and sausage almost blocked out the earthy funk of way-too-strong coffee.

At least it wasn't quite as noisy as usual, with most everyone either half asleep or already out the door to cruel eight A.M. classes. The cafeteria tables were as full as the lounging and study tables were empty, but a few hardy souls crouched over the desks, probably cramming for an exam.

Two kids that he could see were sleeping something off on the ratty sofas shoved against the wall, or else they'd been kicked out of their usual beds over some kind of lover's or roommate's tiff.

For once, he spotted Tammy before she saw him, so he kept walking past the deserted post office with its metal door rolled down over the service window and toward the café.

She'd made the unwise choice of sitting with her back exposed, but he recognized her frilly pink-and-black jacket and hair pulled into an impressive waterfall of a ponytail on top of her head.

He also recognized a guy and a girl—both computer science buddies of his—and Tammy's housemate Christie sitting with her, and they were all leaned forward discussing something. Christie wore her usual preppy outfit, with a little blue alligator embroidered on her blue shirt and some kind of expensive jeans, but she'd been nothing but good to Tammy, and to Paul.

Still, a tingle of unease in his belly warned him to walk away, but not before the guy a year ahead of him in Comp Sci saw him and waved.

All four of them, plus a girl he didn't know sitting beside Tammy, turned to stare, and Tammy's face turned bright red.

"Hey Paul," she said. "Didn't expect to see you here this early."

He slowed his stride, wishing he'd stopped to wait for the post office to open instead.

"Yeah, me neither. Had a few minutes before work, so I figured I'd stop by the PO."

Her blush extended to her neck, but she waved him forward.

"Heard anything from your brother?" She tried to keep her voice low, but the others were too close not to hear.

And nowhere near good enough at acting to pretend not to listen.

"Not a word, but I didn't expect to. Any reason you'd ask about that right now?"

Her eyebrows drew together and she pursed her lips, a sure sign that she caught the irritation he was trying to hide.

"Because I'm worried about you, that's why. And, well, Kit here has a sister studying for the bar exam, and she says—"

"Nice to meet you, Kit," Paul cut in, no longer trying to hide anything. "Tammy, mind if I talk to you for a second? Alone?"

Kit and everyone else at the table looked down at

their empty plates while Tammy stood and followed him several steps away. Her rapid-fire stream of words started before he stopped walking.

"It wasn't me, Paul, those two from your classes saw me first thing and sat down, and they said they were worried about you, and wondered if I knew anything they could do to help, and I ran into Kit last night, so she was already going to talk to you, but then when I..."

She trailed off, taking a deep breath and meeting his glare with one of her own.

"You told *all* of them about me? About my jerk of a brother, about my parents, everything?"

"I'm *worried* about you!" She jabbed a pink-and-black-nail-polished finger at his face. "I know you're not starving to death or anything, but you've got too much going on to put up with Jerry's bullshit. If other people can see it, that has to mean it's getting to you. Kit might be able to help."

Paul leaned away from her finger and she dropped her hand to her side.

"You know I don't want a bunch of people knowing about this. You're right that I'm not starving, but I'm also still pulling all As in my classes, *and* keeping up with extra work right now. Even if it *is* getting to me, it's still none of their business. Don't make me wish I hadn't told you, either."

Now, she jammed her hands on her hips and leaned forward so fast he took a step back.

"But you *did* tell me, Paul Roberts. And those two brought it up to me, not the other way around. We've known each other since what, third grade? Do you really expect me to ignore what's going on with you? You look like you haven't slept more than a couple of hours all week."

Paul let out a breath and stared down as his sneaker-clad feet and Tammy's pink fuzzy slippers. The contrast was too absurd to ignore, but he couldn't quite manage a smile.

"You're right, mostly," he said, still looking down. "I haven't been sleeping much with the library upgrades. But that's partly because they order that greasy stuff from City Pizza and I spend half the night in the bathroom."

He peeked up to see if she cracked a smile herself.

Nope.

Still glaring.

"Your brother's an asshole, but you're being a stubborn jackass yourself. Let Kit or someone else help with this. Not because you *can't*, but because they *can*. And they want to."

He looked back at the group, most of them still waiting but working very hard to keep from watching him and Tammy.

Except Christie, her housemate. Christie kept glancing toward them, her red curls shifting across her back every time.

He was afraid of the answer deep in his guts, but not knowing would be worse.

"Did they really come to you? The two Comp Sci majors?"

"They did, and not like gossips either. I think they're both impressed with you. Or intimidated, maybe. Which is ridiculous but I didn't tell them that."

"At least you didn't tell them *some*thing. I guess I can talk to Kit if the check doesn't show up today. Is Christie pre-law too?"

Tammy waved that away.

"No, she's a psych major, at least for now. She just came over for breakfast at the same time I did. But I'm sure she'd do what she could to help out."

Paul shrugged, wishing he could think of something else to do. He'd made a point of telling Jerry over the summer that the next step was getting their parents' lawyer to step in after going through this crap for two years. Paul doubted the lawyer would charge him, like Tammy said, but he also hated the idea of dragging the woman who'd read the will with honest tears in her eyes into this mess.

Jerry hadn't spoken to him since, but the damned check had been there in September.

Only a week late.

Paul had dared hope that was an end to that particular variety of big-brother bullshit game, but October's was pushing three weeks overdue.

This was a case where an impartial stranger might be exactly what he needed.

"Okay, Tammy. I'll talk to Kit and see what her sister can do. But not right now, and *only* to her, okay? I don't want the others knowing any more about what's going on. Not from me or from you. Can you handle that?"

Her pursed lips made it clear she didn't like the idea, but she nodded.

"I think I can handle it. What should I tell them if they ask?"

Paul jumped when the metal door rolled up in the post office.

"That's up to you. I'm going to have enough trouble facing them in class and pretending I don't know what they know about me. I'm going to check in at the PO and make sure they haven't seen anything, then I've got to run."

He started to turn away, then looked over his shoulder at his friend.

"Thank you for trying to help. And just so you

won't worry quite as much, I think I can probably get an advance from the library to get me through the weekend. They're pretty happy with the work I've been doing lately. But I still don't like...No, never mind that. Thank you."

Tammy blinked back what he sincerely hoped weren't tears before she nodded once.

"You're welcome. I just hope it makes a difference."

Paul walked away without saying anything else. He was still too upset about people he saw in almost every class knowing his messy private business.

He didn't much like knowing it himself.

However, that faded away to mild irritation beside yet again finding nothing but junk mail in his mailbox. Ads for shops in town he couldn't afford, flyers for off-campus events he wouldn't have time to get to even if he had the money, and a pile of credit card offers he would have laughed at on a better day.

He dumped them all and stepped over to the open window, waiting for the girl working this morning to finish her face-splitting yawn.

"Sorry, late night and early morning," she said, rubbing her eyes.

"No problem, same here. I've been waiting for something in the mail for a few weeks, but it's not showing up. I don't mean to sound like a jerk, but is it possible there's a missing mailbag or something like that?"

The girl blinked, then shook her head.

"Probably not, but you might want to check with whoever's supposed to send it. That or file a complaint. I just started here a couple of days ago, so anything's possible. Sorry."

Paul started to walk away, his own cheeks burning now.

Of course he should check with who sent it, that made perfect sense. Except the idea of calling his brother and listening to yet another freaking lecture about how great *Jerry* was doing and how *Paul* kept having to lean on him for help knotted up every nerve and muscle in his body.

Never mind that all Paul wanted was the money their parents had meant for him if the unthinkable happened.

Which it had.

And having to go through this month after month kept forcing Paul to think about it constantly, breaking his heart and shattering his mind over and over again.

He turned back toward the PO and the girl, who was in the middle of another gigantic yawn.

If he was willing to talk to Tammy's friend about

his legal options, it would be pretty damn silly to stop there.

"I'd like to file that complaint after all," he said. "Who the hell knows, it might even help."

After a hectic weekend finishing the library's upgrade, Paul didn't make it back to the union until Tuesday afternoon.

And as soon as he walked in, he knew something was off.

The huge room was as crowded as ever, with kids finishing a late lunch, studying for evening classes, or hanging out together after a full day. Not many seats among the beat-up tables, chairs, and sofas were empty.

But instead of the typical maddening noise, the place was eerily quiet.

The ones who talked did so softly, and even people lingering over what smelled like overly spicy fried chicken hardly made any conversation.

Paul shook his head, reminding himself to ask Tammy if she knew what was happening. She'd been more aware of—and more concerned about—things like this since they were scrawny grade-schoolers running around with bellbottoms and embarrassingly wide lapels.

He'd only stopped by for another futile try at his mailbox before he finally gave in and called his brother one more time. A hurried conversation with Tammy's friend Kit in the library Sunday morning convinced Paul he'd waited long enough to confront Jerry, no matter how much he dreaded it.

Even if Jerry wasn't spending the money on himself and his own family—which Paul more than halfway suspected—he couldn't deny his brother had been breaking the terms of the trust by not sending those checks when they were due.

With the amount of hardship the delays caused Paul, letting his jerk of a brother collect even pennies of interest went way too far.

This time the mailbox was full of junk mail again, but a white envelope and a vivid yellow postcard caught his attention.

He flipped the postcard over first and frowned. It was a note to speak to the postmaster as soon as possible, which he'd never seen before. He didn't even know the college *had* a postmaster.

A quick glance showed the window was open, and a woman he'd never seen before was there doing paperwork of some kind. She was older than most of the students, and she wore the blue uniform of the regular U.S. Post Office instead of the typical college kid's more casual attire.

Paul started that way, then stopped so hard his sneakers squeaked on the bare tile floor.

The envelope wasn't more fake sympathy and concern from his parents' church.

It was from his brother.

Paul's address was written with a scrawl that could only be called aggressive, digging into the white surface so hard it had nearly torn the paper. Both the stamp and the return address label were on crooked too.

Nothing like Jerry's typical neat, almost prim arrangements.

All at once, Paul's heart thudded in his chest, and his fingers shook tearing the edge open.

Even though he wasn't face to face with Jerry or even on the phone, his body seemed convinced the confrontation was still underway.

Inside was a folded sheet of paper, and when he opened it, two checks fluttered out.

He managed to catch one before it could hit the floor, then gasped at the amount.

Jerry had written him a check for ten times what he insisted on calling Paul's "allowance," as if he were the generous parent instead of the reluctant and tight-fisted holder of his younger brother's much-needed educational trust.

Paul flipped open the paper as he reached for the other check.

His cautious elation turned to disgust, confusion, and finally anger as he read handwriting every bit as harsh and furious as the words.

Paul,

I'm sure you'll agree we'll both be a lot happier if I dissolve the trust and give you the whole amount to use or waste or whatever you're going to do. It's not what Mom and Dad wanted, but I'm the only one who seems to care about that.

As far as your pathetic attempt to get me to write you a second check for October, you're out of luck on that one. Best I can do is send you proof that you already cashed it, since you don't yet seem to understand how banking works.

Next time you call a lawyer on me, pal, you'd better be ready to face some adult consequences for a change.

This is as much as I'm willing to send through the mail, especially after what happened this month. How about you finally grow up enough to get your own bank account instead of depending on me to manage your money for you? Send me the numbers, and I'll transfer the rest.

You're on your own, sink or swim, after that.
Best of luck. You're going to need it.
Jerry

Paul forced himself to take a breath, hold it, and let it out as slowly as he could.

Yeah, his brother had proven yet again what a jerk, what an *asshole*, he was, and that hurt a hell of a lot more than Paul wanted to admit.

But if he followed through with dissolving the trust and sending it all, that would solve more problems than Paul had dared to even imagine.

That would be more than enough to get him through the rest of undergrad and a good way through grad school if he decided to continue on. If he was careful, and kept his scholarship, he'd have a good start on living expenses once he graduated either way.

So did it really matter that the only surviving member of his immediate family surely wouldn't bother showing up to see Paul cross that stage?

He finally remembered the second check and took a look.

And grunted in confusion.

It was a cancelled check, made out to him, dated the last week of September.

But the signature on the back was obviously not his. Whoever cashed it hadn't bothered trying, or else they'd never seen his signature to begin with. Even the date was formatted wrong, with dashes instead of slashes between the numbers.

He couldn't imagine the PO or the bank he usually went to cashing this mess.

He caught sight of his watch and forced his feet to get moving. This was a puzzle he had to solve, but it wasn't worth being late for class.

The woman at the post office counter looked up at him suspiciously until she saw the yellow postcard in his hand.

Then her stern face turned compassionate in a hurry.

"This was in my box," Paul said. "I guess I need to know what it's about. Also I kinda doubt you'd be able to cash this, but I figure it's worth asking."

She took the postcard, circled the big twenty-seven on it, and reached for the check.

Paul didn't realize he'd given her both of them until she put them on the counter.

"No, I'm afraid I can't cash this one. You'll have to take it to a bank in town. I think the second one will make it clear why you might want to be more careful getting such a large amount sent through the mail."

"Sorry, I didn't meant to give the other one to you." Paul paused, catching the meaning of her last sentence a beat later, even if he didn't understand why she'd said it. "I think someone else must have cashed it, because I sure didn't."

She pushed the first check across the counter and tapped the other one with her fingernail.

"As for this cancelled one, I believe I can explain what happened. Hopefully the police will be able to take it from there. An officer will be available to meet with you on campus all week."

"The police? What's going on?"

She folded her hands and gazed into his eyes, and he felt like that same ignorant and innocent high school kid who was about to hear horrible news that he'd been on that awful night after his parents' accident.

"We've had an unfortunate situation at this post office that's been going on for a few weeks, and you're one of the victims. It seems a student has been stealing mail from several of the boxes. This check was obviously part of that. I'm not sure of the status of the investigation, but the police will be very interested in seeing it."

Paul blinked and shook his head.

"Stealing? You don't mean one of the kids who *works* here?"

She shook her head.

"Not at all. In fact, they're the ones who gathered

and turned in student complaints of missing mail, which alerted us to the problem. The student in question was opening one of the boxes and reaching through and removing mail from others. Yours was one of the ones they could reach."

Paul opened his mouth to argue, then thought about how the boxes were made. They weren't nearly as deep as the ones he'd seen when he went with his mother to pick up their mail. Those were long enough for more than one envelope to fit inside.

The ones here were barely long enough to hold one.

So if a student was on the thin side, flexible, and determined, that might just work.

"So you know who did it?" he said. "What am I supposed to do now?"

She pushed a piece of paper covered with writing across the counter.

"This is more information about where to meet the officer assigned here, and who to get in touch with at the college for more assistance if you need it. They're as sorry about this as we are, and we all want to do what we can to make it right. They're offering to put a hold on payments due in cases like yours where a check was lost or cashed by someone else."

Paul took it, not bothering to try to make sense of what was printed there. He was having enough trouble keeping up with the storm of thoughts and feelings crashing through his head.

"The kids who worked here didn't get fired, did they?"

The woman smiled for the first time, and Paul surprised himself by smiling back.

"Not at all. We decided it would be best for a postal employee to handle this difficult task instead of them having to explain everything. I'm very sorry this happened to you. And I promise it *will* be taken care of."

Paul gathered the checks and the paper, not quite sure what to do next.

"Okay, thank you for telling me. Have a good day."

"You do the same."

He turned and almost crashed into Tammy, who'd walked up behind him without making a sound.

"Hey Tammy, you'll *never* guess what just..." He frowned at her pale face and red-rimmed eyes. "Are you okay?"

She shook her head, and a few tears spilled over. She didn't bother wiping them away.

"I know what just happened, Paul. At least the general idea. Please tell me your check was one of the ones that got stolen."

"Well yeah, it was. Someone cashed it too, but I have to talk to the police to figure out how. And who. But there's more than that—"

She grabbed his arm a little too hard and walked him away from the PO, into the empty space before the cafeteria tables started. Kids were still eating and hanging out around the desks and chairs, but it was quiet enough to give him the creeps.

Tammy let go, took a deep breath, and blew her bangs away from her forehead.

Paul's heart sank when he finally noticed how flat and dull her hair was, and that she wore drab gray sweats.

"What's going on?"

"This whole thing, it's been *my* fault," she said. "Every last bit of it, and not just with you. I'm so sorry."

"Hang on, that doesn't make sense. Some asshole broke into a bunch of mailboxes, and my brother's as big a jerk as ever. What's that got to do with you?"

She stepped back and held her hands up between them. His heart ached at how gnawed her fingernails were, all traces of care and polish vanished.

"If you'll just let me *talk*, I'll tell you. This isn't exactly easy."

He leaned back against the wall and resolved to keep his mouth shut until she was finished. He had plenty to say, but he was a lot less upset than he'd been for the last few weeks or even ten minutes ago.

He didn't understand why, but *she* was a mess, and right now.

"It wasn't just anybody who stole your check and everyone else's mail, or some random stranger who wandered in off the street. It was my housemate Christie. You know the one, always wearing nice clothes. Nicer than I can afford, anyway."

Paul nodded.

"I gave her..." Tammy squeezed her eyes closed for a second before she went on. "I asked Christie to check my mail when I got busy since this semester started. Only one time, then she started offering every time she came over here. And that's *all* I wanted her to do. Then I find out this morning that she's been using *my* box to steal from a bunch of others. The fucking kicker is yours was one of them. All this time she had your check, even when we were talking about it last week. She knew how much you needed the money, and how much several of us were willing to do to help you get it. But she never said a word."

Paul's brain felt more sludgy and slow than ever, as if he was slogging through nearly dry concrete trying to catch up with Tammy's words.

"I don't want to sound like an idiot, or like I

think you're one. But I'm still not seeing how this is your fault."

She squeezed her hands against her temples and glared at him.

"Because if I hadn't asked her that first time, or if I'd been paying closer attention, none of this would have happened. She hurt a lot of people, Paul, not just you. All because I didn't feel like tromping over here in the rain one day last month."

He stared down at the cancelled check in his hand.

"I still don't see how she could have cashed it. No one here or at the banks in town would have done it."

Tammy rolled her eyes, pushing out a few more tears.

"Oh that's *easy*. She never set foot in a bank, and I doubt she's spent enough time actually talking to someone at the PO this year to remember where the window is, much less ask for help with cashing checks. She set the whole damn thing up with a friend of hers who works at one of the trashy gas stations in town. *That's* who cashed all the checks."

"So now that part makes sense, assuming the police pick up this friend, too. But I'm still not seeing how this is because of you. Sounds to me like *Christie* did it, not you. Not that I have any idea why. She never seemed short of cash."

Tammy rubbed her elbows and looked toward the front door, face tense and fearful as if expecting the police to come charging in and arrest her after all.

"She had cash, and nice clothes, and a good car. I'm not sure whether her parents were hiding money troubles from her or if she did it for fun or just to see if she could." She turned back to him, and now her eyes snapped with anger. "Damn it all to hell, Paul, I *trusted* her. I'm the one who invited her to our house in the first place!"

Paul waited for a second, trying to gauge whether she wanted a hug or if she'd slug him if he tried. He decided to split the difference and touched her arm.

"Then I'd say Christie screwed you and me and a bunch of other people over. That makes you someone else who got hurt. Not the one who did the hurting."

She stepped closer to him, and he shoved everything in his pockets to give her that hug after all.

"Did you already talk to the police?"

She nodded against his chest.

"Then do you want to go with me when I do? For moral support or whatever, or just to get you away from the nonsense inside your head?"

He felt her back rise and fall before she stepped away.

"I guess so. This sucks no matter how you try to frame it to make me feel better."

"Yeah, this does suck. But your friend Kit more than made up for it as far as I'm concerned. She must have already gotten in touch with my brother."

Tammy covered her throat with one hand.

"I *told* her to *wait* until we talked to *you* again! He wasn't angry, was he? The last thing I want is to give him a reason to be even more of a jerk to you."

Paul smiled, feeing a long way closer to his normal, pretty easygoing self.

"Seems to me dear Jerry was furious. He cut me off altogether."

He waited long enough for the lightning to flare in her eyes and her to curl her hands into fists at her sides again before going on.

"He's dissolving the trust and sending it *all* to me, because he thinks I cashed this month's check but I'm trying to trick him into giving me another one."

"But that's not...And he was late all the time unless you practically *begged* him to send *your* money, that you use to stay in college, not going to parties and..." She trailed off, even though her fists stayed clenched. "The whole thing? You mean you won't have to deal with him anymore?"

"Not unless I want to, And I'm sure I don't have to tell you how I feel about that. So look at it this way. If Christie hadn't snatched that check, I might have been forced to put up with Jerry's crap until I turned twenty-one. Which might have driven me insane enough that I wouldn't have cared any more."

Tammy buried her head in her hands, but only long enough for Paul to wonder whether she was laughing or crying.

Laughing, thank goodness. And he couldn't help joining in, even though they did their best to stay quiet in the near-silent room.

"Are you telling me that thieving bitch did you a *favor*?" she said, wiping her eyes.

"If Jerry follows through, and I think he will, she sure did. I'm not ready to put her in charge of my stock portfolio or anything like that. She needs to either go to jail or get help. But she may have changed everything for me. Or what she stole did. So if you're determined to take the blame for Christie, you have to take the credit, too."

Her smile broke through like the sun through heavy clouds, and Paul felt a big chunk of the gloomy, choking weight he'd been carrying for the last few years dissolve at the same time.

"All right then, I will. You've got a break after your next class, right? We can talk to the police tomorrow. I say we need to get out of this slop hall and have a decent meal for a change. My treat."

Paul grinned and shook his head.

"Absolutely not. I'm not about to turn into some kind of flashy moneybags, but you kept me from starving or going crazy trying not to. I can swing a nice dinner for the two of us. You'll have to go home and clean up a little first."

Tammy snorted and looked down at her shabby sweats.

"You don't like my new outfit? My attempt at fitting in with college fashion at last? Fine, but you'll have to dress up yourself, and good luck matching me."

"I wouldn't dare try. See you later."

After another quick hug, Paul headed back out.

He wasn't used to walking on air, and he knew the buoyant sensation wouldn't last forever.

But he was determined to enjoy every minute while it lasted.

And willing to try on the idea that more good days than bad might be in his future.

Especially now that he knew how to find his own kind of family.

Night of the Moto-Men

Robert Jeschonek

If the dead hoarder's house had been Angie Virago's, she would have set fire to it. End of story.

But then, of course, she wouldn't have been hired to clean it out. And these days, with a comatose husband and money issues up to her neck, she needed every bit of work she could get. Especially the kind of robotic labor that would take her mind off things.

As she and her coworker, Big Mike Morrigan, stepped through the front door for the first time, an indoor garbage dump greeted their eyes. Piles of junk and trash filled the living room from floor to ceiling and wall to wall. Animal droppings and rotten food waste littered the piles, drawing flies. A shaggy gray cat lolled on the tiny patch of open floor at Mike's feet, its fur matted with dried blood and excrement.

"This place reeks right through my mask." Big Mike's red mustache rose as he wrinkled his nose behind the clear faceplate of his biohazard suit.

"The masks are airtight," said Angie from inside her own baggy white protective suit. "But yeah, I know what you mean."

"Wasn't Animal Control here already?" asked Big Mike.

"I guess they missed one."

"Oh, God." Big Mike flinched as the cat got up and rubbed its scabby body against his legs. "It does suck to be us right now."

The cleanup began just inside the front door, because that was where the piles started. To clear the exit, Big Mike propped the door open with a cinderblock that had been holding down a chest-high stack of newspapers. Angie worried about the scabby gray cat getting out, but it went in the opposite direction, meandering into the maze of refuse.

How long would it take them to clear out that maze? As they started hauling, Angie could see it was going to take days...maybe a week.

This wasn't the first hoarder house they'd worked on for the cleanup company, but if the second floor and basement were as jam-packed as the first floor, it could turn out to be one of the worst. No one else had touched a thing; the owner, sixty-seven-year-old Helen Fulton, had died without family, friends, heirs...or *answers* of any kind.

Not unless you counted the contents of the overstuffed house.

"Who wants *pizza*?" Big Mike opened a pizza box in front of Angie's faceplate, then laughed as she jerked away.

Instead of decaying food, the box was filled with hairballs—multicolored clumps crammed together and crawling with little bugs.

"Oh, God." Angie wasn't a lightweight, but seeing the hairballs up close triggered her gag reflex. "That is so *gross*."

Big Mike—who'd spent time in prison and had the sense of humor to prove it—pushed the box toward her. "Sure you don't want a slice?"

"I'm sure." Angie turned back to the big biohazard bag she'd been filling with used Chinese takeout containers. There was no way she was going to look inside one of those after her peek inside the pizza box.

"Never ceases to amaze me," said Big Mike as he stuffed the pizza box in his own biohazard bag and reached for a big-scooped shovel he'd propped against a newspaper pile. "I mean, there's being a pack rat, and then there's *this*."

Under the Chinese takeout containers, Angie found a big stack of kids' shirts, fit for a two-year-old, still on the hangers. Grabbing a handful, she chucked them in her bag. "They say we're all just one bad day away from losing it, you know."

Big Mike shoveled what looked like a rotting compost pile slumping against the wall. "Lots of folks have it bad, and they don't turn into this."

"No, they do other crazy things." Angie grabbed another handful of kids' shirts and shoved them in the bag. "Like hurt other people, for example."

"That's true." Big Mike dumped a shovelful of glistening, fibrous compost into his bag. "But this way, you're leaving a big mess for other people to clean up."

"There are lots of ways to leave messes," said Angie.

It was a good thing they were having a cool snap, or the usual mid-July Virginia heat would have roasted Angie in her biohazard suit. She was young—in her early thirties—and in good physical shape, but she was still perpetually soaked with sweat and needed periodic breaks to rehydrate.

Even then, when she stood under the open sky, feeling a gentle breeze stirring her short black hair and sipping water from a plastic bottle, she still saw the refuse from the house when she closed her eyes. She'd been staring at it for so long, it had burned it-self into her retinas.

Her head throbbed with the same, almost-ra-dioactive half-life as the house, the clutter having infected her mind. She groaned, vaguely nauseated by the sickness of it.

Then, not long after she returned from her break, she found something that took her mind off the mess.

Wading into the living room, she bumped into a mannequin wrapped in garlands of tinsel and wearing a long blue wig. The mannequin knocked over the top half of a pile of shoeboxes, dumping them on the floor.

There, amid a scattering of safety pins, lipsticks, and ancient ketchup and mayonnaise packets from fast food restaurants, Angie spotted a folded-up black and white photo.

Unfolded, the eight-by-ten photo depicted a woman in her twenties leaning against an oak tree, her glossy blonde hair tied back in a ponytail. She wore a short-sleeved white sweater and flouncy mid-calf-length black skirt, an outfit that looked like something out of the 1950s.

Over her heart, she held some kind of decoration against her fluffy white sweater—a flat macramé rectangle, six inches long by four inches wide. It looked like a little robot with gears for eyes, a zipper for a mouth, and a body studded with nuts and bits of wire.

"Look at this," she said to Big Mike when he reentered the house from another dumpster run.

Big Mike squinted at the photo. "Helen Fulton back in the day?"

"How do you know?" asked Angie. "There's nothing written on the back."

Big Mike pointed a gloved finger at the robot decoration. "I found some of these in here earlier."

"No kidding."

Big Mike grinned. "She was hot, wasn't she? She could've hoarded me anytime."

He was right. Helen looked perfectly normal—and attractive—in that photo. "I wonder what went wrong?"

Big Mike grabbed the wigged-and-tinseled mannequin and spun it around. "Broken heart, maybe?"

"Could be."

"Let me know when you figure it out." Mike stomped off toward the dumpster with the mannequin under his arm.

Angie and Big Mike weren't supposed to keep anything from the house. It was all considered hazardous and marked for disposal at a special hazmat site.

But Angie folded up the photo and stuck it in a pocket of her suit anyway.

That evening, at the hospital, the nurse didn't bother reporting that there'd been no improvement in Angie's husband's condition. Angie didn't blame her; after all, Gray had been in a coma for almost eight weeks. Nothing had changed medically for him in all that time.

When the nurse had gone, Angie sat for a while and stared at her husband. She barely recognized him anymore, but it wasn't because of the coma or his long absence from her moment-by-moment life. It wasn't because his true self was buried by the weeks of unconsciousness.

It was because his true self had come out more clearly than ever during his long sleep.

With a sigh, Angie got up and walked over to stand beside his bed. "Hello, Gray." Her voice was monotone and affectionless. "Busy day?"

As always, the only reply she got was the beeping of the vital signs monitors.

"By the way, I got a call from another of your floozies yesterday," she told him. "Some girl named Christina. I told her you'd have to call her back later."

Eight weeks after the car crash that had sent Gray into the coma in the first place, girlfriends were still coming out of the woodwork. Surprised as she was by this menagerie, the creditors were more of a shock.

Apparently, Gray had run up some serious debts before the accident. That he'd liked to gamble, Angie had known. That he'd lost half a million dollars at it—staking his bets with cash advances and consumer loans—had blindsided her completely.

Reaching out, she took hold of his hand. With all that she knew about him now, touching him repelled her...but she lived in hope that it might spark an awakening.

"Do you have money socked away somewhere?" she asked him. "Because I really need to pay the bank and the credit card companies."

Angie waited for a response and got nothing...not even a twitch of a finger.

"Please, Gray." She leaned closer. "If I ever meant anything to you, give me a sign. Is there money hidden anywhere?"

Still nothing.

Angie was lost in thought the next morning, obsessing over her problems...but it didn't last. Once she'd suited up at the job site and started digging into the next phase of Helen Fulton's mess, her money worries melted away.

There was just the rhythm of filling the bags and hauling them out to the dumpster in the rain. Fill and haul, fill and haul, fill and haul. The blessed oblivion of manual labor.

Until she found some robot decorations like the one in the photo, that is. There were five of them in a Ziploc bag, each a little different in the arrangement of zippers, gears, nuts, wires, and macramé knots. And there was writing on the label of the bag, scrawled in thick black Sharpie...so finally, she had a name to go with the robots.

"*Moto-Men.*" She read it aloud, slowly, as if the words conveyed the solution of some divine and intimate mystery.

Though, of course, they only deepened the mystery at hand. She turned the bag over in her hands, searching for the answer she craved: what happened to Helen? How did someone so normal go so...crazy?

"How about a break?" Big Mike caught hold of Angie's arm as she shoveled broken glass into her latest bag. "You've been working like a crazy person this morning."

Angie hadn't noticed. "Check this out." She leaned the shovel against a stack of record albums and pulled a macramé robot out of her pocket. "I found out what they're called: 'Moto-Men.'"

"No shit?" As Angie nodded, Big Mike took the Moto-Man and turned it over in his white-gloved paws. "Hey, look." He pulled down a zipper on its back, exposing a wedge of yellowed paper with something printed on it. "Here, read it. I don't have my glasses."

Angie took the Moto-Man from him and held it up to the plastic faceplate of her suit. The lettering on the exposed wedge of paper was tiny but readable. "It says, 'You will meet a tall, dark robot.'"

Big Mike laughed. "What's that, like a fortune cookie?"

"I guess." Angie zipped up the Moto-Man and returned it to her pocket. "Can you let me know if you find any more?"

"Sure," said Big Mike. "Whatever floats your boat, Moto-Woman."

About an hour later, Angie's phone rang, and she hurried outside. To get to the phone, which was in the pocket of her shorts, she had to quickly unzip and shrug out of the top half of her biohazard suit. "Hello?"

"Mrs. Virago? I'm Thomas Barnes, calling on behalf of Exchequer Financial, your home mortgage provider."

Angie knew what was coming next; this wasn't the first call she'd gotten about it. "Cut to the chase. How much time do I have?"

For once, the caller did just that. "Fifteen business days, unless you make payment in the designated amount as stipulated in your contract."

"Thank you for letting me know, Mr. Barnes," said Angie, and then she hung up before he could say anything else. He'd confirmed what she'd already known; any conversation beyond that would just be salt in the wound.

There wasn't any way in hell she could come up with the money, so foreclosure was imminent. Gray had maxed out every line of credit he could get his hands on...and he'd done it in both their names.

Just then, Big Mike stormed out with the latest bag for the dumpster. "Why so gloomy, Gus?"

Angie sighed and pocketed the phone. "No reason."

"Well, I've got just the thing to cheer you up." Big Mike heaved his bag in the dumpster and dusted off his gloves. "I found a couple more of these." He pulled a Moto-Man out of his pocket and tossed it to her.

Angie wasn't supposed to touch the contents of the house without her gloves, but she caught the Moto-Man with her bare hands anyway. Turning it over, she unzipped the back and read aloud the fortune on the wedge of paper there. "'You will be a real robot to riches story.'"

Big Mike laughed. "See? That's good news, isn't it?"

Angie pocketed the Moto-Man. "Best news I've had all day."

Back inside Helen's house, Angie attacked the mess with a speed and intensity that were almost robotic. The whole time, to keep from thinking about the call from the mortgage company, she focused her mind on the woman who'd created this monument to obsession.

The deeper Angie dug, the harder she looked for clues to why Helen Fulton had lived and died the way she had. But as she and Big Mike closed in on the far wall of the living room, nothing offered even the slightest hint.

Instead of telltale photo albums, journals, or scrapbooks, there were laundry baskets of beer cans, shopping bags full of used teabags and coffee filters, and heaps of junk mail. Instead of letters, postcards, or informative keepsakes, there were piles of ancient phone books, crates of doll parts, and jars of dead cockroaches.

Other than a handful of Moto-Men, Angie and Big Mike found nothing to separate Helen from the typical hoarder.

That evening, when Angie went home, she sat cross-legged on the living room floor and fanned out three of the Moto-Men in front of her. She was breaking the rule about taking anything from Helen's house, also flouting her own common sense by bringing items from that contaminated worksite into her own home...but she didn't care. Something about these Moto-Men seemed too important.

So far, nothing else in Helen's personal trash dump offered any insight. Maybe, by examining the Moto-Men in different surroundings, Angie could gain a new perspective on them.

"So, what's the deal, guys?" she asked. "What's so special about you?"

The Moto-Men just stared up at her with their eyes made of gears.

"Did she make you? Did she buy you? Did she sell you?"

The zipper mouths of the Moto-Men remained flatlines, as unreadable as ever...as responsive as co-matose Gray.

"Not talking, huh?" She grabbed a Moto-Man and pulled down the zipper on its back. "Well, maybe you've got some words of wisdom tucked away in here, then."

Holding up the Moto-Man, she peered at the tiny print on the wedge of paper in its back. What she read there surprised her so much that she had to read it again.

Turn off the lights. Don't answer the door.

"What the hell?" Angie had been expecting some robot-themed fortune cookie-style text. Instead, she'd gotten what seemed like a very specific warning.

"Okay, that's just bizarre." She put the open Moto-Man face down on the floor and reached for another.

When she unzipped the next Moto-Man, she got another strange message. She shook her head slowly as she read it.

The end is near, it read. *You should be putting your own house in order, not mine.*

"What is this shit?" The fine hairs on the back of Angie's neck rose with a tingle. The note felt too personal, almost as if it were referring to the cleanup at Helen's. Except it couldn't have been, could it?

Angie shivered as she put the second Moto-Man facedown beside the first one she'd unzipped. Then, she reached for the third and last Moto-Man that she'd brought home. Turning it over, she zipped down the back and read the wedge of paper inside.

Then, she read it again. And again. Each time, she felt more creeped out.

There is only one way out for you, read the note.

The rest of the message, in bigger, boldfaced letters, consisted of a single word: *Burn.*

Angie swallowed hard, trying to make sense of what she saw on that wedge of paper. But the more she thought about it, the less sense it made.

She was so focused on rereading those words that she jumped when the doorbell rang. Her heart, which was already beating fast, jackhammered into overdrive.

Checking her wristwatch, Angie saw it was just after nine. She never got visitors that late; whoever it was, she doubted she was in for good news.

Putting down the latest Moto-Man, the one with the "Burn" message, she got up from the floor and walked over to the front window. When she hesitated, the doorbell rang again.

Pulling aside the window curtain, she peeked out; from there, she could see whoever was on the front stoop.

As soon as she got a look at her visitors, she remembered the Moto-Man message that she'd read just moments earlier: *Turn off the lights. Don't answer the door.*

She should have taken the Moto-Man's advice. There on her stoop was a group of five men—four uniformed police officers and a man in front wearing a dark overcoat.

"Oh my God." Heart pounding, she left the window and stood for a moment with her eyes closed, trying to get her bearings. But the cops wouldn't let her; they pounded on the door again, louder than before.

Shaking, Angie went to the door and opened it. "Yes?"

"Angela Virago?" The man in the overcoat acted like he was in charge, so Angie guessed he was a plainclothes cop. He was a tall guy in his fifties or sixties with wavy silver hair, and he didn't look happy.

"Yes?" said Angie.

"We have a warrant to search the premises." The plainclothes cop handed over a sheet of paper.

Angie didn't read it. "Search for what?"

"Your husband is under investigation for drug-related activities," said the plainclothes cop. "That's all I'm at liberty to say."

When Angie got to Helen's place the next morning, she ripped into the mess with an inhuman intensity. Storming around in her biohazard suit like a manic astronaut, she took out her frustrations from the police visit—from *everything*—on the piles of used adult diapers, the bags of shredded paper, and the fried chicken buckets full of apple cores, heads from action figures, and bones that didn't look like they'd come from fried chicken.

Angie wished the cops had worked this fast the night before at her house; then again, they'd had to sniff out Gray's hiding places under the floorboards and in the basement walls before they could cart out the boxes of secret paperwork and evidence.

There it all was, under her nose—literally—for who knew how long. It was just like all of Gray's secrets, but somehow, this one stung more.

The funny thing was, though, Angie wasn't thinking much about Gray's secret boxes that morning. As important as they were to her future, the mystery of the Moto-Men occupied her mind instead.

The message about not answering the door had been strangely prophetic. What were the chances that Angie would read it at random, out of the various Moto-Men messages excavated from Helen's house, just before the police arrived to raid her own home?

But it was just a coincidence...right? The other two Moto-Man messages she'd read that night weren't prophetic, were they? Did they all have some kind of power to delve into the future and issue warnings?

Or, as Angie thought was more likely, had the pressure of her disintegrating life finally caused her to crack like Helen?

By the end of the workday, Angie and Big Mike had made tremendous progress. The ground floor of Helen's house— living room, kitchen, and dining room —was clear of debris, if not exactly clean.

But Angie was left with no more insight into Helen than she'd had at the start of the job. All she had to show for her efforts was a stack of five Moto-Men plucked from the mess.

Out of her biohazard suit, Angie sat on Helen's

front porch and lined the Moto-Men up on the floorboards like cards in a game of solitaire. As always, they stared silently upward with eyes made of gears and mouths made of zippers.

"Tomorrow, we'll start on the upstairs." Big Mike, in a sweat-soaked white wife-beater t-shirt and jeans, strolled over with two beers from the cooler in his truck. He plunked one of the beers down beside her.

Angie grabbed the beer and had a long drink. "I'll stay and do some more tonight if you will."

Big Mike rubbed his red crewcut and shook his head. "I've got plans."

Angie sighed. The last thing she wanted to do was go home. "You might be able to talk me into tagging along, you know."

Big Mike smiled. "No can do. A buddy of mine's getting out of prison, and I've gotta go pick him up."

"Who's that?"

"Theo." Big Mike leaned down and clinked the neck of his beer bottle against hers. "You know, my former cellmate."

Angie nodded. Mike and Theo had gotten to be good friends behind bars. They'd both done time for drug offenses, though Theo's sentence had run a year longer than Mike's.

"I promised I'd put him up and give him a hand

when he gets out," said Mike. "It's the least I can do, the way he helped me out inside."

"Good for you," said Angie.

The two of them were silent for a moment, swigging their beers while the rain fell. Off in the distance, thunder rumbled like a mighty engine.

Angie reached for one of the Moto-Men on the floorboards and unzipped its back. The message she found was more like the first ones she'd come across.

She read it aloud. "'Your programming will never steer you wrong.'"

Big Mike shrugged. "Whatever that means." He drained his beer and chucked the empty bottle in the dumpster. "Guess I'll see you bright and early tomorrow."

"You betcha." Angie gave him a thumbs-up.

Big Mike drove off in his truck, leaving Angie on her own as the rain intensified. After another swig of beer, she reached for another Moto-Man and unzipped its back. As the printed wedge of paper inside appeared before her, she fully expected another run-of-the-mill robot fortune, like the one she'd just read to Big Mike.

But there was nothing run-of-the-mill about what she found.

I was a prisoner all my life. I built my own prison and hid away inside.

Angie frowned. Another impossible message, one that could have been written by Helen Fulton herself. Hadn't Helen built her own prison in that house, filling it with hoarded refuse and retreating within its rancid depths from the rest of the world?

Setting aside the Moto-Man, Angie reached for another. This one seemed to pick up where the last one left off.

Do you want to be a prisoner forever, like me? Then let the past pile up around you. Let it seal you in.

Angie quickly reached for yet another Moto-Man. She trembled with nervous anticipation for the next note, hoping and dreading another message that seemed directed at her.

She unzipped the Moto-Man's back and read the note there. A lump caught in her throat as the words sank into her mind.

Freedom through fire. Whatever weighs you down, burn it to the ground.

Again, thunder rumbled in the dark sky, and the rain fell harder. *There is only one way out for you. Burn.* That was what another Moto-Man had told her...and now here was that same advice again.

Burn.

Angie gulped; she'd considered doing that exact thing to Helen's house instead of cleaning it out.

Slowly, she put the Moto-Man down on the

porch, her eyes resting on the fifth and last one she had to open. Would it say something to prove that none of the messages had been personalized or prophetic at all? Something to kill what little magic these handmade crafts had injected into her sad life?

She reached for the fifth Moto-Man and tugged down the zipper on its back. Swallowing hard, she read the note inside.

And her eyes snapped open. She dropped the Moto-Man as if it had stung her. For this final robot had shocked her with its power—the exact opposite of her fears.

Instead of killing the magic, it proved itself more magical and personal than she had ever imagined.

See him one last time before the end, it said. *Say goodbye to your husband Gray before the fire sets you free.*

Angie drove straight from the job site to the hospital. She went up to Gray's room on the sixth floor...but she didn't go in. She just watched from the hallway as his chest rose and fell and the monitors blinked and beeped.

Leaning against the doorway, she heaved a shaky

breath as the Moto-Men's messages swirled in her mind. What exactly were they telling her to do?

Whatever weighs you down, burn it to the ground. Did that mean what she thought it meant? Because she knew exactly what was weighing her down the most...and he was right there in front of her.

The last Moto-Man told her to see Gray once more before the fire. Did that mean he was supposed to be *part* of the fire? Was *she*?

Angie sighed. Why give those messages any credence at all? Even if they spoke directly to her, referring to her husband by name, she couldn't blindly follow the advice they offered. She shook her head: all this just because they'd somehow connected with her?

Maybe the smart thing to do was to forget the stupid Moto-Men and move on with her life. She had a nightmare of complications to untangle, thanks to Gray. She was already in a prison from which she probably would never escape.

Every time she went home, all she could think about were the secrets within those walls...all the things he'd kept from her. All the things she'd never known and might never know for as long as she lived, now that Gray was locked in a coma.

He was still just as much a black box to her as Helen Fulton was. He'd left her a mess of his own, a trash dump every bit as toxic as Helen's, one equally lacking in answers.

And Angie was *trapped* in it. *Do you want to be a prisoner forever, like me?* the Moto-Men had asked. *Then let the past pile up around you. Let it seal you in.*

Done and done.

And now the only way out was, what? Burning her husband? Burning herself? As if she could *ever* take Gray's life, even after everything he'd done. And she was nowhere near desperate or lost enough for suicide. Not yet, anyway.

Her eyes burned, and tears rolled down her cheeks. She knew she should go home, but the thought of it made her stomach clench. She couldn't bear feeling those walls closing in around her again, locking her away with no hope of discovering the whole truth behind her life with Gray, no chance to return to normal.

Then, suddenly, she remembered something else the Moto-Men had told her.

You should be putting your own house in order, not mine.

And she knew what to do. She knew what the Moto-Men—or Helen Fulton—had tried to tell her.

It took two and a half more days to empty Helen's house. It might have taken less time if the cool snap hadn't passed, but the returning summer heat was a drag on Angie and Big Mike.

By the time they'd finished, the big orange dumpster was full to overflowing...Helen Fulton's life, just as mysterious in the trash as in the house. The Moto-Men and their messages offered Angie the only glimpse into the woman and what she'd been through. She felt as if she knew her, at least a little, and even identified with her. A prisoner to her own life, to her own house; that, Angie could understand.

"Unbelievable," said Big Mike as he threw a last bag in the dumpster. "I thought we'd *never* finish this job."

"You and me both." Angie leaned against the front porch railing and sipped a beer. "I just hope this next hoarder cleanup isn't so bad."

"I heard it's *worse*." Big Mike laughed and smacked the side of the dumpster. "If you can imagine *that*."

Angie gulped some beer, trying to build the courage to ask him for the favor she needed. Because once the words left her mouth, it would mean she'd made up her mind to follow the Moto-Men's advice as she understood it. It would mean she was committed to a path that felt absolutely crazy and absolutely right at the same time.

Swallowing hard, she got down off the porch and went to him. "Got a question for you."

Big Mike stuck his hands on his hips and grinned. "Shoot."

Angie hesitated, though she felt certain he would have the answer she sought. As an ex-con, he must know all about techniques for committing crimes like the one she planned.

"So, okay." Angie cleared her throat. "There's something I need to know."

Big Mike tipped his head to one side. "What's that?"

Angie met his gaze, and all her nervousness suddenly flew away. She was sure of herself, sure of him, sure she'd made the right decision.

"What's the best way to start a fire?" she asked.

The fire was set in the kitchen of Angie's house and would take a little while to spread. Angie sat in her car down the street and watched to make sure nothing went wrong.

While she waited, she picked up one of the Moto-Men from the stack on the seat beside her—

the handful that she and Big Mike had retrieved from Helen's place during the last two and a half days of the cleanup. She had already unzipped and gone through them...and been totally blown away by what she'd found. Arranged in the right order, their messages told a story, one that Angie hadn't expected. Finally, she had the answers she craved about Helen Fulton and these little robots.

What better story could she reread by the dashboard light as she waited for the climax of her own encounter with the Moto-Men?

As the moments crawled past, and still no flames leaped from the windows of the house, Angie reread the last batch of Moto-Men messages, one after another.

Helen Fulton was lost in her own home. That was how the story started. *She had built walls to keep out the outside world, and they had become a maze with her at the center.*

(Glancing up, Angie thought she saw a flicker behind the sheer kitchen curtains...but no. The house remained as still and dark as Gray's heart.)

When Helen realized how lost she was, she fell into a deep sadness. She cried and cried because she could never escape the maze.

(Again, Angie looked at the kitchen window. Again, all was dark.)

Helen screamed for help, hoping that someone could lead her out of the trap she was in...but no one came to save her.

(Angie checked the window again, and her heart raced with nervous excitement. Finally, she could see the light of flames dancing through the sheers.)

Helen was in that maze for a very long time. Then, one day, a flat little robot made from macramé, zippers, and gears fell out of a pile of books she'd knocked over.

And Helen remembered.

(As Angie watched, the kitchen brightened further, illuminated by fire. Soon, she saw the first snatches of flame flickering in the living room window, too.)

Helen remembered this was one of the Moto-Men, whom she'd made for just such an occasion. The Moto-Men, whom she'd built to rescue her like the good little robots they were.

(Now, the living room was blazing right along with the kitchen...and Gray's office flared with fiery light, as well.)

Sure enough, the Moto-Men did exactly what they'd been designed to do. The message under the zipper on the first one's back was a clue that led to another. When she found the next Moto-Man, it led to the one after that.

(The downstairs windows blew out one after another, starting with the kitchen. Meanwhile, Angie saw the upstairs windows brighten.)

That night, the trail of Moto-Men led Helen right through the maze. Before long, she was pushing the front door open, smiling up at the starry night sky.

(Flames lashed from every window in the house. Watching them made Angie's heart hammer with strange, sweet joy and excitement.)

Helen felt lighter than she had in decades, as if she'd left a great weight behind her. She felt lighter than air, finally free, as if she might float up into the sky at any moment.

(Angie put the car into gear and rolled down the street, eager to leave before the fire trucks arrived.)

The dozens of Moto-Men in Helen's hands beeped and buzzed and twinkled in the bright platinum moonlight shining down from above. They told her, in Moto-Men language, that it was time for the happy ending she deserved.

(Angie smiled as she drove away, watching the blaze consume the house in her rear-view mirror. Did the Moto-Men have some kind of intelligence and power of their own? Or were their voices only Helen's in the end, reaching out from the Great Beyond to save a kindred spirit?)

This time...

(But *had* they saved Angie? Would this one fire really make a difference, given the problems she faced? Or would it just add another problem, if the fire was judged an arson instead of just the latest incident in a long streak of bad luck?)

This time...

(Somehow, Angie thought she would be okay. She felt like this was a turning point, and she could handle whatever came next. All thanks to her gear-eyed friends, who had shown her that the best way out of her personal prison was to burn away what was holding her back without sentimentality.)

(In other words, she had those macramé machine men to thank for showing her how to find her own inner robot.)

This time, the tears running down Helen's face were not hot, salty tears of sorrow or fear. They were Moto-Men tears, cold and shiny as metal shavings.

The Leather Jacket of Doom

Chris Chan

There's a line that my great-grandmother Cornelia told me once that I've often passed on to the young women I take under my wing. "The boy has the fun, the girl has the baby." I get a lot of different reactions to it, ranging from an airy laugh and a nod, along with the reply, "That's so true," to a cold stare and a "That's not funny!" When I told Fiona that quote a year ago, she just sighed and replied, "Well...too late for that warning now, Miss Kaiming."

I was returning from my weekly afternoon faculty meeting when I saw Fiona sitting on the chair outside my office. She had a wad of used tissues in her hand the size of a grapefruit, and her mascara had dribbled down her cheeks, making her face look a bit like a referee's jersey, although I would never have said that in front of her.

When she saw me coming, she jumped up and started rushing towards me. "Miss Kaiming, I need to talk to you right away."

It's always on the days that you most want to go straight home and collapse on the couch in front of a very loud television that your students ask for a little more of your time. I'm not complaining, just stating a fact.

I opened up my office, gestured for her to throw her tissues in my wastepaper basket and take a chair, slung my bag over my chair, and sat down on the edge of my desk. "So, what's wrong?"

The tears were coming back to her eyes, and she plucked a fresh tissue from the box on my desk. "Miss Kaiming, you've been such a big help to me. Thank you."

"You're welcome. What's going on?"

"I would never have been able to stay in high school without your help and your mentoring and your championing me for the scholarship. I really, really appreciate it."

"No problem. It's my job. So what, exactly, is the issue here?"

"I'm coming to you because you're so understanding. I mean, I know that you've been in my shoes. I mean, you had your daughter when you were even younger than me, so you know what it's like to juggle high school and a baby."

"I do indeed. Listen, Fiona, I appreciate your expressions of gratitude, but I've got to drive across town and pick up the interlibrary loan books that just arrived for my dissertation. I know you're distraught right now, but could you please tell me exactly what's bothering you?"

Fiona swallowed and nodded. "It's Parker. You only met him once, but you remember him, right?"

"Of course I do." I was about to say, "He's the

one who knocked you up," but I wisely caught myself in the nick of time, and substituted the words, "He's Tina's father."

"That's right."

"Didn't he say that he didn't want anything to do with you or Tina?"

"I know he didn't handle the news very well when I got pregnant, but he's changed a lot over the past year."

I wasn't convinced, but I managed to reply with a noncommittal, "Good for him."

"I ran into him at a coffee shop near my house a couple of weeks ago, and we started talking, and we decided that we should try to be friends again."

"Did he say that he wanted to take a more active role in his daughter's life?"

"He explained that he wasn't ready for that yet. He did spend a little time with her, but..."

After she paused for a few moments I tried to finish her sentence for her. "He suddenly had somewhere else he needed to be?"

"Well, yes."

I sighed. "Listen. I'm not going to say anything against the father of your daughter. But what's got you so upset?"

Fiona started twitching. "It's Parker."

"I gathered that. What's the problem?"

"He's dead."

Upon hearing that, my stomach twisted into a knot. I slid off my desk and stretched out my arms. Immediately, Fiona leapt out of her chair and rushed towards me for a hug. She started sobbing, and after a quick and gentle adjustment to her head so her tears soaked the tissue I held to her face instead of my white blazer, I patted her back gently while she settled her emotions.

It took about seven minutes before the crying slowed down. "Feel better?" I asked.

"A lot. Thanks."

After we both took a second to settle back down in our chairs, I started to press for more details. "What happened? Was it some kind of accident?"

"Maybe...Not exactly. I don't know."

"Can you please tell me what you do know?"

"They're saying it was a drug overdose."

Fiona must have seen the expression on my face, because she hurriedly added, "But Parker didn't do drugs! He wasn't into that at all! I knew him, and he was clean! He never would've..."

Unfortunately, I've seen too many kids get messed up by addiction to be surprised by anything, but I wasn't about to upset Fiona any more than I had to at the moment.

I tugged a few tissues from the box on my desk

and handed them to her. "Look, start from the beginning. When and where did they find him?"

Fiona shifted uneasily. "That's not really the beginning, actually. I saw him yesterday. After school, the two of us met up to talk. He had the afternoon free because the new sports season won't start until next week."

"All right," I gestured in what I hoped was an encouraging manner. "What did you talk about? Tina?"

"Yes. We went to a frozen yogurt shop around four, and he held Tina for a little while, and I told him about the great things that were going on at Cuthbertson Hall, and he told me that life was still pretty boring at our old high school, and he asked if I was seeing anybody, and...and..." She started sniffling again.

"Let me guess, you told him that with mountains of homework and a ten month-old baby, you don't have time to date."

She nodded vigorously. "Exactly. I think I used almost exactly those words, only I said 'tons' instead of 'mountains.'"

I really didn't care about that point, but I didn't think it was the right time to tell her that.

"Anyway, he was being really sweet and supportive, and he made it clear that he feels really bad about not doing anything to help with raising Tina so far, and he wanted to change for the better."

I was skeptical about that. A guy can claim that he "feels really bad" until he's blue in the face, but it won't change a single diaper.

"So we talked and talked, and he was so earnest and caring that I thought, hey, maybe he is ready to be a father. We walked together for a while, and it suddenly got chilly, so he took off his jacket and let me wear it. I'd left my coat at home because I didn't think I'd need it. Anyway, he'd never done anything thoughtful like that before. We talked all the way home, and he pushed Tina's stroller. When we got to my house he helped put Tina in her crib for a nap, and he hugged me and gave Tina a kiss, and then he left."

"When did he leave your house?"

"A little after five. Maybe five-fifteen."

She paused for a very long time, and I felt it necessary to prompt her for more information. "Okay. Was that the last time you saw him alive?"

"Yes." Fiona dabbed her eyes with a tissue.

"Did you talk to him on the phone or text him or anything?"

"No. The last words he ever said to me were, 'Bye. I'll see you both soon.'"

"How did you find out he..." I didn't want to say

the word "died." I had a feeling that saying that word might provoke Fiona into letting loose with another waterfall of tears, and even though I'm good at comforting my girls during their hours of need, my patience has its limits.

"His mother and my Mom are friends, and she called Mom last night. She was frantic. It was about two hours after I last saw him. Parker had just come back home after hanging out with some friends, and he was helping himself to some leftovers from the fridge. All of a sudden, he started stumbling around the room, looking sick, until he finally collapsed. His mother called an ambulance, and they rushed him to the hospital for tests. Before they could figure out what was wrong with him he..." The tears flowed faster than ever, and I didn't blame her one bit.

Once Fiona got her voice back, she shuddered. "They say it looks like a drug overdose."

"Did they say what it was?" I asked.

"I don't really remember. I think it was phenol."

"Phenol..." I thought about it a moment and suspected that she'd gotten it wrong. "Could it have been 'fentanyl?'"

"Yes! I think you're right!"

"And you don't believe that he was a drug user?"

"No! Definitely not! He's—he was—obsessed with keeping his body in perfect shape. I'm telling you, he was an athlete and once at a game I saw him chewing out one of his teammates who got caught taking steroids or something like that. Just yesterday, we passed by a couple of kids our age who were smoking cigarettes, and he just looked disgusted. He started grumbling about how they were flushing their lives and health down the toilet. He would've had nothing to do with drugs!"

The certainty in her voice convinced me. He may have made Fiona a mom at sixteen, but that didn't make him a junkie. "So, what are you asking me to do here? Do you want me to look into this with my boyfriend?"

"Could you please?" Fiona looked very hopeful. "This is Mr. Funderburke's sort of thing, isn't it?"

I thought about it for a moment. I was planning on spending the evening catching up on my grading and writing at least two more pages of my dissertation. But when one of my girls needs help, I have a hard time saying "no." The fact that I happen to be dating a children's rights lawyer and private investigator who's darned good at his jobs pretty much sealed the deal.

"Sure."

Fiona jumped up and hugged me, and after I managed to extricate myself from her arms I told her to get Tina and hurry home, and I'd call her later tonight with any news that I might have un-earthed.

Five minutes later, I was pulling on my burgundy lambskin trench coat, stuffing some papers and books into my valise, and hurrying downstairs to the faculty parking lot where my boyfriend Funderburke was waiting for me in his fifth-hand thirty-one year-old Volvo that we both love for reasons I can't really explain.

"So we're not going to the library for your dissertation research?" he asked.

I shook my head. "I've got more important matters right now. One of my girls needs me."

Funderburke totally understood. "Which one and what happened?"

"Fiona."

"Long blonde hair, Tammy's mother?"

"No. Tammy is Ginny's daughter. I don't blame you for the mix-up, Fiona and Ginny look a lot alike. Same hair, similar voice, too. No, Fiona is Tina's mother." I took a few minutes and got Funderburke up to speed on the situation regarding Parker's sudden death and potential drug overdose.

By this point, we had driven out of Mequon and into Fox Point. "So, what's Fiona saying?" Funderburke asked. "That since Parker didn't do drugs, ei-ther this was all a freak accident or maybe murder?"

"Well, Fiona's not saying anything—turn left here—except that she wants us to look into it. She knows our reputation for straightening out these situations." I pointed out the window. "The cream house with the blue trim, there. That's Parker's family's house. The Rileys."

About seven cars were parked up and down the road. I figured that the Rileys' friends were paying their respects and offering moral support. We found a spot about four houses down, and we both wrapped our long leather coats around us to protect us from the strong winds.

I was about to ring the bell, but the inner door was already open, and a woman in a pink sweater and jeans inside waved at us, presumably encouraging us to enter.

"Hello," the pink sweater lady greeted us. She was in her mid-to-late thirties, with platinum hair up in a French twist. She scrutinized us for a few moments, trying to see if she recognized our faces, then decided she didn't know us. "I'm Brianna. I'm the Rileys' next-door neighbor. Are you here about Parker?"

"We are."

"Are you his teachers?" Now that we were inside, I'd unbuttoned and untied my trench coat. Brianna surveyed my outfit critically. I have my own preferred style of dressing, and I tend to fall on the flashy side. Flashy but modest, I hasten to qualify. No other teacher I've ever met dresses like I do, and I take an undefinable pleasure in that. "No, you can't be his teachers..."

"Actually, I am a teacher, but I don't work at Parker's school. I teach at Cuthbertson Hall. I'm Nerissa Kaiming, history teacher and director of the Bialowsky Project, which helps teen mothers continue their education. This is my boyfriend and colleague Isaiah Funderburke. He's the student advocate at Cuthbertson. We're here to pay our respects and to pass on the condolences of Fiona Cafaro, who wanted to be here, but right now she's too distraught. You see—"

I stopped because Brianna was nodding vigorously. "Of course. I know the Cafaros, and I've met Fiona many times. I'm not a gossip, but what happened is common knowledge around here."

Whenever someone says that he or she isn't a gossip, that's code for "I know all the dirty secrets of everybody who lives within a mile of me, and I'm just dying to spill the beans." Deciding that Brianna was potentially a treasure trove of information, I leaned in, and gently said, "Fiona's a lovely girl. But she's very upset about what happened, and she doesn't know any of the details. We're very close, and I was hoping that I could find out just what happened to poor, poor Parker, so I could break it to her gently."

Brianna decided that my motives were pure. "Of course. Won't you come sit over here?"

"Excuse me a moment, please," Funderburke stepped away. "Is it all right if I get a glass of water?"

"Oh, of course," Brianna pointed towards a heavily-laden refreshment table. "Help yourself to water or soda or juice. People brought all this food, you might as well eat some of it."

Funderburke gave Brianna his most charming smile, and gave me a little nod to let me know that he was going to work the room and try to extract some information from the mourners.

Brianna led me into a breakfast nook, and as we lowered ourselves into some beautifully carved but horribly uncomfortable wooden chairs, she leaned forward, clearly bursting at the seams with the anticipation of telling me everything she knew. "So, you know all about Parker and Fiona's relationship?"

I nodded. "They broke up right after Fiona realized she was pregnant, and they haven't had too much contact since then, but they were starting to reconcile."

"Were they?" Brianna looked incredulous. "I didn't know that. Parker's been dating one girl after another. I thought he was getting serious—a bit *too* serious—with that girl Lynsey there." Brianna leaned forward and pointed through the dining room, into the living room. Lynsey was a tall, slim girl with a waterfall of wavy blonde hair, wearing a snug black sweater and grey leggings. Even from this distance, I could tell that she'd been crying a lot, and her hands were full of tissues.

"So, Lynsey's his current girlfriend?" I asked.

"Mm-hmm." Brianna pursed her lips, and from the sudden coolness in her voice and eyes, I gathered that Lynsey was not on her list of her top ten favorite people. Or her top hundred or thousand favorite people, for that matter.

A sudden flash of recognition hit me. "I guess Parker had a thing for blondes."

Brianna nodded. "I suppose he did. The other girls he's been seeing the past year, I think that they all had similar appearances. Golden hair, and plenty of it."

"Huh..." I decided it was time to get off the topic of hair and move onto something a bit more pertinent to the investigation. "So...I hope that I'm not prying, but...I'm not clear on how he died. Was it some kind of heart attack or something? Because he was just a teenager..." I figured that pretending to know less about the manner of Parker's death than I actually did would encourage Brianna to tell me everything she knew.

"Oh, no. It wasn't a heart attack or anything like that. It was..." she leaned forward and whispered in my ear. "*A drug overdose.*"

I made my best attempt at a shocked face. "No! But Fiona said that Parker was a real straight arrow!"

"Well, I suppose she was inclined to think the best of him. Anyway, what can you expect from someone who's become a parent at sixteen?"

As someone who became a mother at thirteen, I had a few choice words to say to Brianna, but I decided to hold them in for a little while. In any case, before I could say anything else Brianna continued, "Well, Parker wasn't very straitlaced at all, I can assure you of that. Aside from being...promiscuous..." Brianna took a full five seconds to say that last word. "He liked to experiment with drugs as well. When I moved here two years ago, right after my divorce, I saw him hanging out in his treehouse drinking beers all the time. Lately, I caught him with a liquor bottle. I didn't know how to tell his parents because it wasn't my business, or so I thought. And judging from his pupils and his erratic behavior, I think he was moving on to harder drugs. One time I passed by him on my afternoon run, and I smelled marijuana smoke on him. Just last week I saw him stuffing a little white packet into his jeans. I should have said something, I know. If I had, maybe he'd still be..." Her voice trailed off and tears formed in her eyes.

I handed her a tissue. "So, he was a drug user?"

"Yes," she replied, dabbing her face. "I don't know if he was a full-fledged addict, but he'd been taking all sorts of substances for a very long time."

I was disappointed but not surprised. I'd had the feeling that Fiona was not the best judge of character, especially where the father of her child was concerned, but I'd hoped that I was just being cynical.

I cleared my throat and tried to choose my words carefully, remembering that I was pretending to know less than I did. "Do you know what drug he overdosed on? Was it cocaine or heroin?"

"No. It's called fentanyl. At least, that's what they think it is at the moment. I heard the paramedics as they carried him out of the house. They said his heart rate was very slow, that his blood pressure was dropping, his lips and nails had turned blue, his pupils had contracted to almost nothing..."

"Wait, he had his fatal attack here, at his house? When was this?"

"Yes. He'd just come back home. It was a little after seven. I don't know where he'd been, but he seemed fine right before it happened. I was actually outside, dragging out my garbage bins, when I saw

Parker shuffling home. I spoke to him briefly, just to say hello."

"Did you notice anything odd?"

"Well, he was shaking, but I thought he was just shivering. It was a chilly night, and he had his jacket zipped up and his hands were in his pockets. He looked perfectly fine to me, but it was dark, so I could have overlooked something. I saw him step inside his house, and then just ten minutes later I saw the ambulance pulling up." She started sniffling, so I reached into my pocket and handed her a packet of tissues. I carry a lot of them—it seems like I always keep bumping into people who are crying.

I was about to ask Brianna if she had anything else potentially important to say about Parker's death, but before I could inquire, Brianna hastily stood up and excused herself, informing me that she had to visit the little girls' room.

I started to look around the house, trying to figure out which person would be the best to strike up a conversation with—somebody who knew what was going on, but who had no compunction whatsoever about telling me everything. I looked at a cluster of forty-something women, probably mothers from Parker's school or friends of the family, but they looked like they wouldn't take too kindly to an outsider breaking into their little group and pumping them for details. There were a couple of middle-aged men chatting in a corner, but neither of them looked terribly upset, and I was dubious as to how much either of them actually knew about what happened to Parker. It's been my experience that an unsettling number of fathers have very little idea what their children are up to when daddy's not there. Not all fathers, but the guys in the corner struck me as the "deliberately clueless" type.

Before I could examine the guests further, a burly man came up to me. His head was shaved completely bald, but from the asymmetrical shape of his skull, the totally hairless look was not a good one for him. "I know who you are," he informed me.

"So..." I had the impression that he was trying to intimidate me, and I was not about to give him even a tiny bit of satisfaction. "Wanna tell me your name and make the two of us even?"

I'd shot him what I hoped was my most winning smile, but from his reaction it was pretty clear today just was not my day. "I'm Parker's father. I know that you and your boyfriend are from that fancy prep school, and you both like to play detective."

"Actually, we don't just play detective. We're both fully licensed private investigators and he's also a lawyer—"

"I don't care."

His voice was very blunt, and I immediately realized I needed to switch tactics. "I'm very sorry for your loss, sir."

"No, you're not. If you were, you wouldn't be poking around, sticking your nose where it has no business being."

Given the choice between being on offense or defense, I will choose offense every time. I looked him straight in the eye and said, "I am here at the request of the mother of your grandchild. She is very distraught and has almost no idea what's going on, so out of friendship I came here in order to give her the answers she needs and deserves. If you have any concern at all for your granddaughter's mother, I hope you will please help me by telling me exactly what happened to your son, may he rest in peace."

Parker's father blanched, and then recovered his aggressive demeanor. "That little slut Fiona nearly ruined my son's future. I don't consider that baby my grandchild, and you can tell Fiona that she is not to come to the funeral. I don't want you or Fiona or your boyfriend to come around here again. My son made a lot of bad choices, and taking drugs was one of them. He died from an accidental overdose. Now get the hell out of my house."

I was torn. Part of me wanted to skedaddle and never come back. I didn't like prying into a family dealing with a terrible tragedy. I was pretty sure that there weren't going to be any satisfying answers, just the loss and grief that are happening way too often to families all over the country due to similar circumstances. However, I hate it when people try to intimidate me. Yes, I was in the man's house, but the way Parker's father was standing over me, glaring at me, and talking about Fiona, the contrary aspects of my personality were telling me to plant myself firmly in a chair and refuse to move.

I was this close to saying some decidedly sharp words to a grieving father when I saw Funderburke waving at me through the outside window. I took a deep breath, decided that this was not the time for me to speak my mind, and contented myself to saying a simple, "My condolences, *sir*," and exited the house with all the dignity I could possibly muster.

As I stepped through the front door, I saw Funderburke waving me through a tall wooden gate into the property adjacent to Parker's home. Standing next to him was a short, slightly chubby teenaged boy wearing khakis and a dark grey fleece jacket. I joined them, and Funderburke shut and bolted the gate. We were now standing on a large brick patio, and a quick look assured me that the fence was high enough to prevent the people next door from seeing me, although the top of Funderburke's head was still visible. Still, I reasoned that Parker's father couldn't order us to leave his neighbor's property.

Funderburke gestured to our companion. "Nerissa, this is Remy Cerda. He's Parker's next-door neighbor, and has known him all his life."

"I'm a few years younger than Parker," Remy beamed at me as he shook my hand. I noticed he was blushing a little bit. He looked excited, and didn't seem to be grieving at all.

"Hi! I don't know how much my boyfriend has told you about me—"

Remy interrupted me, but he seemed so happy to be talking to me that I wasn't the least bit upset with him. "Oh! I know all about you. I read Funderburke's blog. I know all about your work for children's rights, I know about those other cases you've solved. I'm a huge fan of you both. It's so cool to finally meet you!"

After dealing with Parker's father, I was delighted to receive such a warm welcome. "It's...nice to be appreciated."

Remy tugged at Funderburke's sleeve. "As soon as I saw a tall man wearing a long black leather coat, and a woman wearing leather pants under a leather trench coat, I knew that you were Isaiah Funderburke and Nerissa Kaiming. I told Lynsey who you were, and that you were probably looking into what happened to Parker."

"That's exactly what we're doing." I abruptly remembered the name. "Lynsey? Is she the blonde in the black sweater who was dating Parker?"

Remy nodded vigorously. "She's my sister. She's three years older than I am. Same as Parker. Have you met our brother Len? He's fourteen months older than Lynsey, but he's in the same class as Lynsey and Parker because he had to repeat a year of kindergarten."

"No, I haven't met him."

Remy shrugged. "Len came with Lynsey and me to pay our respects, but then he disappeared. He does that a lot. Anyway, Len and Parker were best friends. They did everything together."

I started talking without taking the time to think about phrasing my words diplomatically. "When you say 'did everything together,' did that include, well..."

Thankfully, Remy finished my sentence for me. "Drug use? No, not really. Parker was not into drugs, although he liked beer. He and Len have been sneaking beers as long as I can remember. I suspect that Len's been taking drugs for about a year now, but not with Parker. Mom found a bag of pills in his room last week and threatened to send him to rehab, but Dad said that he was already paying through the nose for alimony and child support, and he wasn't going to pay for rehab, too." Remy squirmed a little bit, clearly realizing that he'd spilled a few too many beans.

Personally, I wanted Remy to keep airing out all of the family dirty laundry, but I didn't want to come across as being too eager for salacious details.

Funderburke, sensing that Remy was starting to get a little more reticent, tried to reboot the conversation. "Nerissa, I told Remy that Fiona asked us to look into Parker's death. Now, from what I can tell, everybody seems to think that it was all just a terrible accident. Another kid taking drugs and inadvertently overdosing. But Remy, you seem to be telling us that Parker wasn't a drug user?"

Remy nodded so vigorously I worried he was going to give himself whiplash. "Mm-hmm! I know it's wrong to eavesdrop, but I listened in on a lot of Parker and Len's conversations, as well as what he said to Lynsey, too. Just two nights ago, Parker told Len that he had to quit taking pills, because his grades were dropping, and if he got caught he'd be kicked off the sports teams, and maybe even kicked out of school. Later that evening, I heard Parker telling Lynsey that she should talk to Len, because Len wasn't listening to him, but she—Lynsey—has always known how to get Len to do what she wanted."

Thank God for nosy little brothers.

Funderburke stuck his hands in his pockets and looked thoughtful. "So if Parker wasn't into drugs, then how did he overdose?"

Remy shrugged. "I know. I was wondering about that. Parker has been worried about Len for months. You see, in the last soccer game of the past season, Len got knocked to the ground and this really burly referee accidentally stomped on his leg, and Len needed surgery because of a loose bone fragment, so the doctors gave him painkillers, and I'm afraid he got hooked, and he's been taking pills ever since."

"Opiates?" I asked.

"I'm pretty sure that's what they are."

"Where's he getting them?" Funderburke asked.

"I'm not sure, and I've been trying to figure out for a long time. But the situation's getting worse. Last month, Len demanded that I give him all the money I had saved in my room. He took it all, about a hundred and fifty dollars. He said he'd pay me back, but..." Remy sighed. "I don't need to go into details. You can fill in the blanks. Recently, he asked Lynsey and Parker for money, too, although she told him no, and Parker said that he was pretty much broke. Both of them told Len that they weren't going to enable him by helping him feed his addiction."

Funderburke folded his arms. "But Parker and Len stayed best friends despite everything you've just mentioned?"

"Well...Come to think of it, I think they haven't been hanging out as much the last few weeks. When they talked, they argued about Len's growing dependence on painkillers. Parker was at our house all the time, but he was mostly hanging out with Lynsey."

"How long were Parker and Lynsey dating?" I asked.

"About three months. They were both worried about Len, and I think that brought them together."

I started playing with my hair. I always do that when I have something big on my mind. "What does your mother think about all this?"

Remy looked rather sad. "She hasn't been spending much time at home lately. She has a new boyfriend. She made that one threat about putting Len in rehab, but pretty soon afterwards it seems like she forgot all about it."

"Remy, if Parker was so anti-drug, how do you account for his dying from a fentanyl overdose?" The wind was picking up--Funderburke's hair was starting to blow into his eyes, and his coat was billowing behind him.

"I have no idea. Are they sure it was a drug overdose? I don't know if they've had enough time for a full autopsy. I think that maybe Parker had an aneurysm or a seizure or something, and the doctors misdiagnosed it at first." Remy was shivering. "It's getting chilly. Do you mind if go inside?"

This was fine with both of us, and we followed Remy inside his house. As soon as he entered the living room, Remy jumped and his face turned pale.

"Are you O.K.?"

Remy didn't respond, so Funderburke repeated the question. When he still didn't answer, I put a hand on his shoulder and shook him gently. It seemed to get his attention.

"Huh? What?"

"Funderburke asked you if you were all right, Remy."

"Oh. I'm fine. It's just...I was surprised, that's all."

"By what?"

"That." Remy pointed at a plush blue sofa, although I realized that his gaze was fixed on a black leather jacket that was draped over it.

"What's so disconcerting about a leather jacket?" I was a bit confused. Remy certainly didn't seem to have a problem with the coats that Funderburke and I were wearing.

"That's Parker's jacket. He and Len always throw their jackets on the sofa when they came to hang out here. Well, not that jacket. I never saw Parker wear this leather jacket before yesterday evening. I saw him wearing for the first time yesterday when he walked by our house after school. He usually wore his school letter jacket. I wonder what it's doing here?"

"Could he have left it behind last night?" Funderburke asked.

"No. He didn't stop by our house yesterday. Anyway, it wasn't here an hour ago. I'd swear to that."

"Well, it didn't just walk here." I crossed the room, picked up the jacket, and examined it. It was a very nice jacket, and I know a good quality leather garment when I see one. It was buttery soft and silky, almost certainly lambskin, and was in practically new condition. It was a moto jacket with a racing collar, size medium. I wouldn't have minded getting one like that in a more feminine cut for myself. "How long has he had this?"

"The first time I ever saw him wear it was yesterday. Of course, he could've had it for a while before that. After all, it's been winter coat weather until recently."

I brushed the back of my hand over the material.

"This looks like it could be a pricey item. Look at the designer. Not cheap."

"I thought you said that Parker claimed to be broke," Funderburke commented.

"Well, that's what he said, at least." Remy shrugged.

"Did he have a job?" I asked.

"No, he was too busy with sports and school."

"Then how did he afford this? I'm guessing this would cost at least seven hundred fifty dollars."

Funderburke thought for a moment. "Maybe it was on sale, or perhaps he bought it online. You know better than anybody, Nerissa, how many places there are online where people sell unwanted clothes for a fraction of their store price."

"I suppose so."

Funderburke tapped the jacket's collar. "However he got it, it doesn't explain how it got here."

Our thoughts were interrupted by the sound of water whooshing through plumbing, followed by the noises of hand washing. Soon afterwards, a door down the hall opened, and a taller, slimmer, older version of Remy walked towards us.

It was pretty obvious who he was, so Funderburke didn't bother to ask his name. "Len? My name is Isaiah Funderburke, and this is Nerissa Kaiming. We're looking into the death of your friend Parker."

It was obvious that Len wasn't completely with us. His eyes were cloudy, and he seemed to be in another world. I've known a bunch of students who have struggled with similar addictions, and it was pretty clear that he was under the influence of something fairly strong. "Hey. What's up? I know you guys. My brother talks about you two all the time. He's a big fan of yours." Len walked towards us, but his gait was not very steady.

"Can you tell us anything about how your friend died?" I figured the best strategy was to come straight to the point, without any dithering.

"They say he overdosed, but that's baloney." Len didn't actually say the word "baloney," but my inner censor compels me to bowdlerize his speech to use a less scatological word.

"How do you explain his death, then?"

"I have no idea. That's up to you guys to figure out. That's your thing, isn't it?" Len didn't come across as being snide or confrontational, just a little out of it.

I held up the jacket. "Len, did you bring Parker's jacket over here?"

He wrested it from my hand. "Yes, I did."

"Why?"

"It's mine now. Parker would've wanted me to have it." He wriggled his arms into the sleeves, adjusted the collar, and crossed over to the mirror. "We always shared everything. And it fits me perfectly."

There was something a little macabre about snatching up a dead teen's clothes before the body was even cold, but I got the sense that voicing my disapproval would have the same effect as screaming at a rock. "So...you two were really close?"

"Yep."

"No arguments or disagreements?"

"Not at all. Why? What have you heard?"

From the quietly anxious look on Remy's face, I could tell that he was silently telling me that his brother was lying, and that he was begging me not to tell Len that he had been airing the family dirty laundry. "No reason," I said as calmly as possible. "I'm just trying to get a sense of Parker's mindset during his last few days."

Len turned his attention to the mirror. He stroked the sleeves of the jacket with both hands. Clearly he thought it suited him. "Well, it's weird. He was acting kind of twitchy the last couple of days."

"Can you give us some specifics?" Funderburke asked.

Len shrugged. "I dunno. He looked upset. Maybe he was worried that my sister was going to find out his other girlfriend."

Holy crud, another girlfriend? I managed to

swallow this exclamation, although I don't think I kept all the testiness out of my voice when I said, "So he was cheating on your sister? Do you know who it was?"

"Naw, but come on, Parker liked to get as much as he could, you know what I mean? He wasn't going to tie himself down with one girl. He was bedding two other girls at the same time he knocked up that Fiona chick, you know that?"

I didn't know that, but I wasn't surprised. "Do you know anything that could tell us who his secret girlfriend was?"

"Nuh-uh. Only thing was, it was kind of weird. He told me he'd been with someone else for the last month, maybe more, but he wouldn't tell me who it was. Normally, he gives me all the details. Names, places, number of times, what she said, how she liked it when he—"

"We get the picture." Funderburke's interruption was unnecessarily loud, but he did not want Len to keep going. My boyfriend's a total prude, and I like him that way. Before Len could say anything else, Funderburke continued. "Listen, we're not here to get you in trouble or anything like that. But we are trying to make sense out of all of this, and what you're telling us has led to some seemingly unresolvable contradictions. First of all, everybody's saying Parker died of fentanyl poisoning."

Remy nodded vigorously. "That's true. I heard the police talking about that with Parker's parents about that an hour ago."

"Well, the fentanyl didn't come out of thin air," Funderburke reasoned. "Now please excuse me for asking you to repeat yourself, but once again, Parker didn't take drugs, so he wouldn't have experimented with fentanyl, right?"

"You got it." Len slumped into a plush chair. "He only had the occasional beer. And he wouldn't even have a drink when he was in training. The worst thing he'd take would be those nasty protein shakes he'd make with that powder that smells like old socks."

Funderburke took a couple of steps towards Len. "So if Parker wouldn't take the fentanyl deliberately, that leaves two possibilities. First, he could've taken it accidentally, and we'd have to figure out how that happened. Second, someone could have given it to him deliberately, and in that case we have to figure out who would do that to him."

Len shook his head. "Uh-uh. No way. No one could have poisoned him on purpose. Everybody liked him. I'm telling you, he wasn't murdered. No way."

I re-entered the interrogation. "So rule out intentional poisoning. I've been doing a little Internet research. Fentanyl has been causing a lot of problems for first responders and police officers investigating overdoses. With powdered fentanyl everywhere, the paramedics touch the poison, it gets into their system, and they inadvertently start overdosing themselves."

"I heard about that on the news," chimed in Remy.

"So, if we're thinking an accident, then maybe Parker just got into contact with some fentanyl that had been left somewhere or inadvertently spilled on some surface he touched," I reasoned.

"Makes sense to me." Len looked like he was starting to drift off a bit.

Funderburke bent down, looking at Len at eye level and holding up the hem of his walking coat to keep it off the floor. "Len, I'm going to ask you to please be honest with me. Your answer is not going to leave this room. Please don't take offense."

"What do you want do know?"

"Have you ever used fentanyl?"

There was no trace of anger on Len's face. "No, man. I swear, I only take painkillers."

"Fentanyl is a painkiller," I noted.

"Well, it's not what I take," Len seemed slightly

defiant. "Mine are oxymorphone. I never take any-thing else."

"You don't take fentanyl and you haven't had any contact with it?" I asked.

"Definitely not. I know what you're thinking. I'm telling you, however Parker came across that fen-tanyl, it wasn't from me. I don't take it, I don't buy it, I didn't give it to him or spill it somewhere. Don't try to pin this on me."

"We're not trying to do that," Funderburke said reassuringly. "But can I ask another question, with the promise of confidentiality?"

"O.K."

"Where do you get your oxymorphone tablets?"

For the first time, Len started to look evasive. "Oh, you know..."

"No, I don't know. That's why I just asked you that question."

"From the pharmacy...pharmacies. I have some fake prescriptions and I pick them up from drugstores here and there."

My instincts were sure he was lying, and my in-stincts also told me that any attempts to pump him for more details would be met with more falsehoods. A quarter-second of eye contact with Funderburke told me that he concurred in my assessment of the situation.

I was trying to think of a new approach to extracting information from Len when a chirping noise emanated from his pocket. He whipped out his cell phone, glanced at it, and mumbled something that was probably "Gotta take this. Back soon." With that, he staggered out of the room and stomped up the stairs.

Feeling surprisingly tense, I took a long, slow, deep breath, held it for a few seconds, and released it with enough force to propel a sailboat. "So what now?" I asked Funderburke.

"I think we need to keep digging." Funderburke turned to Remy. "Are there any other friends of Parker who might be willing to talk to us? Anyone who wouldn't make a fuss if we kept digging around?"

Remy's eyebrows pressed closer together. "Actually, I think that most of his closest friends are in Chicago right now for a school day trip. I think that their bus won't be back until pretty late tonight."

"Great." Suddenly I remembered something. "Wait a minute. There's someone else who knew him pretty well."

Funderburke was right with me. "His girlfriend." He nodded at Remy. "Your sister."

Remy beamed. "If we leave her alone she'll just hang around her friends for hours. Let me get her."

Before we could respond Remy burst out of the house with surprising speed, neglecting to shut the door during his hurried exit.

Watching the front door bounce against the wall, I found myself smiling. "I like that kid. He's got spirit."

"I agree."

"Funderburke, do you think that we're wasting our time here?"

"You're trying to help one of your girls. Besides. This isn't the first time we've poked into something everybody said was none of our business." He smiled. "Some of our best dates have centered around helping our students."

"I can't argue with that...but in this case I'm wondering if we're going to do more good than harm. Suppose that what we're hearing is right and Parker didn't take drugs. It was some kind of freak accident. Is it really going to make his aggressive father with a mild case of halitosis less angry?"

"Yeah...but I've got my P.I. instincts telling me to go for door number three."

"What? Explain yourself."

Funderburke leaned against the wall and folded his arms. "Suppose Parker experimenting with drugs and overdosing is door one, and some kind of inadvertent contact with the fentanyl leading to a fatality is door two. That leaves door number three, the option that Len refused to even consider—"

"You mean murder?"

"Is it that much of a stretch? You know the saying—most murders center around money, drugs, or sex. We've got two out of three in play here. First, teen drug use. If Parker was so anti-drug, then maybe he might have done something that upset someone involved in the drug dealing."

"We don't know where Len's getting his painkillers," I mused.

"Right. Now, think about the sex angle. Parker was a player. He's a teen absentee dad. He has a reputation for cheating on his girlfriends. Is it too much to postulate that maybe, just maybe, somebody decided that they didn't like the way he ran his love life? Maybe a spurned lover felt betrayed. A jealous ex-boyfriend, a would-be suitor of one of his conquests, or even an angry parent of a seduced girl decided they didn't like the guy, and figured he needed to die. Not an accidental overdose, but a cold-blooded poisoning."

"Yeah, it's possible...but we'd have to do a lot more digging into Parker's private life before we have enough evidence to even entertain that possibility." I groaned. Suddenly this project was taking up a lot more time than I could spare. With all my work, extracurricular interests, and distractions, I was starting to suspect that I would never finish my dissertation.

"There's one thing I disagree with you about," I informed Funderburke. "You don't have two out of the big three motives in play here. You have all three serving as real factors here. Look. You know me, you know my fashion tastes. That's an expensive jacket. I'm thinking that my initial estimate of seven hundred fifty was actually a little low. That may be a thousand-dollar garment. Where did he get the money to buy it? I know you suggested that he found it cheap online somewhere, but still, who would sell that pricey jacket practically brand new at a fraction of the price? Why take an eighty, ninety percent loss on a barely used—if worn at all—item? I saw the inside of his house. His parents do not have a lot of money. They have enough to live modestly in a nice suburb, but they're watching their pennies. I saw that at least three of their kitchen cupboards were starting to come off the hinges. There was no fancy artwork. Some nice furniture, but not new. Maybe inherited from grandparents or something like that. There was a photograph of Parker and his family standing in front of what I can only assume was their car—and it was at least seven years old with visible rust. They're not rich people, they're just scraping by."

"That's right." Funderburke looked thoughtful. "I overheard someone who I think was a relative talking about how Parker's parents had no idea how they were going to pay for the funeral."

"So if his parents didn't give him the dough, how did Parker get the money to pay for the leather jacket?"

"How'd he get it? He only started wearing it yesterday. Where did it come from? Did he have time to go buy it in a store? Was it mailed to his house? Or...what if he didn't buy it for himself? If that's the case, who gave him the jacket?"

"Good point." I ran my fingers though my hair. "We're going to have to—"

I was interrupted by the return of Remy. He was practically dragging the girl with enormous quantities of blonde hair, black sweater, and grey leggings along with him. She slammed the door shut behind them as he pulled her into the house.

"Mr. Funderburke, Miss Kaiming? This is my sister, Lynsey."

"It's nice to meet you," I said.

"Thanks for talking to us," Funderburke added.

From the cold, dismissive glare on her face, it was pretty obvious that Lynsey wasn't as eager to help us as her younger brother.

"So, you're the one who got knocked up in her

teens and now gives scholarships to other teen mothers at that snotty prep school?" Lynsey was utterly drenched in contempt and defiance.

"Cuthbertson is not snotty." Funderburke is very loyal to his school.

"But otherwise you're correct." I never deny my past. I wanted to smack the smug, supercilious look off her face, but part of being an adult and a teacher is knowing when to use your words. If I wanted to gain control of the situation, I'd have to launch a targeted strike. The best way to put a teenaged girl in her place is to make it absolutely unequivocal who the queen bee is in the room.

I decided to make it damn clear to her who I was and what I was doing here.

"When I was thirteen I was living in L.A. with a single mother who'd had me at an incredibly young age. I was mad at the world, my home life situation was a mess, and I took out my anger by making a serious lapse of judgment. I got pregnant, I had a baby girl. Her father isn't in the picture, but it's not his fault. He was the victim of street violence and is not in full possession of his faculties. Back to me. Then, instead of spiraling downwards I decided that I was going to change up my life. I gathered up every dime I could, I bought a ticket to take my daughter and me to Milwaukee to meet my great-aunt. She's a legend at Cuthbertson Hall. I thought that if there was any chance in hell of my staying off the pole, I was going to have to get out of the rut I'd dug for myself in L.A. and get started on a new path, starting with a great education. And it worked. It was damn challenging and I don't know how I made it, but I managed to scratch and claw my way to the top of my class in high school. A lot of messed-up stuff happened with my family life, but I met some amazing people who adopted me and gave me the love, support, and discipline that I'd never had before I came to Milwaukee. I made great friends in Milwaukee, like Funderburke here. We were classmates long before we started dating. My new family and my great-aunt have been with me every step of the way as I made it through high school, college, my masters, and now my doctorate. I wouldn't have made it in school or as a single mother without a ton of help, and now, thanks to a generous benefactor, I can give back a lot more. I've found a bunch of amazing teenaged girls who have had children, and now I'm giving them a chance to succeed in life, starting with a great education at Cuthbertson Hall. That's what I'm doing with Fiona. She got into a situation that makes it difficult for her to get as far as she'd like in life, and now I've got her back, because I know just how damn much effort it takes to get your high school diploma with a baby at your average school, let alone an amazing, high-pressure institution like Cuthbertson. So that's what I'm doing with Fiona, and why I'm devoting my evening to helping her figure out what happened to the father of her child, who used her for his own personal pleasure, abandoned her when she got pregnant, and who is now dead."

There was a pause as Lynsey stared back at me with a blank face. Funderburke looked more than a little surprised that I'd given her a brief autobiography. Remy was standing with his mouth open. Four silent seconds passed, and then Lynsey clapped her hands to her face and started crying uncontrollably. I wasn't expecting that.

Once again, I counted myself lucky that I kept my pockets full of tissue packets. I tried to hand Lynsey some tissues, but her fingers were fumbling and they fluttered to the ground. Funderburke took her by the shoulders and guided her into a chair, and then we each took a tissue and gently dabbed at her face.

After a minute, the hysterical sobbing ebbed and turned into a mere trickle of tears. A couple of moments later she looked up at me. Her eyes were scared and anxious.

"Fiona's lucky to have a friend like you," Lynsey said quietly.

"Did you know her?"

"Yes. Before she transferred to Cuthbertson, we were really close. I haven't spoken to her in a long time. I haven't seen her at parties or anything."

"She's been busy with school and a baby," I reminded her.

"Yeah, that's true. But I...I dunno, I guess I've been telling myself that now that she's a Cuthbertson girl, Fiona thinks she's too good for her old friends."

Fiona is many things, but she's not arrogant. "That is not the case, Lynsey."

"I guess not..." Lynsey placed her right hand on her stomach and started rubbing it.

"Oh my goodness..." Funderburke blanched.

"What?"

He looked at me, and I saw the gears of his clever brain clicking and turning furiously. "I think I may be leaping to conclusions here, but..."

"But what?"

Before Funderburke could answer me, Lynsey started stammering. "I've been so jealous of her. She's getting a free ride at this prep school..."

"This is hardly a cakewalk for her," I reminded her. "She's at Cuthbertson because—"

"I know! She'll probably get into a great college that doesn't mind having toddlers around the dorms, and I'll...I'll probably have to drop out..."

A glint flashed through Funderburke's eyes, as he got confirmation of his theory, and I realized that history was repeating itself. "Oh."

"What?" Remy didn't see it. "What are you talking about?"

I bent down next to Lynsey, but Funderburke made a quick gesture, hurried over to the side of the room, picked up a wooden chair that was standing in a corner, and set it down next to Lynsey's chair for me to use. He's always looking out for me.

"Lynsey," I said quietly. "Am I right? Are you—"

"Yes."

"And Parker's the—"

"Yes."

"How far along are you?"

"The doctor says just over two months."

Remy finally figured it out. "Ohhhhhhhh." He flopped down on the sofa.

Lynsey gave me a look that I couldn't quite decipher. "You're not what I expected you to be. Either of you."

"What did you expect us to be like?" Funderburke asked.

"I don't know...less nice to me, I guess."

I was a bit offended. "And why is that? Are our reputations that bad?"

"No...It's just that the rumors at school are that

you insisted that Fiona cut off all ties with her old high school and friends."

"Well, that's simply not true." I was bristling on the inside and trying not to show it. "Fiona told me that the other kids were brutal to her once she got pregnant. She couldn't walk down the hall without hearing whispers behind her back, or slut-coughs to her face."

Lynsey looked deeply ashamed. "I know. I was there. I saw and heard all of it. And I didn't do anything to stop it, either." She pulled up her legs and started curling up into a little ball in her chair. "Now, I'm going to get plenty of that."

I put my hand on her shoulder. "Did Parker know?"

She nodded. "I told him three days ago."

"How did he take it?"

"He kind of freaked. He didn't say anything to me, but I know that he was panicking. I told him I was going to keep it, and I'd need his help. I wasn't going to let him just abandon me like he did with Fiona." She paused and bit her lip. "I think that's why he met up with her yesterday. He wanted to see his kid and get his bearings. Did he tell Fiona about me?"

"I highly doubt it. She didn't mention it."

Lynsey started crying again. "I saw them together

yesterday. I thought that Parker wanted to get back together with her. They were walking together, just this perfect little family, and I started worrying that there wouldn't be any place for me in the picture. And I got so angry...I just wanted Fiona out of the way so Parker could focus on me and our baby."

I started to get a really cold feeling in my stomach. "What did you do?"

The tears fell faster and more frequently. "I didn't want to hurt her. I didn't want to hurt anybody. I just...I just thought...I wasn't thinking clearly, but I thought that if Fiona got kicked out of school, then maybe I could get her place at Cuthbertson."

"Wait, you thought that Cuthbertson was this horrible stuck-up place full of snobs, yet you still wanted to go there?" Funderburke has a knack for pointing out contradictions in people's behavior.

"Everybody knows that Cuthbertson grads have a much better chance of getting into top colleges and succeeding in life. If I stayed in my current school, I couldn't face my classmates. I'd probably drop out, and then what would happen to me and the baby?" The tissues in Fiona's hand had reached the point where using them to wipe her face would have only made her face wetter, so I gave her some fresh ones. She tossed the used ones into an empty candy dish, and with a face reflecting both desperation and defiance, said, "Look. I admit I'm not thinking that clearly. With my own issues, dealing with my Dad moving to another state with his new girlfriend and her children, Mom running around, my brother popping pills..." She looked upset. "I shouldn't have told you all the family shameful secrets."

"It's okay," Remy said helpfully. "They already know everything except for Dad moving away."

"Oh...good." Her voice was notably unenthusiastic. "So, I'm making a lot of bad decisions lately."

"Can we please get back to where you were telling us about how you were plotting to get Fiona kicked out of Cuthbertson Hall?" Good for Funderburke for remembering about that. That point had completely slipped my mind.

"Well, I told you I said that I saw Parker and Fiona and the baby together and I just got crazy jealous. That's when I thought of something. A couple of days ago I was telling...someone I know from school, I'm not going to give you his—his or her name, that I was so stressed out. So he—he or she—gave me this little vial of white powder. He said it would help me relax. I tucked it in my purse, but I realized that I couldn't take it. It could've hurt the baby. Plus I didn't know if I was supposed to sniff it or inject it or swallow it..."

"Plus it was, you know, drugs. And you didn't

even know what kind of drug it was." Funderburke made no effort to hide the judgment and disapproval from his voice.

"Right. I know. So I just left it in my purse, and I nearly forgot about it until I got my crazy plan to get Fiona in trouble. I followed them back to Fiona's house without them seeing me, and I snuck into her backyard, looked through the window, and I saw the leather jacket she had been wearing hanging over a chair. The back door was unlocked, so I slipped in, took out the vial of powder, slipped it in one of the pockets, and ran back home. I figured she'd wear the jacket to school tomorrow, and I'd make an anonymous phone call to Cuthbertson and tip them off that Fiona had drugs in her jacket."

I vaguely remembered Fiona mentioning that Parker had given her his jacket to wear. "Of course. Fiona was wearing Parker's leather jacket. Parker hadn't worn the jacket before that day, you didn't know it was his. Fiona and Parker are both tall and lean, the jacket was probably a bit loose on Fiona, but not enough so you'd have suspected it wasn't hers."

"Exactly."

"So why didn't you make the call to report Fiona?" I asked.

"Honestly? I forgot all about it. I mean, I heard

all about what happened to Parker, and my plot to ruin her life completely slipped my mind."

At least Fiona has some *good luck*, I thought to myself.

"Well, we need to have a word with your brother and then we need to dispose of that vial," Funderburke commented with a sigh.

"What do you mean, speak with my brother?"

"Talking about me behind my back?" Len shuffled down the stairs and into the room, with his hands in the pockets of the leather jacket he had just claimed from his late friend's estate.

Lynsey jumped out of her chair. "Len? Where did you get that jacket?"

"It used to be Parker's. It's mine now. He's not going to be using it."

Lynsey started getting frantic. "Take it off! Now?"

"Why should I?" Len's face reflected the defiance older brothers tend to display whenever their little sisters try to tell them what to do.

"Because I don't want you to end up like Parker, that's why! Take off the jacket! Now!"

"What, is something bad going to happen to me because I'm wearing a leather jacket? Are you an animal rights activist now?"

Funderburke was much sharper than the rest of

us. "No. Because she's worried that she's inadvertently poisoned the jacket."

"Poisoned?" Len and Remy said simultaneously.

Funderburke nodded. "Lynsey put a vial of white powder in the pocket, and I'm guessing she thinks that it might be fentanyl."

Lynsey started quivering. "I looked fentanyl up on the Internet. You can overdose just by touching it. The vial must have leaked, some of the fentanyl must have gotten on him when he put his hand in his pocket, and he died! It's my fault! I killed him!"

Len turned as pale as skim milk. Slowly, he withdrew his hands from his pockets, holding a small white vial in his right hand. He yelped, dropped the vial onto a coffee table, ripped off the leather jacket, and threw it on the sofa. "Wait. Wait. Wait. Am I going to die now?"

Funderburke took a step towards him, trying to sound reassuring. "Well, how are you feeling?"

Len started spluttering. "My heart feel like it's going to explode. I... I'm dizzy. I'm sweating. I think I'm going to pass out."

Funderburke had taken out his cell phone as soon as Len said "dizzy."

"911? Please send an ambulance to..." He turned to Remy. "What's the address here?"

Remy stammered out the requested information,

and Funderburke repeated it to the dispatcher. "Possible fentanyl overdose. Please hurry."

Meanwhile, I eased Len into a chair. He was shaking, twitching, and wasn't responding to anything I was saying.

A few tense minutes passed. Remy was crying and Lynsey was hysterical. "I've killed them both. It's all my fault, it's all my fault, it's all my fault..." she kept repeating over and over. I felt bad for her, but she wasn't wrong.

Funderburke's made a career out of defending young people, and even though Lynsey wasn't his client he started treating her like one. Putting his hands on her shoulders and forcing her to look him straight in the eyes, he told her. "Stop that right now. Don't say another word. Not one more word about this being your fault or what you did."

"Will you be her lawyer?" Remy asked hopefully.

Before Funderburke could answer, the ambulance pulled up in front of the house and he rushed to the front door to let them in. As the paramedics did their job, Funderburke hurried Lynsey and Remy into another room.

"Will he be all right?" I asked the paramedics as they carried Len out on a stretcher.

"We'll have to wait and see. His pulse is pretty strong." The taller of the two paramedics told me which hospital they were taking Len to, and I crossed myself and said a quick prayer for Len's recovery. Funderburke saw what I was doing and followed suit.

"Wait." The shorter paramedic picked up the vial of white powder using a little plastic bag, being careful not to actually touch the vial with his hands. Sealing it up, he explained, "We need to run some quick tests on this to confirm it's fentanyl. We don't want to treat him for overdosing on the wrong drug."

"Two teen boys overdosing in two days. What the hell's wrong with the kids on this block?" The first paramedic muttered under his breath, but we all heard him.

Two minutes later, Funderburke and I were driving to the hospital with Remy and a still-hysterical Lynsey in the back seat. I was on my cell, informing my parents about what was going on and why I wouldn't be home for dinner. Soon, the four of us were sitting in the very uncomfortable chairs of a hospital waiting room, waiting for news of Len's condition.

After what felt like hours but was actually only forty minutes, I was surprised and elated to see my parents walking down the corridor, with Dad carrying a big insulated bag. "Dad! Mom!" I rushed up and hugged them. "You didn't have to come here."

"I wanted to make sure you and Funderburke got a decent meal." Mom nodded at the insulated bag. "I made sandwiches with tonight's turkey meatloaf and fresh mozzarella."

"Thank you so much! Are the grandparents watching all the kids?"

"Of course. Who else?"

Dad started handing out sandwiches and cans of seltzer and a thermos of milk with cups, and I was grateful but not surprised that they'd made them for Lynsey and Remy as well. I noticed there was another one in the bag—if Len pulled through, he'd have a decent dinner.

Between bites, Funderburke and I managed to tell my parents the whole story of his unexpectedly hectic and unsettling afternoon. We'd moved across the room from Lynsey and Remy so we could explain some details without them overhearing, and as I stole the occasional glance at them, I noticed that Remy was just nibbling at his sandwich while Lynsey hadn't even unwrapped hers.

Dad followed my gaze. "Has anyone called their parents?"

I nodded. "Remy called them both and left messages. They're both out of town."

"I see."

Funderburke had finished his sandwich ahead of

me, and he wrapped up the narrative while I enjoyed my food, which had been left largely ignored due to my being caught up in telling the story.

As Funderburke explained Lynsey's confession, Dad started to shift uncomfortably. "You realize that we can't just keep this to ourselves?"

"Of course not," Funderburke reassured him. "We're not going to hush this up. If the medical tests confirm everything, we'll have to tell the police everything. But right now, my gut is telling me to wait to make sure of the facts."

"What do you mean, 'make sure of the facts?'" I asked him. "We know what happened."

"Actually, I'm not so sure you do," Mom replied.

"What do you mean, Mom?"

"I listened to your description of Len's symptoms."

"Yeah...And?"

"Well, they don't match the symptoms of an actual fentanyl overdose."

"They don't?" I abruptly realized that I hadn't taken the time to actually perform a basic Internet search for what a fentanyl overdose looks like. I vaguely remembered that Brianna had described Parker's symptoms, but I hadn't thought to compare them to Len's. Normally, I would have Googled the heck out of any subject I wasn't completely aware of.

I must've been tired and distracted. After thinking about it for a quarter-second, I realized that I should be listening to what a medical doctor had to say.

"You said that Len was twitching and hyperventilating," Mom continued. "Did you check his pupils?"

"No, I didn't."

"Did you take his pulse?"

"Yes. I thought his heart was going to burst out of his chest. His pulse was racing."

"Well, that's not a symptom of fentanyl poisoning," Mom replied, adjusting the hem of her skirt. "In a real overdose situation, the pulse drops to dangerously low levels. Hyperventilating isn't a symptom, either. If he'd really overdosed, his breaths would be much shallower. And he wouldn't have been twitching, either. If you overdose on fentanyl, you go limp."

"Wait, seriously?" I was definitely getting confused.

"Of course I'm being serious. Why would I joke about this?"

Funderburke nodded. "That's what I thought. I looked up the symptoms of fentanyl poisoning, shortly after I heard it mentioned, and I noticed they didn't match Len."

I tried to hide my aggravation at Funderburke

being more diligent with his background research than I had been. "Then what happened? How did Len get poisoned? With what?"

Pretty much on cue, a doctor entered the waiting area and walked towards Remy and Lynsey. "Excuse me. Are you Len's siblings?"

Lynsey jumped up. "Yes! Is he alive? Please tell me he's still alive!"

"Yes, he's still alive," the doctor replied as the four of us crossed the room to hear what was being said. "And he's fine."

"Fine? Were you able to get the poison out of his system?" Remy looked both relieved and curious.

"Well..." the doctor looked a bit nonplussed. "He doesn't seem to have been poisoned at all. We noticed right away he didn't have most of the standard symptoms of fentanyl overdosing. His pupils weren't contracted, and his lips and fingernails weren't blue. He seems more or less O.K. right now."

"But...but...the vial of fentanyl," Lynsey stammered.

"We did a quick test of that," the doctor replied. "It's not fentanyl. Our best guess is that it's baby formula."

"Baby formula?" Now I was completely confused. Had Lynsey's drug-taking friend gotten ripped off, having bought baby formula instead of drugs?

"Mm-hmm."

"I don't understand." I was all wound up and I started working off some of the tension by pacing. "What happened? Why did he start convulsing?"

"Could he have been allergic to the baby formula?" Lynsey asked.

"No," Mom said flatly. "My best guess is that this was a psychosomatic reaction. It was all in his head. He'd had his friend's death by fentanyl on his mind, you told him that could be poisoned just by touching the vial, and he had a kind of panic attack in response. It was the placebo effect, in a way. Instead of taking an inactive substance and thinking it's a cure for a condition, Len simply imagined that he'd been poisoned and responded accordingly."

"That's happening a lot," the doctor agreed. "You hear stories about first responders getting fentanyl poisoning themselves after coming into contact when people who've overdosed on fentanyl, but in reality it's highly unlikely someone would overdose simply by getting a little bit of fentanyl powder on them, unless they had an open cut. In some of these cases, the first responders who think they're overdosing through accidental contact with fentanyl go through exactly what Len did—the placebo effect."

"So he's fine?" Lynsey looked as if an elephant had been lifted off her shoulders.

"Well, we need to talk about his use of painkillers, but otherwise—"

I didn't hear the rest because I was too confused. If that vial only contained baby powder, then Parker couldn't possibly have overdosed from it leaking and contaminating his clothing. But if Parker hadn't died from the Leather Jacket of Doom, then what did happen to him?

When I finally snapped out of my mental fog, I heard Remy saying, "So can we see him?"

"In a little bit," the doctor replied. "We'll let you know when he's ready."

The doctor left, and Lynsey and Remy hugged each other. I was happy for them, but I was too confused to celebrate.

I turned to Dad, and asked him, "So what am I supposed to do now?"

He adjusted his glasses and replied, "Well, in theory you could just let this go and let the police try to figure out what happened, but I think we both know that's not going to happen."

"You're correct, it is not." About ten percent of me wanted to go home and collapse on the sofa, while the other ninety percent was not about to rest until I knew exactly what had happened to Parker. "Everything I assumed had happened turned out to be wrong. I still have no idea how he got poisoned.

First, I thought he was a recreational drug user. Then, I thought he might've inadvertently come across some fentanyl somebody spilled."

"But that wouldn't have been likely to have gotten into his system," Mom reminded me.

"I know, I know."

Dad cleared his throat. "Remember what I told you when you started grad school. When you're trying to figure out what happened in the past, it helps to draw up a timeline. What do you know about his last hours?"

Lacking any other ideas, I decided that Dad's timeline idea was my best shot for answers. I asked Remy and Lynsey a few questions, recalled what Fiona had told me, and crafted the following timetable:

PARKER'S LAST HOURS

3 P.M. Leaves school.

3-4 P.M. Unknown.

4-5:15 P.M. Meets with Fiona.

Approx. 5:30. Remy briefly sees Parker walking down the street in front of his house.

Shortly after 7. Brianna sees Parker returning home.

Approx. 7:15. Parker collapses, ambulance takes him to hospital.

I looked over the timetable. Right now, it didn't seem to be much help.

"I'm just wondering what happened to Parker's jacket," Dad mused.

"It's on the sofa at the Cerda house. Len ripped it off when he thought it was poisoning him."

"No, not the leather jacket. The one he had before he got that one."

"That's right," chimed in Remy. "He always wore his letterman's jacket before yesterday."

"He was wearing it at school yesterday," Lynsey informed us. "I saw him wearing it at the end of the day."

I started making a couple of addendums to my timetable. "So...at three P.M. Parker was wearing his letterman's jacket. At four, when he met Fiona at the frozen yogurt shop, he was wearing the leather jacket. So, the big question is, how and when did he get the leather jacket?"

"He could have bought it a while ago and picked it up at home," Funderburke noted. "I mean, he must have gone home. He wasn't carrying his backpack when you saw him walking with Fiona, was he, Lynsey?"

"No. He wasn't. But he had it when he left school. I saw it slung over his shoulder when I said goodbye to him...for the last time. I normally walk home with him, but I had to meet with one of my teachers."

"How long does it take you to walk home from school?" Funderburke asked.

"Just over ten minutes."

"Do you know how long it takes to walk to the frozen yogurt shop from your house?"

"A little under ten minutes," Remy replied instantly. Clearly, he knew that route well.

"All right, so that's twenty minutes gone." Funderburke's fingers were twitching, the way they always do when he's thinking hard. "That leaves forty minutes unaccounted for between school ending and meeting Fiona."

"He could've just been hanging out at home or checking his homework," I noted, "but if he was doing something else, it might be important. Forty minutes..." I thought about the neighborhood and did a little quick math. "He didn't have a car, and walking to a bus stop, waiting for a bus...He wouldn't have time to go a mall or high-end clothing store. They're too far away. He couldn't make it in time. He couldn't have bought the leather jacket then."

"He could've bought it earlier," Lynsey replied.

"No, that doesn't make sense. Remember, I don't think Parker had the kind of disposable income to spend on a luxury clothing item. He told Len he was broke. Even if he found it on sale, why wouldn't he wear it right away? Nobody saw him wearing it before yesterday. Why spend all that money and then just stick it in a closet and suddenly decide to wear it when he met with the mother of his child? A great jacket like that, he'd want to start wearing it as soon as he bought it."

Funderburke reflected on what I just said for a couple of seconds. "You're right. It doesn't make sense."

"I agree," Mom concurred.

"But if Nerissa's right, and I suspect she is," Dad reasoned, "that means he obtained that jacket for the first time during that unaccounted-for forty minutes. I doubt he broke into someone's house and stole it. That just leaves one possibility. Somebody gave him the jacket."

The doctor interrupted us. "Remy? Lynsey? Len's ready to see you now." The siblings hurried out to see their brother, while my parents and Funderburke sank back down into those horribly uncomfortable chairs.

"Nerissa, you said that was a pretty expensive jacket, right?" Funderburke asked, drumming the fingers of his right hand along the left sleeve of his coat.

"Uh-huh. Several hundred dollars, minimum. So if somebody gave it to him, it was a pretty princely gift."

"Someone must've liked him a lot," Mom mused.

"You said he liked to play the field," Dad said, "but the average public high school girl wouldn't have enough money to buy a high-end leather jacket for a boy with a reputation for philandering."

"Exactly, Dad. Whoever bought that jacket had plenty of money to spend, and must've really wanted to impress Parker with it..." Something clicked in my mind. As I turned to look at my parents and boyfriend, I saw Funderburke abruptly sitting bolt upright, and from the expressions on my parents' faces, I figured that they'd reached the same conclusion I did.

"Mom, Dad, I hate to ask, but—"

"We'll stay here and make sure that Len, Lynsey, and Remy get home safe," Dad assured me.

"Thanks so much. You're the best." Funderburke and I made a beeline for his car. As we climbed inside, I said, "If I'm right, we'd better hurry before the killer has time to dispose of the evidence."

"It's been a day. The evidence may already be gone."

"Maybe..." We didn't say much until we were back in Parker's neighborhood. There were a lot more cars on the street, so we had to park even further away. We hurried down the sidewalk and stopped at the house next door to Parker's. I pressed my face against the window, scanning the empty living room, and Funderburke did the same on the other side of the house.

"Nerissa? Look at this." Funderburke pointed. "I think there's something behind the sofa here."

I rushed over to him and peered inside. "Yep. That's a letterman's jacket."

"So, what's our play here?" Funderburke asked.

I whipped out my phone and took a picture of the jacket behind the sofa. "Well, I think we need to—"

"What are you doing?" The two of us whipped around and saw Brianna, looking more fearful than indignant.

I did a little lightning-fast calculus, and I decided that the best course of action was to proceed firmly but not harshly. After all, I was light on proof and heavy on conjecture. It was possible that she could've innocently asked Parker to change a lightbulb on the ceiling and he'd forgotten his jacket. However, the guilt on her face was enough confirm my theories in my own mind.

"I just took a picture of a letterman's jacket behind your couch." I held my phone up so she could see it. Immediately, her knees buckled and she sank down on the wooden bench on her porch.

I have a couple of deaf people in my family, so I know sign language, and Funderburke's learned a little, too. Funderburke quickly signed to me, *She'll respond better to a woman. I'll keep an eye on you.* I nodded, subtly tapped some buttons on my phone to start recording our conversation, and slipped the phone into my pocket. Funderburke disappeared behind the corner of the house, but I knew he was watching us, just in case Brianna turned violent.

I sat down on the bench next to her. "If someone were to go through your credit card records or bank statements, would they find that you've purchased an expensive men's leather jacket recently? A black one, size medium, moto style?"

She froze momentarily, then nodded. "Yes, you know they would."

I didn't think it was shrewd to tell her that I only suspected, I didn't know. I decided to push forward with another general statement that would have a sharp impact on a guilty conscience. I looked at her peroxide-lightened locks pointedly, and told her, "I gather that Parker had a thing for blondes."

She ran her hand over her hair and nodded. "He did. He was pretty open about his tastes in women."

"Hmm." I took a deep breath and plunged forward. "How did it start with the two of you?"

Brianna shrugged and tears started forming in her eyes. I handed her a tissue, quietly thinking that I really had to start charging people for the use of my paper products. "I really don't know," she sighed. "I didn't pay much attention to him at first—he was just a gangly teenager. Then one day a couple of months ago, he helped me shovel the snow off my driveway, I invited him in for a cup of cocoa, and he was so funny and charming...it led to...I'm still recovering from my divorce, and I haven't had much luck on the dating scene."

I decided that I didn't want details. "I see. Could you please tell me what happened yesterday?"

"Parker stopped by my house after school. We'd made plans to meet later that evening, and he just wanted to check and make sure that I was still free. I was. I'd planned to give him a surprise gift then, but I just couldn't wait." She pressed her left palm against her forehead. "He loved the jacket. He looked so handsome in it. He'd thrown his letterman's jacket at the sofa when he came in, I guess it fell at some point, and he just forgot about his old coat."

"Did you know that he was meeting with Fiona? The mother of his child?"

She nodded. "Of course. He was very open about all of his relationships. Fiona, Lynsey...the other girls at his school..."

My blood froze. *How many girls was he dating? Could he have other kids out there?*

My silent questions went unanswered, because Brianna had started unburdening herself, and she couldn't stop herself. "He came back about an hour and a half later, and we...Well, you know."

I knew darn well what they'd done, but I wanted her to be explicit for the recording. "You had sex."

"Yes."

"What happened next?"

"You mean after we..."

"Yes. Did you fight?"

"Yes."

"About Lynsey?"

Brianna looked confused. "Why would we fight about Lynsey? I told you, I knew all about his relationship with her. I knew he wasn't seeing me exclusively, and I was fine with that. I just needed something fun and empowering to get me back in the game after my divorce. I was grateful to him for paying attention to me. That's why I bought him the jacket. As a 'thank you for rekindling my embers' present."

Now, I was confused. "So you weren't upset when you heard he'd gotten Lynsey pregnant?"

From her stunned expression, this was all news to her. "Lynsey is pregnant?"

"Yes...and you didn't know." We were quiet for a few seconds, while I did a few additional mental calculations. I had been sure that the motive was jealousy, but I seemed to be way off. Another unanswered question popped into my head, and I decided to take another swing. "Len's painkillers. He wouldn't say how he got them." I studied her face and knew I was on the right track. "You've been selling drugs to him."

The tears started flowing faster. "Not directly. I don't handle the sales. My ex-husband wiped out our savings with his gambling, and he hasn't paid his alimony in almost a year. A few months ago, someone —I'm not going to say who because I don't want to get her in trouble—came to me with a business proposition. I'd provide her with painkillers from work, she'd sell them, and we'd split the profits. So we did, and it's gotten me out of debt. That's how I was able to afford the jacket."

"And...Parker found out."

"Yes. I was in the shower, and my business partner called me on the phone. Parker answered it, and my partner must've said something that got him suspicious. I don't know what she said to Parker before she realized it wasn't me on the line, but as soon as I stepped out of the bathroom he asked me if I was dealing pills."

"Was he angry?"

"More stunned than angry. He hated drugs. He's seen too many of his friends fall into addiction and drop out over the past two years. At least six of his teammates have developed painkiller addictions. When he found out what I was doing, he was livid."

"So when you told me that Parker liked to experiment with drugs..."

Brianna leaned back and wiped her eyes. "That was all a lie to make you think it was an accidental overdose."

"Tell me about the fentanyl. How did Parker take it?"

"He kept saying that I had to go to the police. He told me that if I turned in Poppy the police would go easy on me, and I probably would only get probation. I don't know why he was so sure about that."

"Poppy?" I asked. This woman was not good at keeping secrets.

"I..." She hesitated, then decided the horse had

left the barn. "Yes. My partner. She's the one who sells the pills. She lives down the block. I don't think you've met her. I'm pretty sure she's Len Cerda's dealer. Anyway, I don't know what I was thinking. I was panicking, and I wanted to stay out of prison. I had this crazy idea that if I could somehow get Parker really high, he might think that the phone call was all a hallucination and forget that I was selling drugs. You know, Parker drank a ton of protein shakes."

"I heard about that, yeah."

"Well...he always liked to have one after lovemaking. He said it 'refueled' him. I calmed him down, I told him I was going to call my lawyer and work out a plea with the authorities. While he was getting dressed I got some fentanyl from the cache where I hide the painkillers I take from work, and slipped a pinch of it into the shake. The shakes taste like chemicals anyway, I figured he wouldn't notice the extra ingredient. He gulped it down, made me promise to call my lawyer as soon as he left, and went back to his house. I don't take drugs myself, I had no idea the lethal dose was so small. I just assumed he'd get high and hoped he'd forget everything. The next thing I knew the ambulance was pulling up..."

She sobbed uncontrollably for three minutes, and I supplied her with tissues. When she was finally able to speak again, I quietly asked her, "So, what do you want to do now?" I hoped she didn't want to run away. It would be hard for me to catch a fleeing killer in the outfit and shoes I was wearing.

Brianna removed her own phone from her purse. "Will you stay here with me, please? I'm going to call the police and turn myself in. If you stay here with me, it'll help me fight the urge to chicken out."

I agreed. That was the first time I've ever put a comforting hand on a poisoner's shoulder while she confessed to the authorities.

A few minutes later, the police arrived. Funderburke rejoined us, and Brianna quietly followed the detectives back into their car. The police didn't announce the charges, but I figured they'd include drug dealing, statutory rape, and either murder or manslaughter; and another car would pick up Poppy soon. Funderburke and I promised to make ourselves available if they had any more questions, and the police car drove away just as my parents arrived with Remy, Lynsey, and Len.

"That police car that we just passed. Was that..." Mom's voice trailed off.

I nodded. "It was Brianna."

"What?" Lynsey and Remy looked stunned. Len still seemed out of it.

"We'll explain in a minute," Funderburke replied.

"Just so you know, on the ride back we told Len

about the team of doctors and therapists that have helped the Cuthbertson students who are fighting their own battles with addiction," Dad informed us. "I made a call, and Len's got an appointment with them after school."

"I promised I'd drive him," Mom added.

"That's great." Funderburke turned to Len. "This will be difficult for you, but if you need moral support, I want you to know you can turn to us."

Len just nodded. He was still in a total fog.

"The police may pick up Parker's jacket for evidence, but they may not need it if there's a confession," Funderburke reflected. "Check with his parents, but there's a fair chance you'll be allowed to keep it."

"On a parallel topic," I stretched my hand out to Lynsey. "Give me your phone. Unlock it first, please." She complied, and I typed my contact information into it. "Just so you know, we're pretty well funded. I don't have a set cutoff for teen moms who want to get a great education. I can't take everybody, but I can recruit the girls who I think have potential. And I think I'd like to work with you." I handed her phone back to her. "Call me tomorrow. We'll set up an interview and a round of testing. If all goes well, you can start going to Cuthbertson next term."

Lynsey looked stunned. "Why are you helping me?"

I shrugged. "You're pregnant, impulsive, and have a history of poor decision making. You remind me of me when I was your age."

"As for you, Remy," Funderburke continued, "Cuthbertson Hall is holding its semi-annual general scholarship testing at the end of the month. If you're interested in coming to Cuthbertson with your sister, please apply. I can't make any promises, but you strike me as the kind of kid we need more of at the Hall."

Remy looked thrilled, but before he could respond, Parker's father came storming out of his house. "Didn't I tell you to get the hell out of here?" he bellowed.

Funderburke turned to him, and as smooth as silk he replied, "We have just found proof that your son was deliberately poisoned. His killer has just been arrested."

Parker's father deflated in an instant. "What?"

"If you'll let me into your home, I can explain everything." Funderburke gestured to the Cerda siblings. "If you want to join us, I'll be able to fill in the gaps in the story for you." He looked at me. "Are you joining us?"

I shook my head. "I'm exhausted. I need to get

home. See you tomorrow." We kissed goodnight, Funderburke said goodbye to my parents, and he led the Cerdas and Parker's father into Parker's house.

"Ready to go home?" Dad asked.

As I was nodding, my phone started ringing. "Hello?" I asked.

"Miss Kaiming? It's Fiona. Have you found out anything?"

I sighed. My sleep would have to wait. "Yes. You live just a few blocks from Parker, right?" When she confirmed this, I looked up her address in my contacts list and said, "I'll be there in two minutes, and I can tell you what really happened."

I looked at my parents pleadingly. "Do you mind—"

Dad nodded. "It's fine. We understand."

I sighed as we all climbed into the minivan. "I wanted to tell her I'd explain everything tomorrow, but I don't think Fiona can bear the wait." Soon, I'd be telling Fiona that the father of her child had been poisoned by his thirty-something drug-peddling lover, and that little Tina was about to have a half-sibling, mothered by an estranged friend of hers.

I do not have an easy job. But I can't think of anything else I'd rather be doing with my life.

Freedom Day

Annie Reed

his year's candle was a tall, thin, ivory taper Millicent bought at one of those cookie-cutter department stores in the mall that featured overpriced cookware branded with the names of celebrity chefs and expensive linens with thread counts fit for a king. The candle was unscented—over the years Millicent had developed ever-more-severe allergies to certain artificial odors—and fit nicely in the one cut crystal candleholder they still owned. The second of the original pair had been lost many years ago, left behind in the rush to stay one step ahead of their past.

Joe set the candle in a place of honor in the center of their mantel next to a framed photograph of their daughter and her family. She lived in Albany now, an associate professor of linguistics gradually working toward her doctorate while raising two small children of her own. Once again, she'd asked her parents to come visit for the holidays as neither she nor her husband, an emergency physician, could get away.

Millicent had said no, of course, even though Joe knew she desperately wanted to see her grandchildren. She'd blamed Joe's discomfort at flying, which was only a partial lie. Neither of them were comfortable with TSA checkpoints or a close examination of their papers.

Were they being too careful? Too paranoid? Perhaps. Today's candle marked the thirty-second year since they'd fled their former lives, although they hadn't always celebrated the day by lighting a candle of remembrance. That hadn't started until their daughter left home for college. Before then, they'd simply sat close together, held hands, and closed their eyes in silent thanksgiving for the life they would be forever grateful to have lived.

Some family secrets were meant to die with the generation that kept them. Joe and Millicent had deliberately kept theirs from their daughter. Better that she grow up believing the only December holidays that mattered were the ones printed in her Day planner and marked with a red-and-white-striped candy cane. Their own childhoods had been stolen, and they didn't want that for their daughter or her children.

Millicent brought two steaming cups of tea into the living room and handed one to Joe. They would have preferred vodka, but he was taking medication that didn't mix well with alcohol and she wouldn't drink without him.

Back in the day, back when they only pretended to be a normal American couple, Joe drank beer because that's what the men he worked with drank. He'd never developed a taste for what he privately called "vile piss water." Millicent used to have an occasional glass of wine whenever she had a girls' night out with the women she'd been ordered to befriend because wine was part of the women's girls' night tradition. Fitting in had been an integral part of their lives. Personal tastes and preferences were irrelevant.

"Why do we still do this?" Millicent asked. "We're not likely to forget the day."

No, he doubted they would. But it was important to remember. Important never to become too complacent. They had before, and it had nearly cost them their lives.

"Tradition," he simply said, knowing she'd understand.

He draped an arm around her shoulders. Her hair had started to turn white only just this year. It had been a soft, luxurious sable when they first met. Her papers had said she was twenty-four years old, and he had no reason to doubt that. His had said he was twenty-six, which was accurate, although his birthdate had been altered. Their birthdates had changed once again before they finally reached their destination—a small, sleepy town in Connecticut.

The birthdays they celebrated now were the ones on the papers they'd obtained on their own. The wedding anniversary they celebrated was the day they had renewed their vows before a Justice of the Peace in that sleepy Connecticut town.

That had been their only real wedding. The marriage certificate they'd been supplied with before they'd arrived at their assignment had been fabricated by their superiors, just like the rest of their papers.

Millicent sighed. "It reminds me of what we've done," she said, gazing at the unlit candle. "I don't like thinking about that."

She laid her head on his shoulder. The old ache was still there along with all the old scars, but he pretended the only thing he felt was the comforting presence of his wife, still with him after all this time.

He didn't like remembering the past either. Lying, stealing, pretending to be someone he wasn't. Fitting in with people he'd been taught were his enemies.

Tradecraft was the American word. He'd long since forgotten the Russian.

"It's important," he said. "We were lucky. We need to remember that."

He put his teacup on the mantel on the other side of their daughter's framed photograph. Using a long-necked lighter he kept for summertime backyard barbecues and to start winter fires in the fireplace of their small home, he lit the wick on the new candle. The wick sputtered as it caught, then the flame burned tall and true, reflecting in the glass that covered their daughter's photograph.

He took his wife's hand and held it as they both gazed at the single tall candle, burning bright.

This was remembrance day.

December 3rd. A day celebrated by two elderly American retirees who'd started their lives as something far different.

The candle marked the day thirty-two years ago when the KGB had been officially dissolved as the government of the Soviet Union continued its collapse.

The day two KGB spies found themselves fleeing for their lives.

***

They weren't supposed to fall in love.

Personal relationships beyond those required for the assignment were forbidden, but Joe and Millicent had been young and healthy and so very much alone when they'd been deposited in a sleepy American town that had little in the way of distractions beyond their covert assignments.

The year had been 1981 when they'd arrived in America. Six months later Joe had gone to work as a civilian employee in a government research facility. His background had been carefully constructed to pass even the most careful scrutiny. He had been rigorously trained not only in the skills he'd need for covert operations, but also in advanced engineering and mathematics. He'd been instructed to pursue advancement within the facility as opportunities arose, but to decline any offers that would require him to transfer to other facilities. Advancement would be rewarded. Demotion—or worse, the loss of his job altogether—would result in severe punishment.

Joe had seen the results of severe punishment during his training. Trainees beaten to within an inch of their lives, broken and left bleeding in the bleak Siberian winter. He was well motivated to perform as expected, and he did as he was told.

Millicent's assignment as Joe's wife was designed to allow her to befriend the wives of other men employed at the facility. Their superiors viewed all American women as decadent gossips. Her assignment was to pass along anything she heard that might be of interest.

It didn't take Millicent long to discover that the wives of the men who worked in the facility with Joe didn't fit that description. While they were outwardly friendly, their friendship had limits. They certainly didn't share the type of gossip worthy of including in any of Joe's coded communications to their superiors. The only gossip she heard was about mundane things—children, shared recipes, what stars had been on Johnny Carson the night before.

The wives were all older than Millicent, and for the most part, they were a conservative bunch, a holdover from generations of American women who were expected to stay home, raise children, and take care of the home while their husbands worked. While Joe was making headway at his assignment, sending what he believed were valuable reports to his superiors, Millicent was continually frustrated with her failure to truly be accepted by the wives. Eventually she came to believe that the wives wouldn't confide in her because they thought she might be one of the new breed of childless liberated women and she was secretly mocking their old-fashioned ways.

"We don't have children," she told Joe one night in late 1984 over a dinner of roast chicken and canned green beans. "They wonder what I do with my days without children to keep me busy. They wonder if I'm an alcoholic, or if I plan to steal their husbands from them."

Millicent could have. She was a Russian beauty, pleasantly round in comparison to the stick-figure-thin American wives.

"You are already married," he said. The papers their superiors had supplied said so.

She made a very unladylike snort. "They watch

too much television. It makes them think all women they don't know well are after their husbands."

She stabbed a piece of chicken on her plate.

Millicent was a trained killer. They both were. Yet here she was, reduced to stabbing roast chicken with a fork while she worried about the vapid wives their superiors were certain would disclose important information if only Millicent truly earned their trust.

Joe watched American football on Sundays so that he could participate in the office betting pool and seem somewhat knowledgeable about the game. They both watched episodes of a television show named *Dallas* and another called *The A-Team* so that they could contribute to conversations about the shows. *The A-Team* seemed especially popular among the mathematicians and engineers.

From what Millicent had told him, *Dallas* was the most popular show among the wives. Apparently infidelity and in-fighting among the wealthy made for good American television. Joe didn't understand the appeal any more than he understood why anyone would drink beer. But shows like *Dallas* indoctrinated Americans as much as the training sessions Joe and Millicent had been subjected to in Russia had instilled a deep-seated loyalty and fear of their homeland.

Millicent didn't have a job. She didn't have children. She occasionally drank wine, but never allowed herself more than one glass. Therefore, in the minds of wives who lived in their own little tight-knit community, Millicent must be a secret drunk who spent her time plotting to seduce their husbands.

As much as Millicent might want to stab something more than a piece of chicken to vent her frustration, there was an undercurrent of fear to her frustration. Her carefully crafted background wasn't helping her to achieve her assignment—it was doing the exact opposite.

Failure to carry out an assignment was unacceptable.

"What is the common denominator?" he asked her. "In their eyes, what is your worst sin?"

He could see her thinking through the problem. Assessing the information, scant as it was, that she had learned from the wives—none of it related to the information their superiors hoped they would obtain —and correlating it to their current situation.

"We don't have children," she finally said. All of his co-workers had children. It was another area where Millicent didn't fit in. "Therefore I need to do something visible that will keep me as busy as their children keep them busy. We must ask permission for me to obtain employment outside of the home."

Millicent's suggestion made sense. If their superiors had rounded out their family with a young child before Joe and Millicent had arrived in Connecticut, no one would have questioned what Millicent did with her days. Moscow certainly had plenty of orphaned children to choose from. Moscow could not provide them with a child now without raising suspicions.

Joe included both the difficulties Millicent had encountered in carrying out her assigned tasks as well as her suggestion of how to cure those difficulties in his next report to their superiors. Millicent worried that he'd said too much. That admitting she hadn't been entirely successful in her assignment might result in her reassignment—or removal in a more permanent manner.

When they did not receive an immediate response, they began to wonder if someone had been sent to dispose of them both. Joe didn't believe even the KGB would be bold enough to kill him while he was inside the facility, but he became hypervigilant whenever he was outside of work. Millicent limited her solo outings and kept her firearm with her at all times she was alone in the house.

Joe's work began to suffer as he and Millicent slept in shifts, one always awake with a firearm in easy reach. They discussed how to disappear should the possibility of a visit by an assassin become a reality.

Neither of them doubted their ability to survive an assassination attempt. They had both been thoroughly trained to be the best at what they did.

An answer to their concerns finally arrived three weeks later and not in the form of a KBG assassin.

The directive was short and to the point and, like all their orders, came written in deliberately shaky block letters on a scrap of notebook paper inserted inside their bulky Sunday newspaper delivery. Complete compliance was not only expected but demanded.

Conceive a child. Raise it as your own. Further failure will not be tolerated.

When the order from Moscow arrived directing them to conceive a child—and they had no doubt that the decision had been made at the highest levels of their Directorate—Joe and Millicent had been posing as husband and wife for over three years. They slept in the same bed, but that was all they had done. Sleep.

During that time, Joe had been promoted three times at the facility where he worked. The last promotion had been to a middle management position, which afforded him the ability to review a great deal of sensitive data. The data would have been incomprehensible to a layman, but with Joe's engineering and mathematics training, he'd been able to sort through the stacks of paperwork and provide the salient information in his reports to his superiors. He came to believe that the only reason the two of them had been spared from reassignment—or assassination—was his position at the facility and the information he provided Moscow.

Although Millicent had been raised in a different state-sponsored program than Joe—a program meant to turn orphaned girls into obedient operatives—he knew she never questioned Moscow's order to conceive a child. She went to the local library and checked out books on conception and pregnancy, and made sure one of the wives saw her do it.

"I want them to think we've been trying to have a child," she told Joe. She said she hoped it would make the wives more sympathetic to their situation.

It did.

The wives started sharing helpful hints and old wives' tales with Millicent, most focusing on the best way to get pregnant. Joe's co-workers started slapping him on the back and telling him to keep on trying. "You're going to have a lot of great sex," more than one of them told him. "And the best thing is, she's going to want it all the time."

She did, but not the way Joe's co-workers hinted at.

At least, not at first.

"Conceiving is now part of my assignment," she told him, and she executed that assignment with the same precision and dedication she brought to the rest of her assignments.

If Moscow wanted her to have a child, she would have a child.

But something happened along the way. Something unexpected.

They began to develop feelings for each other.

The little touches they'd engaged in when in public before—the brush of a hand against the small of a back, the drape of Joe's arm around Millicent's shoulder as they sat next to each other on a co-worker's sofa and the way she leaned into him in response—changed from calculated actions designed to simulate interactions between spouses to the natural responses of two people who cared for each other.

For the first time in his life, Joe began to wonder if he was falling in love.

One night after they had completed their latest attempt at conceiving a child, Millicent rolled toward him and draped a leg over his. She placed a gentle kiss on his shoulder. Her hair was draped over one side of her face, but he saw her eyes glittering in the dim light of the digital readout on their clock radio.

She smiled at him, the tenderest smile she had ever given him.

"I think that was it," she said. "I think we did it this time."

He shifted until he could wrap his arms around her. "Are you certain? How can you tell?"

He'd skimmed through some of the books she'd brought home from the library, but nothing he'd read indicated women could tell when conception actually began.

"Are you that eager to proceed with the next step of your assignment?" he asked. That would no doubt end this phase of their relationship. He felt bitter disappointment at the thought. He didn't want to go back to simply being colleagues, two agents embedded in a foreign land, able to rely only on each other for support.

She lifted her head up until she was gazing directly into his eyes. "This stopped being merely an assignment long ago."

She kissed him tenderly on the lips, but the kiss didn't stay tender for long. It turned wild and passionate, and a new feeling shot through him. A need like none he'd ever experienced, tempered only by his love for the woman in his arms.

When they were done, she stayed in his arms. She placed another soft kiss on his skin, this one on his chest just below his collarbone on the side that ached whenever the weather turned cold and damp. He'd been injured long ago as a part of a hand-to-hand fight training. He hadn't blocked an incoming blow correctly, and instead of pulling back, his instructor had followed through and broken Joe's collarbone. As a lesson in failure, the instructor had said.

"I love you," Millicent whispered in the dark of their bedroom, with the only light from their clock radio as a witness. "Husband."

Joe's heart swelled with such tenderness it almost choked him. "I love you, wife." His voice was so rough with emotion he almost couldn't get the words out.

They weren't supposed to fall in love. Their superiors had failed to anticipate this new development, even though they should have.

When Millicent visited the doctor several weeks later and discovered that they had, indeed, conceived a child, Joe dutifully included that fact in his report to his superiors. He omitted any mention of the fact that the two of them had no plans to stop doing more than merely sleeping in their bed.

It was the first thing that Joe deliberately omitted from his reports.

It wouldn't be the last.

"We're in trouble," Joe told Millicent after dinner one night in November of 1991.

Their daughter, a bright and brilliant six-year-old with her father's blue eyes and her mother's thick, sable-brown hair, was playing with her dolls in the living room. From Joe's vantage point, it looked like Barbie was getting a new hairdo to go along with the new outfit Joe had bought on an after-work visit to a neighborhood toy store, the one all his co-workers shopped at.

He'd wanted to make sure his daughter was distracted so that he and Millicent could have a private conversation without young ears overhearing. He'd never been around young children when he'd been young himself—he'd been an only child who'd been orphaned at ten—and had been somewhat surprised to discover what his daughter picked up on. Like the curse word he'd used when he'd burned himself on a frying pan one evening.

That word had become his daughter's favorite for a week. Thank goodness he hadn't cursed in Russian.

Millicent stood at the kitchen sink washing dishes while Joe used a dishtowel older than their daughter to dry them. The dish soap had a flowery scent that made his wife sneeze if she used too much. He'd told her to replace it with an unscented brand, but she insisted on not wasting what she'd already bought.

Ever since their daughter had been born, Millicent had been saving what money she could, stashing it beneath a loose floorboard in their bedroom in case some day they needed to disappear. It looked like that day might be coming very soon.

"I read the paper," Millicent said. "That's what you're talking about?"

The Soviet Union, their homeland—the country they'd secretly worked for all these years—was tearing itself apart. Political machinations were nothing new, but there'd been a failed coup in August, and since then republics had been seceding from the union. For the first time, articles in this morning's newspaper had referred to their country as the "former Soviet Union."

When Joe read those words, an icy cold spike of fear had shot down his spine.

What would the KGB do with its spies when there was no longer a country to work for? Would they be eliminated? Joe and Millicent had spied on the United States for years. Stolen its secrets. Betrayed the people who'd befriended them. Would the

KGB have them killed to prevent the United States from learning who they really were and what they'd done?

It had been years since Joe had worried about assassination, but now it looked like a real possibility.

Or would they be repatriated to whatever new form of government took the place of the "former" Soviet Union? The possibility of being separated from Millicent chilled him to the bone. After their daughter had been born, Joe and Millicent had "renewed" their vows in front of their friends, including the wives who'd finally accepted Millicent as one of their own. As far as Joe and Millicent were concerned, they'd finally been officially married on that day. Joe did not want to lose his wife.

But worse by far was the question of what would become of their daughter.

Joe had never known the kind of love that had nearly broken him when he held his infant daughter for the first time on the day she'd been born. He loved his wife, and he'd been overwhelmed the first time he'd felt his unborn child move within his wife's swollen belly.

But actually holding his newborn daughter? That was a miracle he'd never expected to experience in his life. Spies didn't have families of their own. They might infiltrate a family, become friends with someone else's children. But spies weren't supposed to have children of their own.

The people who had trained him called children a distraction, but that was far from the whole truth.

Children owned their parents' hearts. Children demanded—and deserved—total loyalty. Children came first, pure and simple.

Joe loved his wife, but if a choice came down to saving her or saving his daughter, he would choose his daughter. Millicent could defend herself. His daughter—their daughter—was an innocent. He would not see the KGB take his daughter and put her in a program like the one Millicent had grown up in. He'd seen the scars on his wife's body from the beatings she'd endured "to build character," she'd told him. But far worse had been the psychological scars from years of humiliation meant to break her before she could be remade in the form of a perfect spy.

He could not, *would* not, let that happen to their daughter.

"How much have we saved?" he asked his wife as he finished drying a dinner plate. The plate had a chip along one edge where their daughter had thrown her sippy cup when she'd been two and registering her dislike of certain foods. Like strained peas.

"Enough, I think, at least to get us started." Millicent handed him another dish, this one the serving dish for the mashed potatoes she'd made from scratch. "Do we leave now?"

Joe had been thinking of that all day. The newspapers might refer to their homeland as the former Soviet Union, but the KGB was still a formidable presence even though its chief had been involved in the failed coup and had been subsequently detained.

Ever since the August coup, Joe had become hypervigilant again. He'd become so fully assimilated into American life, thanks to his daughter, that he sometimes forgot he wasn't a simple middle-class American with a wife and one child to support and a backyard barbecue where he cooked hamburgers and hotdogs on the weekends.

The only reminder of who he actually was came every other week when he submitted his coded reports and his superiors acknowledged receipt through a note rolled into his Sunday newspaper. Their superiors still treated Joe and Millicent as they had all these years: as covert assets, no more, no less.

If they ran now, if they attempted to disappear, would the KGB still be strong enough, still organized enough—still motivated enough—to find them?

Their daughter shrieked from where she was playing in the living room.

Joe's heart skipped a beat before it pounded double-time in his chest. He dropped the dish he'd been drying. It shattered on the kitchen floor as he ran into the living room, his wife on his heels, sudsy water dripping from her hands.

Then his daughter giggled.

Joe stopped so fast that Millicent ran into his back.

"She's fine," he said. "She's only playing."

The little girl turned her head toward where her parents stood just inside the archway between the dining room and the living room. She was sitting on the faded avocado carpet, Barbie and her accessories spread out around her.

"Look what Barbie can do!" she said. "She can fly!"

She proceeded to throw her doll high in the air, shrieking in delight as Barbie reached the highest part of her flight, and then almost catching her when she fell back to the floor.

"That's great, sweetheart," Millicent said, her voice breathless. "Let's use our inside voices though so you don't scare Mommy and Daddy."

"Okay." She picked up her doll. "Don't scream so loud, Barbie. You scared Mommy." Her voice sounded eerily like Millicent's.

Joe shared a look with his wife. There'd been no play time in the programs he and Millicent had been raised in. There'd been no joy, just day after day of drudgery interspersed with sheer terror. Both of them would do anything to save their daughter's innocence from the people who had stolen theirs.

But they had to pick the optimal time to disappear, and now wasn't it.

"Soon," he said. "We'll leave soon. Just not yet."

He hoped that by waiting for the right moment to disappear, he could save his daughter from the kind of life he'd had as a child. If the KGB even kept her alive instead of killing her outright.

Above all, he hoped that the right moment would actually come.

The KGB was officially dissolved on the third day of December, 1991.

Even though they'd been shocked by the events that put an end to the government they'd worked for, that had caused news reports to refer to their homeland as the "former" Soviet Union, the formal dissolution of a state organization as powerful, as ruthless as the KGB shocked them both to their core.

They'd invested in a small radio for the kitchen, even though Millicent hadn't wanted to spend the money. Joe had found the radio in a neighborhood thrift shop, and they kept it tuned to various news programs almost constantly.

"It's not gone," Millicent said, her face pale, her eyes wide. She was gripping her morning cup of coffee so tightly that her knuckles had turned white. "It can't be gone. They will rename it something else. It will become something else."

Something worse. She didn't have to say it. Joe had already thought the same thing.

"We'll leave tonight," he said. "After work. Pick me up as usual. Leave the lights on. Make it look like we're coming back. Maybe leave a casserole in the refrigerator and the radio on."

They only had the one car, a station wagon—more of their cost-cutting measures—so Millicent took him to work every morning and picked him up at night, like most of his co-workers' wives.

He couldn't simply not show up to work. The facility where Joe worked had an important deadline and had cancelled all vacations. "If you call in sick, you better be in the hospital," his boss had told Joe's entire team. If they left this morning, his boss might actually send someone to the house to get him, and their disappearance would be discovered too quickly. By leaving tonight, Joe wouldn't be missed until the next morning, and by then they'd be miles away.

But he wasn't the only one who had someplace

to be. Their daughter was enrolled in public school, and public schools had rules about attendance. He didn't want to leave their daughter alone with virtual strangers. Not today.

"Call the school," he said. "Tell them she's sick, then take her someplace public. Someplace busy. Stay visible."

He didn't have to tell his wife to stay vigilant.

She nodded her agreement. Before she could tell him where she planned to go, he held up his hand. "Just come get me at the usual time. I don't want to know where you'll be."

If he didn't know, he couldn't tell anyone else, even if he was tortured for the information.

Millicent nodded again. Her face was getting some color back, but she was still frightened. Not for herself, he knew, but for him and their daughter.

"We'll be fine," he said. "We should have a day, two at most, before any orders go out concerning us. By that time, we'll be far away."

It was a good plan. A solid plan. A workable plan.

It had but a single flaw.

And that flaw nearly destroyed his family.

For the first time in his life, Joe made a serious miscalculation.

He forgot that the KGB was a bureaucracy in and of itself. Bureaucracies ran on plans. They ran on redundancies. They ran on contingencies after contingencies.

Before the public announcement was ever made, before the law had been issued that reorganized state security bodies including the KGB, plans had been set in motion regarding the agency's covert operatives.

All of the agency's covert operatives, including Joe and Millicent.

The operatives knew too much, that was a given. The operatives embedded in the United States were intimately involved with operations the KGB had carried out for years right under the noses of the Americans. They knew what information had been of great enough interest to Moscow to risk their discovery.

State secrets could not be risked. Assets could be replaced, the security of Moscow's intelligence agencies could not. New generations of assets were already being trained. Current assets were a liability, and liabilities would not be tolerated.

On the morning of December 3, 1991, when the world woke up to the news that the KGB had been dissolved, plans had already been set in motion. Contingencies had been discussed. Redundancies accounted for. Orders issued.

Skilled operatives given new assignments.

The bureaucracy was reinventing itself. New management was taking over.

Before Joe had even taken the first sip of his morning coffee, the fate of his family had been decided by men he had never met.

When Millicent dropped him off at work, kissing him goodbye as she did every morning, he had no idea that it was already too late.

Millicent wasn't waiting for Joe after his shift.

The gated employee parking area at the facility where he worked required the swipe of a keycard for entry. Since the only car they owned was the station wagon Millicent drove, they kept the keycard in the car, attached to a lanyard and stored in the glove box. With the keycard, she had access to not only the parking area but also the employee common areas, such as the cafeteria and the restrooms right off the cafeteria.

Access to those restrooms had been necessary on more than one occasion when their daughter was still an infant and required an emergency diaper change. On one such occasion, Joe had met his wife inside the family restroom and used his daughter's diaper bag to remove classified documents from the building.

With the December holidays fast approaching, Joe's co-workers always had things to do immediately after work. Those who drove themselves had already left and no one besides Joe was waiting outside the employee entrance to the building.

A chill ran down his spine. At this time of year it was always dark when he left work. While his overcoat protected him from all but the coldest nights, tonight the dark seemed ominous. Almost like a living thing, and he couldn't seem to get warm.

The only vehicles still in the lot belonged to his supervisor, a single man who worked nearly sixty hours a week and never mingled with the people who worked directly for him, and a middle-aged woman in Human Resources. The few times Joe had met with her, she'd seemed outwardly friendly but her eyes held no warmth. Office gossip attributed that to the sudden death of her husband at a young age and the fact that she'd never remarried. She lived for her work, the gossips said, some with pity, but most with fear. When you were called in for a meeting with H.R., the reasons were rarely good.

He didn't see Millicent or their car anywhere.

One of the streetlights that illuminated the parking lot near the far corner of the facility's main building was dark. It could have burned out, those things happened, but the hair on the back of Joe's neck rose.

He had no weapons with him. He and Millicent had handguns, but security in the facility was too tight for him to bring a firearm to work, even secreted in his briefcase. Millicent would have packed both guns in the car along with a few—a very few—of their belongings and the money she had stashed at the house they wouldn't be going back to.

Something was very wrong.

He'd been standing on the sidewalk next to the parking lot, a husband waiting for his wife to pick him up. A wife who was late. Any other husband would return to his office and call his house to see if his wife had left, so Joe started to walk back toward the employee entrance. Not that he would be able to call Millicent. If she followed the plan, she wouldn't be at the house, but he needed to act as if everything was normal even though his belly was a hard knot of worry.

He tried to tell himself that if something had happened to Millicent—if something had happened to their daughter—he would know. Wasn't that what was supposed to happen? If something happened to those you loved, weren't you just supposed to know?

He was halfway to the employee entrance when a shadowy figure detached itself from the corner of the main building.

Joe would have recognized his wife's figure any-where, and relief flooded through him.

Until she raised her arm and pointed a gun at him.

"Millicent?"

Her hand was steady on the gun. Gone was the gentleness he'd grown to expect from his wife. From the mother of their child. This was the hardened op-erative he'd met all those years ago. The one who had only pretended affection for him in public.

He wished he could see her eyes, but the parking lot was too dark. The night created deep shadows on her face, and he couldn't see her eyes.

"The money's gone," she said. "Every cent. It was there last week, but not today. Today I only found orders in its place. I am to do this thing if I want our daughter to be safe. I have no choice."

Her voice quavered on the last few words, and he understood. She was a skilled operative, but she was also a mother. Not to a child who had simply been placed with her, but a child she had given birth to. Moscow knew that by threatening to kill her daughter, they could make her do as they ordered.

Moscow would not keep its promise. Millicent might be allowed to leave tonight, but another skilled operative would come for her one day. Come for her and their daughter.

"In your heart, you must know they're lying," he said. "If it serves their interests, they'll kill you too—and our daughter—without hesitation."

Now her hand did shake. "This buys her today," she said. "This lets me take her and disappear, don't you understand? It gives me *today*. If I don't... there is no today, no possibility of tomorrow. *They knew what we planned.* They must have known all along."

Joe's mouth went dry.

He'd been stupid. He hadn't considered the obvious.

Someone had been watching them. Someone else in the employ of the KGB.

It could be anyone. One of their neighbors. One of the people he worked with. The man who delivered their mail. One of the clerks at the grocery store where Millicent shopped. Or someone they had never met, had never seen, but who'd been watching them closely.

He had never met the person who picked up his reports. He handwrote them at night at the dining room table, reports written in code that would be gibberish to anyone who might glance at them. He delivered his reports in a series of blind drops, never at the same place twice, yet always at a place a suburban family man might be expected to occasionally go.

For all he knew, different operatives picked up his reports every time.

For all he knew, *anyone* could be watching them.

If that was the case, why force Millicent to kill him?

Was the watcher even still here? The last time she'd checked the money was last week. She'd done her grocery shopping and always added whatever money was left from her food budget to the money hidden beneath the bedroom floor.

But Millicent left the house at some point almost every day. They had no alarm system. No one in their neighborhood did, and they could not afford to stand out by getting one. A skilled operative would have had no trouble breaking in and taking the money at any time. Joe could have done it in his sleep.

Whoever had been watching them, had been collecting Joe's reports, could be long gone by now. Why else would Moscow have given Millicent these orders? To prove her continued loyalty? That ship had already sailed, as the American saying went. It had for him, and he was certain it had for his wife as well.

"We can still run," he said. "We can still survive. Our daughter deserves to grow up with both her parents."

His wife's gun hand was shaking badly now. He couldn't see her eyes, but he could see the tracks of tears running down her cheeks.

"Promise me," she said. "Promise me we can keep her safe."

"I promise," he said.

Perhaps he said it too quickly or he said it too glibly. Or perhaps even if he'd said it with all the heartfelt emotion of which he was capable, it wouldn't have mattered. Promises like the one she demanded could never be kept, not in their world. For spies, safety wasn't something that could be guaranteed. Maybe it couldn't be guaranteed for anyone else either, but Joe had never been anyone else.

He saw her take a deep breath. "I wish I could believe you," she said.

And then she pulled the trigger.

Joe opened his eyes and took a deep breath.

The candle on the mantle had burned halfway down. The tea Millicent had brought had cooled while they sat side by side on their sofa. She no longer rested her head on his shoulder. She knew that the old injuries pained him worse in the winter when even in the central California valley the nights grew cold. She held his hand instead, but gently. Her arthritis wasn't as bad as his, but fingers that had done hard work for decades were showing their age in swollen, stiff joints.

Remembrance day was hardest on her. For the both of them it meant the day they had claimed their freedom, but for her it was also the day she had almost killed him.

When she'd fired her gun that long ago night, the bullet had hit him high in the shoulder. The same shoulder where an instructor had broken his collarbone years before to teach him a lesson.

The impact had knocked Joe down, the shock of it had almost knocked him senseless.

When she fired again, he thought the second shot would kill him.

Instead, Millicent's second shot killed the woman from H.R.

Joe and Millicent had both been trained in threat assessment. Trained to make split second decisions.

Trained to take appropriate actions without hesitation.

Millicent had seen the woman approaching the two of them from the opposite side of the building. She'd been prepared to lower her gun when she'd seen the woman raise a gun of her own.

Millicent hadn't hesitated. She fired, only her aim was off because her hand still hadn't been steady. Instead of hitting the woman coming up behind Joe, she'd hit Joe. When he'd fallen down, she had a clear target and she fired instantaneously.

Her shot had impacted the woman center mass. The woman pulled the trigger on her own gun a split second too late. Her shot went wild. She was dead before she hit the ground.

Joe hadn't needed anyone to tell him that the H.R. woman had been the person assigned by the KGB to watch them. She had been in the perfect position to make sure he maintained his job, that he survived cutbacks that had seen countless co-workers given their termination notices, and that Joe was cleared for advancements. But she didn't have the education to understand the science like Joe did. She was merely a middleman. Someone that Moscow would have needed to eliminate as well. He wondered if she'd ever realized that.

The few pain-filled days after December 3, 1991,

were a blur in Joe's memory. Millicent got them—all three of them: Joe, Millicent, and their daughter—out of the parking lot before the police arrived. She dug the bullet out of his shoulder and tended his wound. Somehow she managed to get penicillin for him, and she drove through three states while he slept under blankets in the back of their station wagon.

They survived that first bad year. A year of no money except what they could steal or earn with short-term, low-paying jobs. A year of living out of their station wagon and eating in soup kitchens.

But once again, they managed to fit in. America was suffering through a recession, and they weren't the only family without a home. They shopped for clothes in charity shops. They changed their identities more than once. But no matter how hard life became, Millicent refused to part with their one remaining cut crystal candleholder.

Someday there will be light again, she'd said.

And she'd been right.

By 1993 the economy had begun to recover. Joe got a job in a store selling home computers. They still looked over their shoulders in public, but they began to relax, just a little. They stayed in one place long enough for Joe to establish a track record in the home computer field before they relocated and relocated again.

By the time their daughter was ready for high school, both Joe and Millicent were working from home. Telecommuting allowed them to live wherever they wanted and still earn a decent living. Millicent found she had a knack for computer languages, just as she'd had a knack for foreign languages, something her handlers in Moscow had recognized but had never exploited. She wrote computer programs the way the wives she used to share girls' nights out with had done needlework or puttered in their flower gardens. It relaxed her, but it also had a purpose. Using her skills, she managed to eradicate every trace of their former lives that her little electronic bits and bytes discovered, no matter where that information was stored.

But they still didn't feel entirely safe.

Because it wasn't just their lives they were protecting.

They had a daughter, and now she had a husband and children of her own.

Joe got up from the sofa and blew out the candle. Then he reached for the framed photograph of his daughter and her children, touching each of their faces gently with a callused fingertip.

It would be such a long way to go to visit them. They would have to traverse the entire country.

But how many more years did he and Millicent have? The hard years—years of deprivation and hardship and constant physical and mental abuse in the Soviet Union, the years of living out of their car, the years of constant vigilance—had taken a toll. Arthritis had advanced from his hands and knees into his elbows and one hip, forcing him to walk now with a cane for support and to guard against a sudden fall. The constant ache in his collarbone, the one that had been broken during his training all those decades ago, worsened during the damp winter months. Millicent's heart was not as strong or steady as it had once been, and she tired easily.

How many more birthdays and holidays and special days with their daughter and her children—grandchildren they had never met in person—were left for two former spies living out their remaining days in obscurity? He didn't expect that either of them would live more than a handful more years.

Air travel was still out of the question. Millicent had done her best work erasing their past and creating their present, but he had no doubt the American government's own intelligence services, as maligned as they had been in recent years, were still far better than his self-taught wife. He did not want to test the limits of their new identities. Trains might be problematic as well due to a lack of control, as would busses.

That left driving. They had a reliable if unremarkable car, a gray sedan that blended in with all the other gray sedans that shared the road with oversized pickup trucks and SUVs.

Could they drive cross-country, just the two of them? The distance seemed so vast, but the reward... the reward would be incredible.

He turned to face his wife. She sat holding her half-empty teacup. She was looking into the middle distance, but he knew she wasn't looking at anything in their living room. Their house was small and theirs only thanks to a long-term lease and a landlord who left them alone, just the way they liked it.

"We should go," he said.

She looked up at him in alarm. "Have we been found? What do you know?"

"To New York," he said. To Albany, where their daughter lived.

She tilted her head. He had never suggested such a thing before, and he'd confused her.

"If we're careful, if we take our time... avoid the storms..." He'd read how vicious winter storms could be, and they would have to cross the Rockies at some point or risk going south through places where pcople could be unkind to strangers. "We can make it in time."

"In time...."

Her voice trailed off, and he saw realization dawn on her face. Realization and hope, but they died quickly and she shook her head.

"It's too dangerous," she said. "We can't."

"It has been three decades," he said. "If they'd found us, we'd be dead by now."

Her mouth thinned to a straight line. "It's not just us."

No, it wasn't. But if they'd been found, their daughter would have been found as well. And their daughter had never known about their double life. She'd always lived her adult life in the open. Taken only the normal precautions a woman should take in American society.

He laughed and spread his arms wide. "We no longer matter! Disinformation. Opinion control. That's what matters today. No one cares what we were or what we did."

"Some would care," she said, and he knew she wasn't talking about Moscow. "We are not rich or powerful."

Rich and powerful men had always been able to write their own rules. Game the system, as the Americans said. Rich and powerful men could make friends with the enemy, share secrets with the enemy, and still escape punishment. At least in America. In other parts of the world? Even the rich and powerful, if they crossed the wrong person, could be eliminated in convenient accidents.

He sat down on the sofa next to her and took her hands in both of his. Her fingers were cold.

"We can still be careful," he said. "We have had a lifetime being careful. We know how."

She looked at his hand for a long time, then her gaze shifted to the half-burned candle on the mantle. "It never burns all the way," she said. "We never let it."

No, they didn't. A single taper took a long time to burn. They never lit their remembrance candles at any other time of the year, and they always bought a new one every year. It seemed bad luck somehow not to.

She got up from the sofa and picked up the lighter. "We remember what we were, but we never let the candle finish its job." She lit the wick. The flame kicked up high, illuminating their daughter's face in the framed photograph. "We never let it take the memories away. Perhaps we should." She turned to face him. "Celebrate who we've become. Let ourselves truly be free."

"Freedom day." He turned the words over in his

mind. They sounded right. They sounded like how he felt. How he wanted to feel for as many years as were left to him. To the both of them.

This time when they sat next to each other on the sofa, they didn't close their eyes and relive the past. They didn't do penance for their sins. This time they looked at their daughter's photograph. They talked about how long it would take for the drive, what routes they should take. What gifts they should buy for their grandchildren.

This time they let the candle burn until the flame guttered in the cut crystal holder.

Would they buy another candle next year? Celebrate their new holiday the way they had the old?

Only time would tell.

For two elderly spies who'd never expected to live this long, another year of life—of freedom—deserved more than a single candle.

Maybe next year they would buy two.

TROUBLED WATER

DONALEE MOULTON

There is a knot in my stomach that tightens every time I press the start button.

And nothing happens.

The Keurig coffeemaker refuses to cooperate. It simply sits there blinking blue. Now the knot is moving further up my abdomen and across my kidneys and lodging in my lower back.

When I was the police chief in Humboldt, Saskatchewan, I could just duck out the door to the nearest Walmart and have a replacement in mere minutes. But I'm currently a police chief in the Canadian north, a mere 2,000 miles from the Arctic Circle, and there is no Walmart. There is no department store of any kind. Amazon delivers in three to five days (it used to be three weeks), but coffee in a climate where temperatures can routinely hit -13 degrees Fahrenheit is not simply nice to have, it is essential.

There is a Facebook marketplace that might be the best option. I turn to ask Ahnah Friesen, the Iqaluit Constabulary's exceptional executive assistant, what she'd recommend we do in this crisis. Before I can say anything, however, our front door swings open and David Picco, the member of the legislative assembly for Rankin Inlet, strides in.

"Got a minute," he says heading for my office. It is not a request.

David Picco is the man responsible for getting

the local police force established – a first for the territory of Nunavut – and the person responsible for me being here in Iqaluit without a coffeemaker. He's also a mentor and a friend.

I'm right behind him. Coffeeless. "What's up?" I ask before the door shuts behind me, something we rarely do here and a harbinger of bad news to come.

"I'd like you to come with me," David says. "We have a situation. It doesn't appear to be a police matter, but I'd like your input."

"Of course," I say without hesitation. "How can I help?"

"Not sure," says David. "I'll tell you what I do know on the way."

We're heading down Mivvik and turning on to Queen Elizabeth past the post office. David is clearly rattled about something. I wait silently. My training as a cop in the south has taught me that. Lack of caffeine makes it easier.

"A young man has died," David finally says. "It might be the water."

"Shit," I say sitting up straighter. The knot is back.

Water is a hot-button issue in Iqaluit. Residents have repeatedly complained about the smell of fuel every time they turned on their taps, and last year the city's 8,000 residents had to use bottled water for two months when it was confirmed something potentially toxic was in the water. That something was fuel. It turns out a 60-year-old underground fuel tank was buried next to the water-treatment plant. Remediation and cleaning are under way, but many people in town feel efforts are too little, too late.

David brings the Ram 1500 to an abrupt halt in front of a green and grey apartment building on Aiviq Street. The coroner's Subaru Crosstek and the city's one ambulance are parked out front. "Second floor," David says.

"I don't want to influence what you see," he adds by way of explanation. "And I don't want to see that room again unless I have to."

There is no elevator, not unusual in Iqaluit, and the stairs have seen better days, also not unusual. There is a group of people outside the third apartment on the left. "Doug Brumal," I say by way of introduction. "Police chief."

That creates a stir. A clear voice from inside yells out, "What the hell are you doing here?"

That would be Kari Frost, the chief coroner. I make my away around two paramedics, one gurney, and a clutch of what I presume are other tenants. Kari is on her knees in front of a motionless man. A stethoscope dangles from her neck. Kari nods in my direction as if answering my unasked question.

I step in closer, mindful not to contaminate what might be a crime scene, although with the crowd and the chaos inside the apartment, I fear that ship has sailed. "David Picco thought I might be able to help. He's outside in his truck."

That got me a raised eyebrow, and this response. "I'll meet you both at your office in 15 minutes."

I take a quick look around. The apartment is a mess—but not from efforts to save the young man lying dead on the floor. Dirty dishes overflow the sink and the counter and have made their way into the small living area that includes a Formica dining table with mismatched chairs and a sea-green sofa with purple cushions and two bed pillows. I realize for the first time that there is a young man on the sofa. He is so still I didn't see him until now. The first thing I notice: he's breathing.

"Doug Brumal," I say by way of introduction. I'm now standing in front of him. He's Caucasian and I'd guess around 6'1" and 140 pounds. He's lean–and he's nervous. This could simply be the aftershock of seeing someone die, someone I presume who may be close to him. The young man nods but barely looks up.

"I'm the police chief," I add. Now that gets me a response. Mr. Lean with the Save-Our-Planet T-shirt looks up quickly and seems to spasm. Again, I'm not sure if this is shock or something more.

"Jakob," he says. "But everybody calls me Peanut."

I hear a not-so-subtle cough behind me. I take a quick look at my watch. There's ten minutes left before Kari descends on the police station. I head for outside and fill David in. Like most Inuit I know, he has been waiting patiently and without impatience.

"What do you think?" he asks.

"I think there is a dead man on the floor and something Kari wants us to know," I say. Frankly, it's all I've got at this point.

We stop at the only Tim Horton's in Iqaluit on the way back to my office and stock up on coffee for everyone. I jokingly ask the server if she has an extra coffeemaker she could sell me. The joke falls flat, although I get a polite smile. Inuit must think people from the south are strange.

We're met with a rousing round of applause when we enter the station. That's for the coffee and the box of Timbits. I'm on my third bite-size doughnut when Kari marches in. "Thank god," Iqaluit's coroner says. "I'm starving. Death has that effect on me."

A southerner from Calgary, Kari has lived in Iqaluit for five years, a lifetime for many people who move to a place where the land is permanently frozen, the sun dips below the horizon for months, and a head of lettuce can cost you as much as $6. This is her home, but she has brought the south with her. Haven't we all.

"Sorry guys," she says looking at Ahnah and my two constables, Kallik Redfern and Willie Appaqaq, "but this will have to be a closed-door meeting for now."

Kari grabs a coffee, takes a long swallow, and lets out a big sigh. "Guys, this might be a mess. A big mess."

We wait for her to continue. I want to dive in and ask, "What might be a mess?" "What do you mean by mess?" "Why are we discussing this behind closed doors?"

But I have learned a little forbearance since moving to Nunavut six months ago. The Inuit are a thoughtful people. They don't jump into conversations, interrupt, or even respond immediately. They reflect, if only for several vital seconds.

Kari takes another swallow. Her 5'3" frame seems to deflate a little. "I think the kid died of benzene poisoning."

It's clear from the expressions on David's face and my face that we have no idea what this pronouncement means. That confusion is quickly replaced with concern. "Benzene is a petroleum-based chemical," says Kari. "The last water test results from the chief medical health officer showed concentrations 600 times higher than the maximum set in the *Guidelines for Canadian Drinking Water Quality*."

"Shit," David says quietly.

Water issues have been contentious and ongoing in Iqaluit, but they have not been fatal. Until now. "Are you sure?" I ask.

"Not in the least," says Kari. "I won't be sure until we get blood results back from Edmonton."

"You can't test here?" David asks quickly. Having to ship blood cultures 2,800 kilometres away takes time and wastes time. It also increases the number of people privy to what is being tested.

"No," says Kari. We accept her answer. The coroner knows what is at stake, and she knows what resources are available in her field here. In a small community that is closer to the north pole than a major city, resources can be hard to come by.

"What makes you think it's benzene?" I ask hoping we might find a flaw in Kari's reasoning.

"The symptoms the paramedics witnessed–vomiting, abdominal pain, convulsions," Kari says. "He also smelled sweet."

She sees our uncertainty. "Benzene has a sweet smell."

"This isn't good," says David. You can see the concern etched on his face. "I need to contact the environmental health officer and fill them in. Then we'll need to inform the city council and the government executive." In Nunavut, the territorial government is run by consensus. Decisions do not have to be endorsed unanimously but they must be carefully thought through and presented. The member from Rankin Inlet is in for a long few days, maybe weeks.

"Doug, will you dig up everything you can on this young man, and keep me apprised," David adds as he makes his way to my office door. "Kari, please push for the blood results."

There are only a few hours left in the work day, and my team is in full swing. This is new to us. First, almost everything is new to us. The Iqaluit Constabulary has officially been up and running for fewer than three months. Second, we usually investigate what is a suspected crime not a suspected accidental death.

The young man now has a name: Erik Whetton. What we know so far is that he's 27, originally from Bakersfield, CA, and has been living in Iqaluit for the past six months. Willie is reaching out to the deceased's family for further background. Kallik is going through the apartment, taking photos and samples, as appropriate. Ahnah and I are meeting with the roommate/lover/husband in 40 minutes.

Jakob Brandt is prompt. Ahnah has made the interrogation room as friendly and welcoming as possible. The lights are not on full beam, there is bottled water on the table, and biscuits I suspect were a treat for me from Kallick's mom. It's not usually my style to jointly interview suspects, witnesses, or others, but somehow Ahnah has become integral to this process. I'm not sure how this happened; I suspect Ahnah knows exactly how it happened.

Brandt lowers his lanky frame into one of the three metal chairs in the room. He overflows the back of the chair and his legs protrude almost to the edge of the table that is in front of us. Today his T-shirt says, "Save the whales."

"Thanks for coming, Jakob," I say trying to sound friendly. I'm actually trying to be friendly. It is a technique I've learned from the Inuit, but to them it is not a technique.

"Peanut," says the lanky man with the long legs. "It's Peanut."

I can sense Ahnah's confusion. She's trying to take notes but a grown man with the name of a snack food makes no sense to her. It's something I'll try to explain later, although I'm not sure how. "We're trying to find out what happened to Erik," I explain, "and hoping you can help."

"I'll try," says Peanut. It's more of a mumble. Again, not sure if he's nervous or shy. Or something else.

"We have the report from the paramedics," I note. "It indicates you called fire and emergency." Iqaluit does not have a 911 system.

Peanut nods. He obviously does not want to re-live this moment, but to his credit, he sits taller and says, "We were working on some stuff. Erik got up to get a glass of water. A couple of minutes later he's flailing on the floor, throwing up, and clutching his stomach."

"Do you have any idea what happened?" I ask.

"Whatever it was, it killed him," Peanut says. So the young man has an edge.

"What were you working on?" I ask.

Peanut looks surprised. "What do you mean?"

"You mentioned you were working on 'some stuff.' I'm wondering what that might be."

It turned out to be stuff Peanut is passionate about. It appears he was not alone in that fervor. I have a friend who contends there are three types of people who are drawn to the northernmost territory in North America: mercenaries, missionaries, and misfits. Whetton appeared to fall into the second cat-

cgory, or at least a sub-category. A staunch environmentalist, Whetton, Peanut tells us, came to Iqaluit
to work with a non-profit group called Nuna
Anaana. Their focus is on climate change, specifically
permafrost degradation and increased coastal erosion
caused by the late freezing of sea ice.

"You know a lot about this," I say by way of
making conversation and making Peanut feel at ease.
I need to learn more, then I can figure out what is
relevant and what isn't. Ahnah tilts her head and
gives me a quizzical look. I'll explain later.

"I'm an environmental engineer," says Peanut.

"What was Erik's background?" I ask.

"He just cared about the planet," says Peanut.
There is a hint of defensiveness.

"Were you two roommates, or friends, or..." I let
the sentence dangle.

Peanut sighs. "We're both straight. We're friends,
and we're broke. We lived together to save money and
because we like each other's company."

"So let me get this straight," I say switching gears
abruptly, "Erik takes a drink of water, then he dies."

Peanut is sitting up straight now. Can't tell if he's
miffed or anxious. "Well, it wasn't quite that quick,
but close enough."

"You think he died because he drank the water," I
say. I can feel Ahnah flinch.

"I do," says Peanut. "That water has been killing people in this community for decades. It just usually takes longer."

Indeed, it does.

I spent a restless night. Listened to a little Elvis and opted for a Jack Daniel's. Neat. It's a little past 8 a.m., and my office door is closed. Again. Inside are David, Kari, me. On the table is hot coffee and two equally hot issues. Jakob Brandt has gone to the local paper to discuss the untimely death of his friend, who is described as an avid environmentalist whose mission in life was to make the planet healthy and safe for all living creatures.

We knew the story was coming out. A reputable, indeed award-winning, newspaper, the *Nunatsiaq News* reached out to confirm Brandt's allegations before publishing. Municipal officials are quoted in the piece, as is Kari.

What wasn't anticipated was the life or the reach of the story. Frontpage news and social media fodder here, the story has become a national story. Media attention from outside the territory is unusual and often unwelcome, at least for the government.

David drops the paper on the coffee table.

"Nothing we can do about this. It's not going to go away until we deal with the problem."

That brings us to the second issue. Kari has the blood results. Whetton's blood has a benzene level 1,200 times above the recommended maximum.

"I've never heard of anything like this," says Kari. She's looking frazzled. Wisps of her curly brown hair protrude at unusual angles, and there are circles under her eyes that weren't there the last time we met behind closed doors.

"Is it the water?" David asks.

"What else could it be?" Kari replies.

"Let's find out," I suggest. Two faces turn to look at me in confusion. "Let's test the water."

"That won't help us," says Kari. "We'd need to test water from the day Erik Whetton died. Benzene levels fluctuate."

"Would it help us to test Peanut's blood?" I ask. "He and Whetton lived in the same apartment, drank the same water. Surely his levels should be elevated."

"We could do that," Kari agrees, "but where does it get us. If his levels are high, it only means he got lucky or didn't drink the apartment water on that day."

"Why would the levels be so much higher in one part of town than another?" David wonders. I'm not sure if he's talking to us or to himself.

"The underground tank leaked fuel unevenly. Some areas are more contaminated than others, and because it's in the groundwater it's hard to predict where levels are highest or how the treatment plant is adding to the issue," says Kari.

"Still," she adds almost as an afterthought, "no one else has died from benzene poisoning that we know of. I checked with the hospital. No one is even diagnosed with this. Of course, we also weren't looking for it."

"Are we saying this might not be accidental?" I ask.

David and Kari look at me in surprise. "What do you mean?" David says at the same time Kari asks, "How could it not be accidental?"

Now I'm thinking like a cop, not a supportive friend and colleague. "Let's just focus on what we know and see where it leads us."

Here's where we end up. Erik Whetton died of benzene poisoning, of that there is no doubt. Where the doubt creeps in is whether he died by drinking tap water himself or at someone else's hand. If it's the latter, it's murder.

There is really only one suspect: Jakob Brandt. It takes Kallik less than an hour to find a credit card receipt for the purchase of benzene, which we discover is easily available online for lawful purchase. Credentials are required, however, and Peanut has these. He's an environmental engineer. And right now he's sitting in our interrogation room.

Ahnah has made sure there are no niceties this time. The camera light shines a steady red glow on the stainless steel table. Ahnah is on one side of the table taking notes, even though the interview is being recorded. I'm on the other side, next to Peanut, the better to see his movements and his reactions.

"There's been a development," I say without preamble and toss a copy of the credit card receipt on the table.

Peanut looks at it and cannot hide the recognition in his eyes—or the implication of what he's looking at.

"You bought benzene," I say, "and your friend died of benzene poisoning."

"So what?" Peanut says. He tries to sound full of bluster. He fails.

"You can connect the dots," I respond. "You're bright, and you're in a lot of trouble unless you can explain this purchase."

"I was conducting some experiments on benzene

in soil," Peanut says. "I have my notes to prove that."

"What will the notes prove," I want to know.

"I've accounted for all the benzene I've purchased. I did not kill my friend," says Peanut. He stands up. "We're done here."

It's been two days since Erik Whetton died. The whole Iqaluit Constabulary—all four of us—are in the station meeting room. There's a whiteboard, which is very white at the moment, a fresh pot of coffee, and homemade bannock, compliments of Kallick's grandmother. There is also molasses, but it is not getting a warm reception. I've encouraged my team to try this on the traditional deep-fried bread, but it is not catching on as a taste treat here. Ahnah has put some on her plate to be polite, but she is making sure to keep her bannock as far away from it as possible.

We take time for a few bites, a slurp or two of coffee, and some pleasantries before we dive in. Peanut has buried us in data and documentation, most of it indecipherable squiggles on paper and spreadsheets that spread in all directions. We're each taking a stack, making notes, and passing our stack to the person on our left when we're through. Three hours later we put on a fresh pot of coffee—Willie has brought his coffeemakcr from home–and settle in for a review.

As far as we can tell, Peanut has accounted for all of the 500 ml of benzene he purchased legally from a lab in Arizona. The chemical, it appears, was used in soil samples to assess evaporation levels and absorption rates and reach.

"We don't have much soil," Ahnah points out. "Why spend all this time and effort examining benzene in soil?" It's a good question. In Nunavut, most of the land is tundra, which means it is bare, rocky, and treeless. And it is also locked in permafrost. Only a few inches of soil subsist in parts of the region.

Willie writes Ahnah's question on the board and puts it in a column under Peanut's name and Kari Frost's name. "Even if he used the benzene in the soil like he said, could he then have put the soil in water and given it to Whetton?" Willie asks. "That way he would account for the benzene he bought."

"Would you drink dirty water?" Kallick asks. Still, Willie puts the question under Kari's name. "Could he have faked the numbers?"

That is the key question. I feel a surge of pride at how far this team has come and how quickly. "Either Peanut used the benzene as he documented, he fudged the figures, or there is another source of benzene," I say. "Let's check with Kari."

As if on cue, the coroner walks through the door. I look at Ahnah.

"I texted her when we began," she says quietly.

Of course, you did.

Kari spies the bannock–and the molasses. "Oh my god. It's been so long since I've had molasses on my bannock." My team looks at her like she has two heads. Kari doesn't notice. She piles a plate high with bread and drowns it in the black syrup. We wait while she eats–and reads our no-longer-white board.

"I can answer your questions, but I'm not sure if it helps," Kari says. We're informed that Iqaluit's water treatment plant sits on a bed of contaminated soil, so Peanut could have been investigating the impact of benzene on groundwater. The benzene in the soil could have been dissolved in a glass of water but this would be time intensive and result in a very dirty liquid. Even though people in Iqaluit are used to water that smells funny, brown water is not the norm. In fact, many people don't even drink tap water.

The last question is the most problematic: is the data genuine. "I don't have expertise in this area, but what I'm reading in Mr. Brandt's notes appears complete and authentic," Kari says.

"So we have a dead man and no suspects," I say, more to myself.

"Or you have an accidental death caused by benzene in the drinking water," says Kari.

"We're back to where we started," says Ahnah.

"Then we start over again," I say.

The best place to start over is with Peanut. This time I head to his place. Ahnah asks if she can tag along. Peanut doesn't seem surprised to see us, more resigned.

"What do you want?" he asks.

"To find out why your friend died," I answer. That seems to dispense with the attitude. Well, almost. Peanut invites us in and offers us a glass of water. We decline.

"Your research is impressive," I say. Lying.

"How would you know?" Peanut counters.

"Coroner," I say simply and wait a few seconds. "I'm trying to figure out why Erik got sick from the water and you didn't."

"I drink bottled water," says Peanut. "Erik refused to. He said bottled water wasn't affordable for everyone and it deflected us from the real issue–that the water here is contaminated."

"He sounds committed to the cause," I say, more to keep the conversation going.

"More than anyone I've ever met," says Peanut. "Erik believed we were killing the planet and nowhere faster or more profoundly than in the north. He dedicated his life to fixing that."

I asked Peanut a few more perfunctory questions and got the expected answers. Ahnah and I thanked him and headed for my truck.

"What did you think?" I ask her. Our executive assistant is insightful and reflective.

"I believed him," she says.

Me too.

Ahnah hesitates a second, then asks. "Is there anything you're willing to die for?"

Dammit. There it is, the thing that has been eluding us. "We need to go back," I say turning quickly and heading into Peanut's building. If he's surprised to see us back so quickly, he doesn't show it. Just shrugs and ushers us in.

"What kind of friend was Erik?" I ask without preamble.

Now Peanut does look surprised. "What do you mean?"

"Would he ever hang you out to dry?" I ask. "Let you take the blame for something he did?"

"Never," says Peanut firmly and quickly.

"We need to search your apartment if that's okay with you." Peanut nods his assent. I turn to

Ahnah. "Can you get Kallick and Willie over here."

"I've already texted them," she says. Of course you have.

I explain to the team that we're looking for the equivalent of a suicide note. Something that will make it clear Peanut did not harm his friend and his roommate. Three blank stares greet my request.

"This is part process of elimination," I explain, "and part profiling. It's unlikely drinking tap water killed Erik. We've never had levels that high, and no one else died that day. No one even got sick. So that means this was deliberate. Someone needed access to benzene and Erik Whetton."

"That's Peanut," says Willie, "but we ruled Peanut out."

"That leaves us with only one suspect," I say.

"He killed himself," says Ahnah quietly.

"Why would he do that?" Willie asks.

"Because no one was taking the water issue seriously," says a voice in the background. I had almost forgotten Peanut was here, sitting quietly on the couch. I suspect that was a role he often played with Erik Whetton.

"Could Erik have taken some benzene out of your container and replaced it with water?"

Peanut nods. "He wouldn't need much, and a little dilution wouldn't be noticeable in my work."

"But he would know, or at least assume, that you could be blamed for his death," says Ahnah. We all turn to look at her. I can't help but smile.

"Suicide note," I say, and we dive in. Couches and chairs are pulled apart, vents are opened, ceiling squares are removed, and mattresses upended. After 40 minutes, I hold up my hand. "We're going about this all wrong,"

My team, which for now also seems to include Peanut, looks at me. In Humboldt, we call this the look of a deer in headlights. "We're searching for something that would exonerate Peanut in case he was ever accused of killing his friend. Whetton wouldn't have made it almost impossible to find. It has to be somewhere obvious but not obvious."

Peanut nods. "Erik had a great sense of humor. Maybe it was because his work was so heavy, but he loved to laugh."

"Water," I say. "It has to have something to do with water."

"What's funny about water?" Willie wants to know.

"Funny ironic," says Ahnah. Some day this woman will be police chief.

"What was in the freezer?" I ask.

We take inventory: four frozen dinners, two caribou roasts, one serving of char, a water bottle, two containers of ice cubes, and one bedraggled ice cream container. The frozen dinners appear intact, but we open them anyway. Nothing. The ice cream container is immersed in hot water. Still nothing.

"What's in the water bottle?" I ask.

"Water," says Kallick. He tries not to smile. "Ice actually."

"Melt it," I say. In the middle of the small water puddle that results sits a clear plastic tube with a lid. (Both made of recycled material Peanut tells us.) Inside is a thumb drive.

We won't know for several hours exactly what's on the thumb drive, but we all know what's on the thumb drive. Erik Whetton's last act in life–before giving his life to help save this community and this planet–was to protect his friend.

Peanut is in tears. He reaches for the bottle, and I stop him. "We'll need to keep this for evidence. At least for a little while."

"Read the bottom," he says.

There in black letters is the brand name of the bottle manufacturer: Water Protector.

Your Mother's a Whore!

David H. Hendrickson

WARNING: This story comes with an R rating.

If I'd known what a whore was, I'd have known my mother was one before I even entered kindergarten. Not in the sense of the taunt "Your mother's a whore!" That can mean anything from she's promiscuous to nothing at all, I'm just trying to piss you off.

No, my mother was a whore. Literally.

Use all the euphemisms you want, but that's what she was. It took me a few years to figure out the plumbing. I didn't have a grasp of that sort of thing when I was all kindergarten and first-grade innocence.

Misplaced innocence.

I saw, but didn't see, the bloodstains on the sidewalks. Saw, but didn't see, the rats as big as dogs outside our apartment building, a three-decker just outside the projects, its white paint all but peeled off and its rickety porches unsafe to venture out on. Heard, but didn't hear, the constant wailing of police sirens each night through the neighborhood.

I was all innocence and sweetness with my Barbie lunchbox, curly brown pigtails, pink dress, and black patent leather shoes. I knew that boys went to the boys' room and I went to the girls', but I didn't piece the birds and the bees together—that the boy's thing gets put in the girl's thing—for quite a few years.

I just knew that at night my mother put on a

short, black leather skirt, fishnet stockings, bright red lipstick, strong perfume that almost made my eyes water, and a blonde wig. She'd tell me to go to bed by my bedtime—it was just the two of us, so I had my own tiny bedroom that I only had to share with the cockroaches—and she warned that if I called her cell phone for anything less than to tell her the apartment was on fire or I was dying, she'd spank my bare bottom so hard I wouldn't be able to sit down for a month.

So I never called.

When I woke up in the morning, she was always back home, asleep in her bedroom, almost always alone, but every so often with a stranger in bed beside her. Either way, I was never to wake her. Just eat some Cheerios, get myself dressed, and on school days, get on the bus. And I'd better not be late and miss it or young lady, you will regret the day you were born. So I knew she wasn't like any of the other mothers in our neighborhood.

I just didn't know that she was a whore.

I should have figured it out the night I walked into her bedroom a little after midnight and she wasn't alone. She and this scrawny, old, bald man were doing stuff on the bed without any clothes on. Naked as a jaybird. Whatever a jaybird is. The man on top of my mother, bouncing really fast, squeezing his wrinkled behind.

"Katie, go back to your room!" was all she said.

That's how I figured out the birds and the bees.

But I was so dumb it still didn't dawn on me that she was a whore. Did I know at some primal level, but didn't want to admit it to myself? Perhaps, but I think I was just so dumb, so oblivious to what was right in front of me that I still didn't get it.

I didn't piece the She's-A-Whore puzzle together —even though the interlocking pieces should have been painfully obvious to me by then—until I heard those words on the playground at Grover Cleveland Elementary during recess.

I was on the see-saw with Rolanda Thomas, a Black friend in my class with a sunny smile and pretty red ribbons in her Afro. My fall jacket was zippered tight to shield me from the cold and the brisk wind that stung my face. Up into the air I'd go, then back down. My feet would push off the rock-hard ground and up I'd go again, then back down. Up and down, up and down. Our bright laughter filled the air. I'd just eaten my snack of a Twinkie and could still taste the remnants of the sweet cream. It was a happy time.

Then Sammy McWilliams sauntered up, a freckle-faced, butterball of a kid two or three grades older than Rolanda and me. He and his friends, all of them white, always seemed to be fighting with groups of either Black or Spanish kids, but today they'd just been watching Jeannie Jones hanging up-side down on the jungle gym while wearing a dress so the boys could see her underpants. They liked that and were disappointed when she climbed down.

That was when Sammy came over with four of his friends. Red-faced and wearing a shit-eating grin, he got to within ten feet and stopped.

"Your mother's a whore!" he hollered, pointing at me. He laughed, then turned to his friends for their approval. When he saw that they were laughing and clapping just like when they were looking at Jeannie Jones's underpants, he yelled it again. "Your mother's a whore!"

My face burned, even though I still didn't get it, because it sounded mean. Rolanda and I stopped laughing. Our rhythmic bouncing up and down on the see-saw slowed, robbed of its joyful enthusiasm.

Soon, it was a chorus of Sammy and his friends. "Your mother's a whore! Your mother's a whore!"

Over and over.

Even in my ignorance, I was horrified.

The boys kept it up for what felt like hours but was probably more like the longest minute of my life. Finally, they got bored and went away.

"What did they mean?" I whispered to Rolanda when we slid off the see-saw. "What's a whore?"

"You know," Rolanda said, shrinking away as if I had a disease.

"No, I don't know. Tell me!"

"It's...." She looked away and shrugged. "You really don't know?"

"No!"

"It's... it's a dirty woman," Rolanda said, and looked at me, eyebrows raised, to see if that was enough.

It wasn't. She winced.

"It's a dirty woman who does, you know... does bad things with men," Rolanda said. She looked at me hopefully. When she didn't see what she was looking for, she leaned close, looked away and whispered, "Has *sex* with them for money."

The light finally dawned. It blasted all over me, covering me with shame. The black leather miniskirts. The fishnet stockings. The strange men. I knew now what Sammy McWilliams and presumably the entire world knew.

My mother was a whore.

My face burned as hot as Hell even as the cold wind whipped into it. I wanted to die of shame. I wished the ground beneath me would open up like in the movies and swallow me.

A long, heavy silence hung between Rolanda and me.

It seemed to go on and on. I couldn't break it. I couldn't speak. It felt like I had a baseball lodged down my throat.

"Sammy's just a jerk and so are his friends," Rolanda finally said. "Don't listen to him. He's just saying that to be mean."

I nodded wordlessly and fought back tears. I could barely breathe.

"Ignore him. It isn't true," Rolanda said, then perhaps seeing the truth written all over my face, she asked in disbelief, "Is it?"

Long seconds passed before I could speak. I just shook my head numbly.

"Of course not," I finally said, my voice shaking.

But it was true. And I finally knew it.

My mother was a dirty, filthy whore. *My mother!*

I suddenly hated her with every ounce of my trembling, tiny body. With every beat of my broken heart. With every jagged breath I took, trying to hold back the tears.

I wished she were dead.

I wished I were dead.

Over the next few years, the taunts and catcalls grew worse. Of course, they did. The pack always turns on its weakest one and devours it. It's the law of the jungle. Sometimes even other girls joined in.

Girls that had been my friends suddenly distanced themselves from me. Even, saddest of all, Rolanda. Until finally I had no friends at all.

Simply the object of ridicule. The one to torment so the others don't instead torment you.

The pariah. The leper. Of no value at all, except to myself.

And then, even that was gone.

"What'll you do for a dollar?" Sammy McWilliams asked one day on the playground, smirking. Soon the question was ringing in my ears from other boys. And even Suzie Winslow.

"Will you blow me for my lunch money?" became the next catcall.

So when Jimmy Dixon pressed a quarter in my palm in the school hallway to pay for a feel of my butt between classes, I couldn't just put my head down, stifle my tears, and try to ignore him like I'd tried to ignore everyone and everything else.

I gave him a feel all right. I let him know how it felt to get a knee in his balls. He howled and started bawling his eyes out. *How does that feel, Jimmy?*

I got detention.

At home, I said nothing of my humiliation for years. It wasn't as though my mother was going to find out at parent-teacher conferences. Instead, I built a rock-hard wall of hatred between us, adding a fresh layer with every new day, with every new degradation.

Hatred for who she was. Hatred for what she was. But most of all, hatred for how it had destroyed me.

I never threw the "W" word at her. I pretended not to notice the leather miniskirt and fishnet stockings she wore out every night, the cheap perfume, and the strange men she brought back home to her bed.

I let her drown in her denial.

Somehow, my abstinence toward the "W" word felt more satisfying than letting her know my pain, than letting her know that I saw everything now. I knew it all and would never, ever forgive her. And each time I denied myself use of that word added another impenetrable layer of hatred to that wall.

I called her by her first name, Sharon. She hated it and said it was disrespectful. Yup, you whore, that's the point. Never again "Mom," or "Ma," or "Mother." You don't deserve that. I sassed back every chance I got, but never used the "W" word. And every time she slapped my face for my sassing or spanked my bare ass, I applied another ever so satisfying layer to the wall.

I wished so badly that she were dead. I wondered at times if I could kill her myself.

She'd be just another dead whore. No one would miss her. Least of all, me.

Finally one night, the word shot out of my mouth before I could stop it. Perhaps I just couldn't bear to hold it in any longer. We were eating our usual four o'clock dinner seated opposite each other at the rickety kitchen table. The meal was even more disgusting than usual, TV dinners of Salisbury steak, a meat too disgusting to even feed to animals, coated in a salty, clumpy gravy.

When she told me to eat my peas and stop complaining about it, the forbidden word and plenty others shot out of my mouth like puss from an infected pimple.

"What do you care?" I snapped. "You're not a *real* mother. You're just a *whore!*"

She rocketed out of her chair and leaned across the table. The hard slap to my face knocked me onto the floor. Light flashed across my eyes. I tasted blood on my lips.

My mother towered over me, her eyes practically bulging out of their sockets. "How *dare* you!"

But there she was in her black leather miniskirt,

fishnet stockings, and blonde wig. She wasn't dressed like that to go work at McDonald's. Suddenly every humiliation I'd ever suffered because of what she was exploded out of me.

"Look at you!" I screamed. "Of course you're a whore! Just a cheap *fucking* whore! What else could you be?"

As she wound up to hit me again, only harder this time, I delivered my own knockout blow. "I bet you don't even know who my father is!"

She froze. Blinked rapidly. Then began to wobble on her feet. She staggered backwards, then collapsed into her chair almost knocking it over.

I felt like the heavyweight champion of the world. I popped to my feet, euphoric, and looked down at her. Defeated. Broken.

Take that, you *whore*! How do you like it?

The clock on the wall ticked loudly in the silence. *Tick, tick, tick.*

"Don't you ever say that again," my mother finally said, shaking her head, her breaths coming in short gasps. "Of course I know who your asshole father is. But he left as soon as I told him I was pregnant. Left and didn't exactly leave behind a forwarding address.

"He might be dead for all I know, but it's tough to kill a rat. So he's probably out there somewhere. I just don't know where. We were living together, and he left me without a red cent, behind on the rent and all the bills. Just evaporated into thin air."

She pushed herself back onto her feet, got in my face, and put her hands on her hips. Flames of anger roared in her eyes. Her nostrils flared.

"So yes, I am a whore!" she yelled. "Are you happy now, you ungrateful little shit? I'm a whore, I'm a whore, I'm a whore! I'm not proud of it. I hate it! But it's the best I can do. I have no skills and flipping burgers won't pay the bills."

A single tear leaked down her face.

"I'm a horrible mother," she said, her voice suddenly soft and her eyes distant. "I'm a horrible everything. The only thing I do well is suck a dick!"

I guess I was supposed to feel sorry for her. Feel an outpouring of love. Feel *something*.

But all of that was long gone. Ripped out of me years earlier with the chants of "Your mother's a whore!" and everything that followed. My total isolation and disdain from everyone around me.

Just me and my wall of hatred, towering to the sky, rock hard and unbreakable.

So our Cold War began. My mother and I didn't

speak or eat together or interact at all. She even stopped trying to hide what she was. Instead of servicing most of the men in their cars, as she had done, she now brought many of them back to her bedroom, especially her regulars. She even convinced Louie, her pimp, to send them straight up to our apartment so she wouldn't have to go out and walk the mean streets.

Just lay on her back and take it like a whore.

One after another.

I said nothing about this change or the sounds coming through the thin wall between our bedrooms. But I knew the true benefit for my-mother-the-whore was not for convenience on either her part or the men's. It was a flagrant fuck-you to me. If I was going to call her a whore, I'd have to listen to her earning her trade.

My hatred burned even hotter. But I wouldn't be powerless forever. I'd get the last laugh.

―――――

I sent my own fuck-you when, for my fourteenth birthday, I sold my virginity to the highest bidder.

Louie, my mother's pimp, was a scary-looking, hulking man of about six-five and close to three hundred pounds. He had long, tangled, black hair, a ragged beard, tattoos all over his neck, arms, and shoulders broken only by a jagged scar from his right ear down to his collarbone. He almost always wore his black Hells Angels leather jacket and black boots. He and his friends not only controlled the whores in this neighborhood and the projects but also the drug trade.

He didn't come by the apartment often, but when I heard the roar of his Harley outside, I rushed to my bedroom and locked the door. My mother had told him to stay away from me. I was off-limits both as a piece of ass to sell and as a customer of his product. But that didn't stop him from trying.

With increasing frequency, he'd be sitting on his Harley outside our three-decker, waiting for me when I got home from school. Mostly alone but sometimes with his friends, also astride their Harleys. I'd try to rush by on the sidewalk as if I didn't even see him—as if it would even be possible to miss that mountain of a man and his bike—but he'd call out playfully.

"Hey, little girl, lighten up," he'd say in his gravely voice. "I don't bite. I know you're sad. Your life is fucked up. But I got stuff that'll brighten up your day."

I just kept walking, my head down and my heart pounding, fearful he'd climb off his bike and grab me. Perhaps do to me all the things the boys at school just talked about. Sneered that I should do for their lunch money because like mother, like daughter. Only Louie wouldn't be all talk, and he wouldn't be asking or paying. Just taking what he wanted.

But as I'd race on by and up the steps, Louie would only laugh and say, "Someday, little girl. Someday. It'll make you feel so good."

Then one day, he was alone and said words that finally made me stop.

"I'll bet you're still a virgin," he said, straddling his Harley and facing me. "Cause you hate your mother and you don't want to be anything like her."

Instead of staring at the ground, shaking my head to whatever he was offering, and rushing on by, I stopped and looked at him. For only a second, but that was long enough.

"Bullseye," he said with a coarse laugh. "You hate your mother's guts. I don't blame you. I would too in your shoes."

I stared at him, frozen in my tracks.

"Don't blame you one bit," he continued. "And I bet you seen a hundred TV shows about guys like me getting girls like you hooked on stuff, and next thing you know, they're no different than your mother. Trapped."

My eyes widened. It was like he could read my

mind.

He held his hands up as if in surrender. "I mighta thought about it with you some time ago, but you're too smart for that. You're a smart one. Not at all like your mother. So I just want you to think about something."

I waited, wide-eyed.

"How old are you?" he asked.

"Thirteen," I said, my mouth as dry as cotton. Somehow, I managed to swallow. "Turn fourteen next month."

He nodded. "Sooner or later, you're going to let some boy at school pop your cherry. And you're going to just give it to him for free. And he won't even appreciate that gift." Louie shook his head sadly. "But a sweet thing like you has choices. You can let me find you a man every bit as handsome and charming as that kid in your school, and you can give that sweet gift to him in a nice hotel room with candle lights and satin sheets instead of in the sweaty backseat of some kid's car. Strictly high class. And he'll reward you richly for the treasure of your gift."

Louie then quoted a dollar figure that took my breath away.

"Give it away," he said, spreading his hands out, palms up. "Or let me find the highest bidder."

I suddenly realized what he was saying. I mean,

I'd known all along what he was saying, but now the full reality hit me. I felt sick to my stomach. This was the very thing the boys had taunted me about. That my mother was a whore and soon enough, I would be too. Only a matter of time.

Like mother, like daughter.

"I... I couldn't," I said, unable to move, barely able to breathe. "I'm not like that."

"This ain't like your momma," Louie said, as if he was reading my mind. "Forget that shit. She's just a cheap street whore. You'd be strictly high class. A high class escort. You can practically name your price."

"I'm just thirteen," I said softly, struggling to get the words out.

"But like you said, almost fourteen," Louie said, then shrugged as if it didn't make any difference to him. "Hey, if you're too afraid, I get it. But every day you wait, little girl, the value of that cherry of yours goes down."

"I'm only thirteen," I said again, unable to think of anything else, for the first time in my life in no hurry for that next birthday or any of the others to follow. "Thirteen."

I turned to get away. I reached the stairs. First step. Second step. My legs felt like concrete. I was moving in slow motion. Third step.

I glanced over my shoulder, heart racing, afraid Louie was coming after me. But he was still sitting there on his Harley, his thick arms crossed, that jagged scar on his neck the only break in the tattoos.

He was smiling.

"Think about it," he said. "But don't wait too long. Don't let fear cost you too much money. You're worth more as a thirteen-year-old, even thirteen years and eleven months, than at fourteen. Don't wait until that birthday. The price is dropping even as I speak."

———

I never thought I'd say yes. But that night, I began to wonder as I listened to my mother—probably just to piss me off—egg her men on.

"Oh yeah," she groaned. "Give it to me. Harder! Harder!"

Just one "Fuck you, Katie" after another sent my way.

No need to share them with the cockroaches that came out when I turned off the lights, or with the critters in the walls I liked to think of as mice even if I knew they probably were rats.

No, my mother's fuck-yous were all mine, in-evitable since the say I called her a whore to her face and said that I doubted she ever knew who my father was.

God, how I hated her. And that burning hatred helped me give Louie his answer.

I'd take the money for my virginity from the highest bidder under one condition. I had to be stealing away one of my mother's best customers.

Pretty soon, that was the drug I couldn't get enough of, the drug for which I couldn't control my craving. I always needed more.

At first, I stole away her best customer for just that one night. Then again. And again. And then he was mine forever.

"*What do you think you're doing?*" my mother screamed at me the morning she found out.

I was sitting at the kitchen table where we always had our best screaming matches, eating my Cheerios, the clock on the wall loudly ticking. *Tick, tick, tick.*

I smiled with a sense of intense satisfaction that warmed my heart. It even gave me a strange tingle between my legs.

"Same fucking thing you're doing," I said. "But getting paid a whole lot more."

"This was never supposed to happen!" my

mother yelled. "You were supposed to have a better life than me!"

"I do," I said. "I get paid more from one man than you get from ten."

Her slap sent me flying to the floor, but I bounced right back up. "You better never do that again, or I'll tell Louie and he'll beat the living shit out of you."

She stared at me in disbelief.

"Don't believe me?" I said, taunting her, enjoying the thrill of finally being on this end of a taunt. "Do it again and find out." I stabbed my index finger into my chest. "*I'm* the valuable property in this household now."

She began to cry.

Boo-hoo.

It was too late for me to give a shit. Far too late. I couldn't even remember back when I last gave a shit.

"You were supposed to go to college," she said. "Get out of this cesspool."

"How? With what?" I demanded. "Your massive savings? Or the special scholarships available for the daughters of cheap whores?"

"Stop it! This is killing me!"

"*Good!*"

She looked at me as tears streamed down her face. "Stop now! Get out before it's too late."

"No!" I said, and felt a thrill at turning her down that I guessed might be near orgasmic.

"I'm begging you," she said. "You're still my little girl."

"Oh, fuck off!" I said, and left for my bedroom, slamming the door behind me.

The next day, I poached her second best customer. Her third and fourth best called me jailbait and told me to come back when I was legal. So I moved on down the line. If they wouldn't, or couldn't, pay a premium, I took them anyway. It was enough to steal my mother's best.

Soon, I was leaving the filthy bitch only the bottom of her own disgusting barrel.

And when I fucked the best of her old customers, I fucked them in my own bedroom where, for a change, *she* had to hear the action through the thin walls. I'd goad the men to be louder. Louder! *Louder!*

Payback was a delightful bitch.

Suddenly awash in money, even after Louie's cut, I decided to party after all. You only live once and life is short. Party hardy! So my profits starting going up my nose.

And when my dear, beloved mother asked for a cut, first of my profits and then of the coke, I told her to go fuck herself. I'd paid a share of the rent, but if she wanted to get by, she'd just have to work harder to beat the competition.

Me.

Our apartment became a busy two-woman brothel. I was the star attraction. The high-priced headliner. The classy, pampered, adored, under-aged escort, never to be confused with my mother, the cheap street whore. The lowliest of fucks. What men resigned themselves to when they couldn't get any better.

The only thing I shared with her was my last name. And if I knew who my father was, I'd change my name to take his. My mother and I no longer ate together, not after a succession of meals resulted in screaming matches and even fights.

The first time she gave me a black eye was her last. Louie stood up for me. Of course he did. I was his high-priced meal ticket. So he made that bitch pay so bad she was screaming for mercy. Even the super on the first floor, who overlooked everything because he, too, was Louie's customer, complained until Louie shut him up fast.

The black eye cost me and Louie both money. It wasn't the look of a high-priced escort, even one living in a dump of an apartment. But I covered it up as best I could until it went away, and it never happened again.

Not a word was spoken between my mother and me. Our eyes never even met as we passed each other, one leaving the bathroom and the other entering, or one of us heating up a meal only for ourself.

I couldn't legally drop out of school until I was sixteen and didn't want to attract the attention of any social workers, so I attended only enough to stay under the radar. When I was there, I paid no attention at all. This wasn't the pricey suburbs or the elite city magnet schools, so I fit right in. Except, of course, blowing Mr. Snyder so he'd give me a passing grade in Math.

The days went by. I snorted more and more coke. I fucked more and more clients. And hated my dear, beloved mother more and more than the day before.

Until the day I came home from school and found her dead in the bathtub.

Suicide by overdose. Lifeless eyes open as if to stare at me one last time.

I almost threw up, not because I suddenly gave a shit, but because in death she'd shit herself something fierce and the bathroom reeked of the stench. She left me a note taped to her red, flowered blouse so I wouldn't miss it.

Her one final fuck-you to me.

I can't take it anymore. When you were little, you were the one joy in my life. Now, I don't even have that. You hate me and I can't hardly blame you. I can't imagine you'll ever forgive me, but I hope someday you do. If the priests are right and there is a Heaven and Hell, I know where I'm going. But it can't be any worse than here. Get out before it's too late.

Louie moved in and somehow convinced the authorities, who didn't seem very motivated to find out the truth, that he was my mother's common law husband. Since I had no known relatives, he became my legal guardian. Throughout the process, he was the ventriloquist and I was his dummy. I said whatever he wanted me to say.

And why not? He'd always been my protector. I'd been the ventriloquist and he the dummy. I was his classy, high-priced meal ticket, and he acted accordingly.

Until he stopped.

Soon after my mother's death, I switched from snorting blow to horse. And maybe I got sloppy. Or maybe being around me in the apartment changed things. He couldn't keep his hands off me.

I resisted for a while, but finally, he took what he wanted.

After that, the mystique was gone. I wasn't special to him anymore. I still dressed up like a little girl, wore pigtails, and had teddy bears on my bed when clients came into my bedroom, but my "little girl" illusion that worked for them was lost on Louie.

When I turned sixteen, it all seemed to change overnight. I could drop out of school—yay! about fucking time!—but I was no longer jailbait. We could pretend for customers that I was still fifteen even as my breasts grew more pronounced, my days as an A-cup far from over, but we couldn't fool all of them and even the fools couldn't be fooled forever.

For some, now that I was legal, the allure was gone. I was no longer special. And as Louie had said a lifetime ago, every day I aged, the price dropped.

Or maybe it was just that my hatred for my dear, beloved old mother no longer fueled me. I wasn't driven to make more noise in my bedroom that she'd have to hear in hers. That primal urge to goad her old customers into louder and more frenzied expressions of their enthusiasm was gone.

At times, I had all I could do just to lay there and feign any interest at all. One customer even did me a favor and made of habit of me pretending to be dead.

In the blur of snorting more horse and fucking more and more customers—dipping deeper and deeper toward the bottom scum of what had been my mother's disgusting barrel—I became no more special than any other whore. When I tried meth, I got acne that wouldn't go away and my teeth began to rot.

Overnight, I had fallen from the pinnacle of a high-priced escort. I became just another hooker. And then what felt like just another overnight later, I went from just another hooker to just another cheap street whore.

I became my mother.

Like mother, like daughter.

The realization made my skin crawl. I denied it for as long as I could, but I stared at the mirror and saw what I had become. I used to be young and pretty. Still sixteen, I no longer looked young. Or pretty.

I began to lose my best customers, first in a trickle and then in droves. Somewhere out on the streets, an unknown-to-me, younger, still-attractive girl, who still fancied herself a high-priced escort in charge of her life, began skimming away the cream of my crop just like I had done to my mother. This unknown girl and I didn't know each other, so she got none of the vicious satisfaction I took out of the theft of a client, but I felt the same helpless hatred toward whomever this girl was.

Soon, the death spiral quickened its flushing of me down life's toilet. And I found I didn't really care. Louie could beat me, and I didn't care. Customers could beat me, and I didn't care. I would come close to accidental overdoses, and I didn't care.

I'd been fueled for so long by hatred for my mother that now I had no fuel left to keep me going. Hatred toward Louie or toward my customers didn't work any better than diesel fuel in a gasoline engine.

I just didn't care. Not even when Louie sold me to a room full of men. He listened through the thin walls and never came to my rescue, even when I screamed.

I wasn't worth saving.

And yet somehow that was not my personal rock bottom. My point of no return came when I opened my bedroom door to an old familiar face.

Sammy McWilliams. The first one to yell "You're mother's a whore!" The one that gave me that first push toward life's cliff. And every time I stumbled to my feet, he'd knock me back down. "What'll you do for a dollar?" he had asked when there was still a hint of sweetness and innocence left in me. And then "Will you blow me for my lunch money?"

Now eighteen or so, he was still a freckle-faced

tub of lard. And still an asshole. He looked about my bedroom, at the teddy bears that no longer seemed appropriate for a whore who looked closer to a hundred years old than fourteen, and then at me.

"Finally, I get that piece of you I've been wanting all these years," he said. But then he grimaced as if smelling week-old garbage. "I just wish you'd given it before you turned to shit. You look awful."

Not that that stopped him.

"That's okay," he said. "I'll close my eyes and remember back when you were pretty."

And he slapped me. Hard. And again.

"I paid a little extra to the big guy so I could do this," Sammy said.

And he slapped me again. Then he switched to his fists. When I lay on the floor, unable to get back up, he got the rest of what he paid for.

And then some.

He treated me like the cheap street whore that I am.

Worthless. Just like my mother.

Soon, maybe tomorrow, maybe even today, it will be time to join her. Because she was right about one thing.

Even if there's a Hell, it can't be worse than this.

A New Q

Leah R Cutter

Albert loved BBQ competitions. Or at least that was what he reminded himself as he drove up the interstate, leaving Texas for Oregon, of all places. He was going to take part in the first year of the Salmon Wilde BBQ competition, organized by the Left Coast BBQ Association (LCBA).

Most *real* BBQ competitions took place out east, in places that had a true BBQ tradition, like in Kentucky or even Alabama. (Though honestly, did white sauce even qualify as a BBQ sauce?) Hell, even Texas had its own style of BBQ—plain salt and pepper, letting the meat and the smoke do all the talking.

Oregon? What in God's name did they have for BBQ?

Nothing that originated there, that was the truth.

However, here was Albert in his RV, hauling Betty, his long off-set smoker, up the highway, heading toward another contest. He was only in his mid-forties, so the long drive wasn't going to be too bad. Plus, the family member he most resembled was his Great Uncle Willis, who was still alive and kicking at eighty-four. Sure, it meant that Albert's lanky brown hair would thin out (more), his glacial-blue eyes had needed glasses since he was twelve, his white skin burned worse than bacon if he stayed out in the sun too long, and his chin had definitely receded some.

But he was hearty and hale and rarely ever sick. He'd take that for the win.

Might be the only thing he had going for him at this time.

It was true that Albert and his team—Smoking Good Q—had lost the last couple of BBQ competitions they'd signed up for.

Maybe more than a couple.

Things kept going wrong: Betty ran out of fuel that one time, Albert had used salt instead of sugar in a rub another time, then there was the time they missed turning in their smoked meat to the judges by five minutes because the clock next to the smoker had been set wrong.

When Paulo, Albert's number one pit monkey, had suggested that maybe they needed a change of pace, to try a new contest, Albert had agreed.

Which was why he was barreling up the interstate at the end of September for almost three days, though he was making good time, heading to Hawksville, on the Oregon coast.

Albert always liked to get to a contest area early, to do one or two test smokes on Betty before the actual competition started. Never knew what the weather was going to be like, and that applied to every city he'd ever cooked in. Might go in thinking that since it was July in Memphis it was going to be warm and sticky, only to be drenched in hail and cold. Or be prepared for frost in Kentucky in October, and be stuck in a heatwave.

Since Hawksville was a coastal town, Albert assumed humidity and wind, but that might not be the case. Maybe the contest itself wasn't in sight of the water, was set inland a ways, so was warmer and drier. But it was also the end of September, so who knew how much rain they'd get?

It didn't matter. This time, Albert was going to win at least one category in a contest. Bring home another trophy for the food truck he ran in Dallas. Albert had joked about getting a second truck just to hold the trophies and ribbons. Though some of his crew had warned about that bringing bad luck, it hadn't. Not for the first five years.

Not until recently, when his winning streak had stopped.

Albert shook himself, staring out at the highway as the old RV ate up the miles. Normally, he traveled with at least one other member of his crew. However, Paulo was already on location, as he'd gone up early. Had family in the area, or something. They'd drive back together.

Everything had to go right this time. They didn't have their usual group of onlookers to cheer them on, as none of their regular BBQ family was making this long drive.

Nope. It was just Albert and Paulo. Men against meat.

Despite the name, the Salmon Wilde BBQ contest didn't have a fish category. Instead, they'd chosen to do the traditional four meats of BBQ competitions: brisket, pork shoulder, ribs, and chicken.

Albert wasn't going to fuss too much with the chicken. He regularly made the top ten in that category, frequently snagging one of the top three spots that came with a trophy and a cash prize. Chicken was hard to do correctly, with the pieces uniform, the skin perfectly tender and melting into the meat, everything juicy and flavorful.

He didn't bother doing in the truck, just at competitions.

Ribs could also be finicky, but Albert had had good success in the past with those meats, often placing and occasionally winning contests.

Pork shoulder and brisket were his specialties. He had the perfect injection for his brisket that enhanced the meat flavor. Most competition cooks injected their pork as well, but Albert didn't. His rub and his cooking techniques were good enough that he didn't need to. He almost always placed high in those categories.

Except for recently, when all his tried-and-true recipes had failed him.

What he really needed right now as a win.

Hopefully, Oregon would get him back on his streak again.

The campground next to the park where the BBQ contest was being held was beautiful. Albert had no other words to describe it. Instead of a bare open space with concrete and each RV parked within two feet of its neighbor, all the campsites were tucked away under huge pine trees. The crisp air smelled like baked earth, with a hint of the ocean underneath. The weather forecast predicted sunshine all through the weekend—Albert had arrived on Thursday night, and the contest didn't really start until Saturday. But weather was changeable, and those people who predicted it had a lousy average most of the time.

Albert texted Paulo that he'd arrived, let him know the campsite he'd been assigned, then went to take care of Betty.

Betty was a long, offset smoker. She looked as though someone had taken three large oil barrels, laid them on their sides, then riveted them together. Hanging off the left side of the long metal body was the firebox, for the wood Albert burned. (Hence, offset, as the heat wasn't directly in the main cooking body.) On the right side, a large chimney jutted out. Sturdy legs with heavy-duty wheels supported the entire structure.

Each of the three barrels had lid as well as a built-in thermometer. Albert knew Betty well, where her hot and cold spots were, the best places to cook a particular cut of meat, how to get exactly the right amount of heat and smoke.

Generally, underneath the main grate that took up most of the interior, he stuck a large pan filled with water, to ensure moisture throughout the entire offset.

That afternoon, Albert left Betty up on her trailer, as he was going to have to haul her to the competition area Saturday morning, which was in the park just across the street from the campground. The LCBA had sold tickets to the locals, for Saturday and Sunday, promising real BBQ. There'd be a band playing both Saturday and Sunday, and a number of local breweries would also have stands, mixed in between the BBQ establishments.

Albert stoked up the wood in Betty's fire box, getting a nice burn going, letting the smoker heat up before he put on his dinner—porkchops and baked apples. The meat had a rub of his own making, with lavender, rosemary, lemon peel, coarse salt and black pepper. Toward the end of the cook, he also threw on sauerkraut—store bought, but warming it up on Betty made it amazing.

Sure, it was a bit much, heating up the long smoker just for a short while. However, he wanted to make sure she was all right after the long haul. Plus, a short cook like pork chops was a good test for how she'd handle in this location.

Albert had managed to stay friends with his ex-wife, even after she remarried and started popping out kids. (It had been one of the reasons why they'd gotten a divorce—Albert honestly couldn't stand kids, and Rebecca had wanted a slew of them.)

One of her girls had turned out to be allergic to onions and garlic. Albert would have just as soon stopped living if he'd had to give up such flavors.

However, when Rebecca had challenged him to create something for Patricia, Albert had risen to the occasion and upped his spice game. Now, he frequently made his rubs that didn't contain the usual ingredients.

So at times like this, he experimented. He'd started adding lavender as a way to increase the lightness of a rub—what some snootily called the floral notes. Cloves were another of his secret ingredients: they added the earthiness of pepper without the heat.

The pork was perfect when he pulled it off the grill. Seared and tender, with just a kiss of smoke. The apples were fantastic as well. He'd done two of them, cored out and wrapped in tinfoil: one savory, with rosemary, thyme, and sage, while the other was sweet, stuffed with brown sugar and cinnamon. Plus, both had a generous serving of butter melted with all the other goodness.

Albert ate alone at his park-provided picnic table instead of inside his RV, enjoying being outside for the time being. The evening had turned much colder as the sun set. Some brave cicadas still sang in the grass off to the side. Maybe if it grew quiet enough he'd be able to hear the ocean off in the distance.

After he finished his stupendous meal, he poured himself a shot of whiskey and added it to his decaf coffee, wishing for the moment that maybe he had some hot chocolate instead. He tended not to like things that were too sweet, which was why he didn't have any.

It was so peaceful up here, out in the woods. Albert could feel himself recharging after three long-ass days of driving.

And Betty was working great after all that travel. So well, in fact, he couldn't imagine losing. Not this time. Not in this place.

Nope. That losing streak of his was over.

Paulo showed up midafternoon on Friday. He looked happier than he had been, down in Texas, his dark brown eyes softer, his grin wider. Even his dark Hispanic skin seemed lighter. He wore his usual stuffy, long-sleeved shirt, looking like a business-man, with a blue bandana holding his dark curls back.

"Hey, stranger," Albert said as opened the door to the RV when Paulo knocked.

"Howdy, boss," Paulo said with a grin. "See you got all set up."

"Yup," Albert said. He'd brought more than one grill, of course. While last night had been Betty's turn, this morning he'd started up the barrel smoker and made himself a slew of eggs and sausages, with a little of the sauerkraut from the night before thrown in, plus cheese, of course.

The barrel smoker was made from a single, modi-fied barrel that stood upright. The bottom of it had a drawer that could be easily slid out for adding more charcoal or wood. Just above that was a second drawer that held a water pan. Then there were three layers of wire racks for smoking. The removable top of it was flat, with a chimney sticking out of the middle of it.

Albert's barrel smoker was painted black, with flames at the bottom of it and his logo—Smoking Good Q—on the side, just below the thermometer. The smoker was good advertisement, and it made really good meat. Plus, the guys who'd made it were sponsors of Albert, so the smoker itself hadn't cost him anything.

Sure, there was a cooktop in the RV. Albert might use it to start a sauce or something. The rest of the time, though, one of the smokers or grills that he'd brought would do all the work.

"You doing okay? Family okay?" Albert asked.

The grin he got in response told him all that he needed to know. "They're all good," Paulo assured him. "Any trouble getting up here?"

"Nope. GPS is a wonder, y'know? And Betty did just fine," Albert assured him.

"Oh, yeah, that's right," Paulo said.

His cheery nature seemed to diminish. The smile he showed to Albert was suddenly forced.

"Hey, we'll win this time. I can feel it, y'know? New place. New start," Albert assured him.

Paulo looked off, over the trees, then nodded. "Yes. New place. It'll be a fresh start."

Then he looked back at Albert, a determined look in his eyes. "Let's get Betty moved over to the competition grounds."

"What, now?" Albert asked, then he shook his head. "Nope. I don't want to take a chance, leaving her all alone at night. We'll stay here tonight, then we'll move her tomorrow morning, first thing."

"We might have to use the RV then, to move her," Paulo said. Turned out that he'd borrowed a truck from his brother that they could use to haul Betty's trailer, as Paulo himself had flown up.

"No, no, that just doesn't feel right," Albert said. "She stays here. Besides, I'm already cooking half-a-dozen pork butts on her, seeing how she does here. We'll be serving customers tastes of that tomorrow, before we start cooking the competition meats."

Paulo looked so disappointed, Albert added, "Let's go over to the competition area, check in, like that."

"All right," Paulo said, though he shook his head and didn't seem pleased with the notion.

The pair of them walked along the paved trail, past other RVs and some of their competitors. Albert didn't recognize many of the names—pit crews that were new to him. Still, he waved at the three women standing around the long offset who had a banner across their RV that read, *Las Chicas de Carne*, as well as the young man with the egg-shaped smoker with a banner proclaiming him *King of Cool Smoke*.

To get to registration, they had to walk through

the area set up for the contest. The competitors were arranged in a horseshoe around the edges of a large, cleared field—at least as long as a football field. A stage was being assembled at the open end. Standing next to the stage, to the right, were a couple of long tents, with signs indicating meat turn-in stations.

"This is much bigger than I thought it'd be," Albert admitted as they looked across the open field.

"Think it'll be full of competitors?" Paulo said.

Albert nodded. There were stakes marking out each competitor's area all around the field. "I do," he said. "It also won't matter a lick. We got this."

Paulo nodded. "Yup," he said, though he didn't sound convinced in the least.

That was okay. Albert felt their chances were good.

The people running registration appeared to have a clue about what was going on and how to run a competition (unlike that one event they vowed to never return to, in Kansas). The Smoking Good Q team was assigned a spot in the field, their competition number, when they should set up their offset on the field, and a window during which the meat inspector would come visit them to inspect the meat they'd brought for the contest.

Albert was glad they hadn't brought Betty down.

It wasn't that she'd be lonely out on the field all by herself, but it would have made her a target to any mischief makers.

Paulo and Albert went over their strategy for Saturday and Sunday, how they were going to get Betty over to the competition area, the timing of the meats they were cooking, rubs and spices.

Paulo insisted that the judges here weren't brainwashed by the Kansas City Barbeque Association (KCBA), that they didn't need the extreme sweetness preferred by some of the east coast judges.

It was part of why Albert had wanted to try a LCBA contest. He'd read the same things on the online BBQ forums he lurked on.

Now, he wasn't about to go hog wild and give them one of his Chinese five-spice rubs on the pork shoulder.

However, Oregon, or at least Portland, was all about coffee.

Maybe he should use one of his coffee rubs, like on the pork. It had instant espresso powder, thyme, tarragon, smoked paprika, and sage.

Just as they were finishing up their planning, another RV pulled in, right beside them.

Albert couldn't help but grimace. It was a group of idiots that he recognized from some of the KCBA contests that he'd attended. They called themselves HOT Grill Action.

Real competitors might have a shot of whiskey, or even a beer or two, during a contest. Chances were, though, they were completely sober and didn't drink a drop until after they'd turned in all their proteins.

When you had to get up at three or four in the morning to start cooking your brisket, you didn't drink heavily the night before. Or stay up all night. That was for amateurs.

HOT Grill Action was made up of a group of rowdy frat boys, at least as far as Albert was concerned. All twenty somethings who'd just started competition grilling that year. Professional teams had two or three members. These yahoos had twice that, and would only turn in one or two meats.

He would grudgingly admit that they'd had some success.

Beginner's luck.

They had no skill, no finesse, and no endurance. He bet they'd go down hard at a double, when you cooked the same four proteins two nights in a row.

"Wonder when the real competition will arrive," Albert said dryly.

When Paulo didn't reply, Albert glanced over at him.

He'd gone completely pale, as though he'd covered his face in ash for *dia de la muerta*.

"You okay?" Albert asked, tapping his elbow against Paulo's forearm.

Paulo shook his head. "What? Yes." He stared ahead again. "I'm so sorry."

"What the hell you got to be sorry for?" Albert asked. "Those punks ain't gonna beat us."

Paulo visibly gulped. "Yes, yes, you're right. It's going to be fine."

Albert wasn't convinced, and he was damned sure that Paulo wasn't convinced either.

Everything was *not* going to be fine, but Albert had no idea what was wrong, what had spooked Paulo so badly, or how he could fix this.

While still regaining his winning streak.

After Paulo left, Albert stuck to the campsite, never leaving. Even when the idiots across the way started in with their loud rap music.

Gansta rap, despite being as pale as Albert.

As if. They were just a bunch of punks. Would probably piss themselves if they wandered into a real barfight.

Albert felt like a fool going out twice that night

to check on Betty, to make sure that she was still there, still in prime condition.

However, Paulo had gotten Albert spooked.

He felt like less of a fool when the redneck alarm he'd set up—a series of tin cans tied together with a string, attached to one Betty's legs—jangled at three AM.

No one was there by the time Albert made it out the door of the RV.

But he would swear that Betty had been moved. Maybe just an inch to the side of the platform.

Like all good rednecks, Albert kept his granddaddy's old Government Issue Colt in his safe box in the RV.

He wasn't about to pull it out, though, or do something foolish like store it in his boot, unlike that jackass up in Tennessee who blew his own damned foot off.

He reset his redneck alarm, tying the cans to a different leg and making it impossible to move Betty without some sort of noise. Then he tried going back to sleep, but kept waking up every time he heard wind blowing through the trees or the sound of pine needles softly falling on the roof of the RV.

Paulo arrived early, before seven. He was able to borrow his brother's truck again so they could easily transport Betty over to the competition area. Their space was on the lower curve of the horseshoe. If the stage was noon, they were in the five o'clock position.

Albert came prepared with tents, camp chairs, tables, the barrel smoker, and all the cooking and serving gear he needed. Paulo and Albert had set up this sort of stand before, a place where they could meet and talk with customers who came through to try their BBQ. He had the big banners for Smoking Good Q hanging nicely over the tents, along with signs with the QR codes that people could use to get to the food truck's website.

Just that summer, Albert had started selling a few of his rubs. He'd named his line, "Nuthin but Taste" as he'd focused on those recipes that didn't contain nightshades, garlic, or onion. None of them contained gluten, of course, and a bunch were sugar-free as well.

Sure, a few of his competitors thought he'd gone over the bend and was too *foo-foo* to be serving anything good.

Seemed, though, that an awful lot of people wanted to buy those sorts of rubs. Particularly after they tried it at a show.

He'd gotten a food seller's permit for Oregon through the LCBA so he'd brought a wide range of rubs available for people to try, along with the pork butts he'd smoked the day before.

Everything was going to be just fine.

And it was, as the crowds came wandering by, tempted to taste the pork he'd cooked that was melt-in-your-mouth tender. They sold a good number of the jars of rub he'd brought as well.

Albert sent Paulo up back to the RV a few times for forgotten items, though honestly, Albert didn't need them. He just wanted someone going back to the campsite at odd times so that no one would try to do something stupid and sabotage it.

An older, heavy-set woman with salt-and-pepper wild curls came by around two PM. "Hi there. I'm Sally Barker," she said as way of introduction. "Your meat inspector."

Albert shook her hand, impressed by how strong she appeared to be. She'd not spent her life inside, typing on a computer, that was for damned sure, especially based on her ruddy cheeks and weathered skin. She wore a comfortable gray hand-knit cardigan over jeans and heavy boots.

Albert brought her back to the rear of his setup and showed her the coolers where he'd kept the competition meat. Sally professionally examined every piece, making sure that it was being kept at a safe temperature, was still in the original packaging, and that nothing had been added to it, like some sort of marinade.

Sally chatted easily as she went about her business, asking about where they'd come from, how long they'd been doing competitions, the different types of smokers they'd be using.

It wasn't until after the inspection was over and she'd handed them their certificate that she asked about the rubs. She appeared impressed that Albert had the "Nuthin but Taste" line.

"Got a niece who I swear is allergic to just about everything but water," she commented as Albert explained the basic rub that was free of the eight most common allergen.

"I hear you," Albert commented. "Have a stepdaughter who's the same way, who inspired most of this line."

Sally put down the rub with a sigh. "I need to finish my rounds, first. But I'm coming back for that."

"I'll put aside a jar for you," Albert told her. He knew he couldn't just offer it to her, as that might be seen as a bribe.

Everything had to be on the up-and-up. Particularly as he was planning on replacing his losing streak with a winning one.

Late in the afternoon, he made the decision that he'd stay down in the competition area, with Betty, all night. He made Paulo bring down a cot and a sleeping bag and they rearranged the cooking schedule, so that Albert could take care of the meat.

Pork butts were going on first, as he tended to cook his for sixteen hours. Next, the brisket would go on at three AM, as it also needed a lot of time to cook. After that came the ribs, then the chicken last. The judging would be blind, meaning the judges would have no idea who turned in what box.

The contest turn-in times for when the meats had to be ready for the judges were varied. Chicken at noon on Sunday, ribs at twelve-thirty, brisket at one, and pork at one-thirty. Turn-in times were tightly controlled, and a contestant only had a ten-minute window to get their boxes turned in.

It would mean a lot of work in the middle of the day, as Albert tried to schedule everything exactly, getting the boxes set up and delivering those at the perfect time, so the meat would still be warm and appetizing for the judges.

Then, Albert could relax a little. While he was busy with the cooking, Paulo would be handling the crowds coming through, talking with customers, handing out samples, selling rubs.

If Albert could have afforded it, he'd have three people, like *Las Chicas de Carnes* who were just a couple of stands away from him, closer to the six o'clock location. That way, he could have two people prepping boxes while the third handled everything else.

However, Oregon was a long-ass haul from Texas, and he didn't expect anyone to come along for free.

As his dad had drilled into his head, if your business model depends on slave wages, it ain't much of a business model. The only way Albert had been able to afford this trip was because Paolo had volunteered to go to Oregon on his own.

Hopefully, they'd sell enough rubs and place high enough in the various categories that Albert would show a profit. Competitions were mainly for the prestige, advertising, and the sponsorships. As he was based in Texas, he wouldn't see a bump in his food truck business by coming all the way out here.

However, maybe the online store would.

The day drew to a close and the crowds of customers dwindled. Albert had already put the pork butts on Betty, at the far end of the offset, so they'd cook low and slow all night.

The firebox was heavily insulated so once it got hot, it stayed hot. However, the smoker itself wasn't insulated. As the temperature dropped, Albert put Betty's coat on her—a bright red thermal blanket that had been tailored to fit the offset perfectly. This would keep the temperature more even along the long barrel, and he'd need less fuel.

For this cook, he was starting with mesquite wood, as that was plentiful and cheap in Texas, but would be an exotic flavor up here in Oregon. It added a lovely, sweeter smoke, which would be perfect for the pork. Later on, when he put the brisket into Betty, he would start adding more hickory to the firebox, to give the smoke a more robust flavor, appropriate for beef.

He'd cook both the ribs and the chicken on the barrel smoker. For this contest, he'd use natural charcoal instead of wood, as both meats would have sauces. All that he needed to develop taste-wise was a kiss of smoke. The flavor of the smoke would be less important.

Finally, Albert sent Paulo back to his family, not allowing the other man to stick around, even though they'd originally set up the schedule with Paulo doing the first shift and Albert doing the second.

No, Albert needed to spend the night tending to Betty. Particularly after the redneck alarm had gone off the night before.

Paulo had questioned whether or not the wind had just blown the tin cans over.

Albert was convinced, though, that Betty had been moved.

At least staying here, at the event space, meant he wasn't subjected to that stupid rap that the HOT Grill Action team was playing. They had played it for a short while until one of the women from *Las Chicas de Carne* went over and talked with them. She reported back that their player had gotten too hot and burned out, or something like that.

Albert spent some time that evening hanging out with *Las Chicas*, Gabby, Cecilia, and Elenore. Nice women, totally into BBQ. They had a food truck down in San Francisco and had done more than one LCBA event. They'd assured him that what he'd heard was correct—the LCBA judges didn't need the sweetness that the KCBA judges preferred.

When he got back to his camp, he did an inspection of everything, Betty, the barrel smoker, all his equipment.

It all seemed to be just fine.

He arranged the redneck alarm again, set his alarm for an hour ahead of when he actually needed to get up to put on the brisket, and went to sleep quickly, given the night before hadn't been great, his dreams filled with sweet smoke and sweeter victory.

Albert awoke with a start, before the alarm went off.

Someone was there, at the site, with him.

He quietly slipped out of his sleeping bag, snagging his flashlight but not turning it on, then walked toward the figure standing at the back of Betty.

A ripping sound filled the quiet night.

Albert flipped on his light.

Paulo stood there with a knife in hand.

"What are you doing?" Albert asked quietly.

He'd had his suspicions. Some of the bad luck he'd been having had been just that.

However, too many time it had seemed as though someone was out to get him.

Sometimes, it isn't just paranoia.

Paulo stood frozen, his face pale in the harsh light.

"I'm sorry, boss," he said softly. "I didn't want to."

Albert nodded. "Someone is making you."

Paulo stood silent, still frozen.

"Blackmail?" Albert guessed. It was the only thing he could think of that would turn one of his crew against him.

Finally, Paulo moved, giving Albert a sharp nod.

Albert took a deep breath, letting it out in a white fog cloud.

"Come on," he said quietly. "Let's make some coffee. Then you can tell me all about it."

Paulo shook his head. "I can't."

"Yes, you can," Albert said. "You don't want to betray me, or the crew. I know that. Otherwise, you would have been more efficient at stopping me. What did you do this time, by the way?"

"Sliced through Betty's coat," Paulo said. "So the temperature wouldn't stay up."

"I'm going to come over and see the damage," Albert said softly. "Then we're having coffee together. Understand me?"

Though Paulo still looked as though he wanted to bolt, he stayed where he was.

At least Albert had gotten there quick enough that only a single slash marred the back of Betty's coat. Some duck-tape would hold that together just fine.

After doing a quick repair, Albert made them some coffee, then put out two chairs.

Paulo still looked as though he wanted to run. But he stayed, slumping down into the chair, looking like a dog afraid that he was about to be beaten. Again.

"I didn't want to betray you," Paulo said after the coffee had warmed them both up a touch.

"I know that," Albert said. "That's why I only had my flashlight and not my gun."

Paulo gave him a watery smile. "See? You're so

much smarter than I am."

Albert snorted at that. He was a redneck, and could figure stuff out sometimes. Not smart at all.

Just look at his past with Rebecca and others.

As deep as a mud-puddle, she'd said once.

Paulo seemed stuck, still trying to find the words, so Albert asked, "Is it the HOT Grill Action crew? Do they have something on you?"

Paulo shivered. "Yeah. They do."

"What?" Albert asked, possibly a bit sharply. His patience was only going to last so long. "Tell me so that we can fix this."

"You aren't going to want to help me after I tell you," Paulo warned.

"Let me be the judge of that," Albert said.

Paulo looked off across the dark field for a few moments, gathering together his courage, before he finally said all in a rush, "I'm gay."

Albert waited for a moment, waiting for the other shoe. Finally, he said, "So?"

Paulo wrenched his head back and stared hard at Albert. "What do you mean, 'so'?"

Albert shrugged. "You do know my older brother's gay, right?"

Paulo looked shocked. "No! I thought he was married!"

"He was," Albert said, nodding. "Absolute witch

of a woman. Probably married her as some sort of punishment for himself. Finally divorced her and admitted his true nature. He still has awful tastes in partners though." Albert paused, thinking for a few moments. "You dating anyone?"

Paulo snorted. "No."

"Remind me to introduce you to Ellis at some point," Albert said, nodding.

Paulo blinked, still in shock. "That's it? You don't care?"

"I may look like a redneck who'd be comfortable wearing sheets and singing to Hitler, but I'm a grown adult and able to make my decisions," Albert said firmly.

"Wow," Paulo said, shaking head. He obviously hadn't been expecting this reaction at all.

"I honestly don't care who you're sleeping with. As long as it's all consenting adults, I'm fine." Albert paused, then added, "No, aslong as it isn't a vegetarian. Or god forbid, a vegan."

Paulo finally started laughing at that. A little hysterically to start with, for sure, but the laughter faded and he ended with a true smile on his face. "You truly don't care."

"That's right. I don't. So what does the HOT Grill Action team have on you? A video? Pictures?"

"Something like that, yeah," Paulo said. "They recorded me in the men's restroom in Georgia."

"All right, so first off, act like an adult and get a room next time, okay?" Albert said.

Paulo nodded, abashed. "My family didn't know, either," he said softly. "It's why I came up. They were mostly like you, though my *abela* said she'd always known and that it was about time I came out."

"Grandmothers know everything," Albert said. His own had been a scary woman who he'd sworn more than once had had the ability to read minds, though she claimed it was just auras she saw.

"What type of device did they record you on?" Albert asked after a few moments.

"Camera," Paulo admitted. "It was kind of weird. Like they were all prepared or something."

"Uhm, was that restroom something of a pickup spot?" Albert said, not sure if he wanted to hear the answer or not.

"It is!" Paulo said enthusiastically. "See, the end stall is just the right size—"

"Spare me the details." Albert sat for a few moments, drumming his fingers on the arm of his chair. "Every accusation is a confession, or so I've been told. Do you think there's any chance that when they went in there, they'd been planning on taking advantage of the, uhm, accommodations, themselves?"

"Maybe," Paulo said. "I wasn't really paying attention to them."

"Do you think you could persuade one of them into a dalliance? So that I could come in and record it?" While Albert didn't really want to see such an act, he also really couldn't think of any way else of getting Paulo out from under this thing.

Until Paulo came out to everyone, and decided that he just didn't care anymore.

He shook his head. "That's a good way of getting my ass kicked." Then he paused. "But maybe, if I just went to talk with Erik, alone…"

"You think on that," Albert said. "I'll see if I can figure out some other way to get some dirt on them."

Paulo jumped up out of his chair. "I'm going to go take a better look at the restrooms here. See if there's a good place for a hookup."

"All right," Albert said. He glanced at his watch. "May as well start the fire in Betty, get her ready for the brisket."

The fire caught nicely—no problems starting her at all. Had Paulo been responsible for that one time when she wouldn't light and stay lit? Possibly.

Albert was concerned when Paulo didn't come back right away.

Surely he wasn't stupid enough to "try out" those "accommodations" tonight, was he?

Finally, Paulo came bursting back into the camp.

"You'll never guess who I found already 'using'

the restroom!" he exclaimed, explaining how he'd found two of the HOT Grill Action team in "action" and had recorded them on his phone before they'd realized he was there.

"Good!" Albert said. He was happy he hadn't had to go and do that part himself. "So, tomorrow, you, me, and maybe Gabby from *Las Chicas* need to go and confront those idiots."

Paulo blinked in surprise. "Why bring in an outsider?"

Albert just grinned at him. "While Gabby and Cecelia are sisters, Elanore is Gabby's girlfriend."

"Oh. Oh!" Paulo said. He paused for a moment. "You really aren't bothered by this."

"When I was young and stupid, I might have been," Albert admitted. "But hopefully, we all grow up at some point and realize that it's absolutely none of our business."

Paulo nodded and eventually left, Albert still tending the fires while Paulo went up to the RV to sleep. Tomorrow would be another busy day, and they both needed to be at their best.

Albert hoped that without the sabotage, he really would regain his winning streak.

Meeting with the HOT Grill Action team had gone better than Albert could have hoped. The members of the team started accusing each other of all sorts of lewd behavior, shouting and shoving each other around, like the rowdy frat boys they were.

They didn't end up disqualifying themselves, though it was touch and go for a while, particularly after the contest officials got involved due to the prolonged shouting match going on.

However, they didn't place high in the ranks at all, much to Albert's satisfaction. He hoped it would be the last he saw of them for quite a while.

Las Chicas placed well, taking first in ribs, seventh in brisket, tenth in pork, and way down in the bottom for chicken.

Gabby and Albert commiserated, as he hadn't even reached the top ten in chicken either.

It was just such a hard protein to get right!

However, the rest of the Smoking Good Q scores were right in line with where they should be: fifth in ribs, third in brisket, and second in pork.

The team who scored the highest in all four categories was awarded the Grand Champion trophy for the entire competition. Though Albert had snagged more than one of those in previous contests, he only made third overall this time.

Still, not bad for an inaugural run of a competition, as well as his first time with the LCBA.

As Albert drove away from Oregon on Monday morning, Paulo quietly riding in the passenger seat, Albert reflected again on how he loved BBQ competition.

Going to them, competing in them, and then, winning them.

READ MORE!

Never miss an issue of Mystery, Crime, and Mayhem! Get yourself a subscription!

https://www.mysterycrimeandmayhem.com/product/mcm-subscription/

For the latest news, sign up for the newsletter here:

https://www.mysterycrimeandmayhem.com/never-miss-a-release/

In addition to learning about all the great issues, you'll also get a free copy of the *MCM Criminally Good Anthology.*

Our Friends

Friends of MCM
    Knottted Road Press
    PubShare
    BookFunnel
    Thrill Ride the Magazine
    WMG Publishing
    Sisters in Crime
    I Found This Great Book
    Crime Writers of Color
    One House Productions

Milton Keynes UK
Ingram Content Group UK Ltd.
UKHW011814090224
437558UK00013B/641